Year of the Smoke Girl

a novel

by

Olivia J. Boler

Dry Bones Press
Roseville, CA 95678

Year of the Smoke Girl
by Olivia J. Boler

Copyright 2000 Olivia J. Boler

Library of Congress Card Number: 00–102848

Dry Bones Press, Inc.
P. O. Box 597
Roseville, CA 95678

(415) 707–2129

http://www.drybones.com/

Publisher's Cataloging–in–Publication Data
FICTION
Boler, Olivia J. —
Year of the Smoke Girl / by Olivia J. Boler
Series: New Voices in American Fiction
p   cm.
ISBN 1–883938–78–3
1. Chinese language and culture.   2. Chinese in
America.   3. Lesbians and lesbianism.
I. Author   II. Title

For my parents, *Lucy S. C. Yang*, and *Paul J. Boler III*, with love.

At last the secret is out, as it always must come in the end,
The delicious story is ripe to tell to the intimate friend;
Over the tea–cups and in the square the tonge has its desire;
Still waters run deep, my dear, there's never smoke without fire.

—W. H. Auden

What a blessing this smoking is! Perhaps the greatest that we owe to the discovery of America.

—Sir Arthur Helps

Part I

Prologue

It was not the last time she would see her mother alive, alive as one could be in the last stages of cancer. On that very last day, her mother lay in the bed as if she were sleeping while the family watched at her side. Coma: a cavernous word, a word as deep as the instability of regulated, eyes–closed existence it described.

But today, they were alone, and her mother was still conscious, although she was weak and frail. Scared. Her emotions were not numbed as her body was by the morphine cocktail dripping from her I.V. into the pierced vein. Everything floated in a painless, liquid fog, and her daughter was never sure if her mother was completely present.

They could not know this was the last time they would speak to each other.

The young woman sat by the bed, twisting a pen in her hands to keep them occupied. The nurses left the TV on during daylight hours to simulate liveliness in the room, but her mother had requested the sound turned down. The box hung above them, suspended in the corner of the room over the door, at once a surveillance monitor into make–believe worlds and also an eye guarding their real life progress.

"I want to tell you something." She spoke from the hospital bed. The daughter wondered if they should raise the back of it so she could sit up; perhaps she needed to clear her throat, to feel dignified.

"Listen to me. I want to tell you…" Her voice retreated into a cough, the sound making the young woman's eyes water. She tried to ignore it.

"What is it, Mom?"

"You and your brother." Her voice strained, hissing like a snake gargling pebbles. Since she got sick, it was parched and grainy. The doctors had removed some of her vocal chords a month ago.

7

"Yes, Mom?"

"You've always thought you and your brother didn't have middle names. But you do. They're not on your birth certificates, but you do have them."

The young woman tucked the pen behind her right ear.

"What are you talking about?"

"I gave you Chinese names. Yours is *Wu Shan*." Her voice lowered as she pronounced the words: "It means 'Foggy Hills.' To remind me of my hometown."

"Foggy Hills." San Francisco. They had never visited this place together.

"Or Misty Hills. That's prettier. Don't you think so?"

"Yes." The girl paused; she was not used to talking about her Chinese side. She rarely thought about it. "What's Porter's name?"

Her mother gazed at the ceiling for a while. This was not unusual. Sometimes she did not blink for many minutes.

"Diligent Scholar."

Her daughter smiled at the irony of her younger brother's Chinese name.

"Those are nice," she said.

"My mother suggested it when I was a girl."

"She knew Chinese?" For some reason, the thought of a white person knowing Chinese struck her as odd. But why not? Millions of Chinese people knew English. She blushed at her ignorance.

"I've wanted to tell you..." Her mother closed her eyes and stayed silent for a few moments. She breathed in and out as if it were a new habit. "Your father and I love you, you know. But you've been content. You've had a good youth?" She posed it as a question. "Your life will continue to be...prosperous."

The daughter shifted her hips in the vinyl chair and looked out the window.

"I've wanted to tell you for so long..." Her voice faded, swallowed, along with the pain, by the drugs.

8

Her eyes closed, and her daughter willed them to open again but let her be, tentatively touching her mother's hand, the plain wedding band as dull as her dried out skin, once silky like rose petals.

After her mother had died, she tried to remember how to say Misty Hills in Chinese, but the raspy, knocking sounds were lost to her. She decided it did not matter; at least she remembered the name in English, and that was something with which to begin.

Chapter One

The banister of the old porch stairs creaked as she leaned the small of her back into it, squinting at the sky, trying to find the Pleiades. Stars were grounding stones: they were always somewhere above, even when the sun was shining.

Khatia Quigley gave up and lowered her eyes, staring into her wine glass, looking for the sky's backward reflection. All she found was a swirl of fractured whiteness. The whiteness was actually her maudlin eyes, and she thought, If there is one word I would use to describe myself, it would be "rootless." Boundlessly Groundless, not Drippy Mountains, or whatever it was, should have been her middle name. The stars opposed her: they belonged exactly where they were. She could not say the same for herself.

The phone rang inside and she jumped a little. Even though she knew Estella would not hear its clanging, Khatia hurried inside to stop the noise. The old black dial phone sat on its doily–protected table, a relic from the Fifties.

"Hello?"

"Hey, it's me."

"Shoshonah!" she said, and sat in the old cane chair.

"I've met a lot of Eskimos here. They look like you. Sure you're not Inuit?"

"Ha, ha."

"Hey, what's the difference. You know some of your Asiatic ancestors probably came across the old land bridge at *some* time or another. Oh yes." Her voice took on the tone of an evangelist. "We're all cousins in the end. We're all *monkeys*. How are you?"

"Oh, fine. I was just about to toast the moon."

"What for?"

10

"I can't remember."

"Typical of you. Selective memory."

There was phone–silence, and over the nearly imperceptible hum, she could hear Shoshonah's hair falling against her nylon parka. Wires whirred rhythmically on the line.

"I was just thinking about you this afternoon as I faxed Greenland Oil requesting some documents. I was thinking, 'In the inlets of Alaska, Shoshonah is catching fish and slicing them up on a boat called *the Narwhal.* I wonder if she's seen any.'"

"Seen any what?"

"Narwhals."

"I have."

"Your last letter smelled of unwashed labia." Khatia imagined Shoshonah bending over a sink of soapy water at night, trying to get the stink of fish out of her fingers.

"That's just lovely. You kiss your Aunt Estella with that mouth?"

Khatia curled the cord around her finger. "*Kinky* fantasy. What has it been, two months since we last spoke? Have you been out to sea that long?"

"We had one stop a couple of weeks ago, but there wasn't a pay–phone."

"Oh." She began pinching the dying chintz cover of Estella's address book, wondering how long Shoshonah's hair was now. She had cut it short before sneaking off to Alaska almost a year ago.

"So, I did it," Shoshonah said.

"Did what?"

"Saved up money. Paid off over half my loans. I'm coming home."

"To Vermont? Shosh, that's excellent! You'll visit me of course."

"I'm not staying for very long."

"What do you mean?" The fabric tore away from its cardboard backing, the thread sticking under her nails as evidence, and she stopped picking.

"I *mean*..." Shoshonah's let her voice trail off suspensefully. "That

11

I'mmm...

"What? What! *Dis*–moi."

"...Going to go...to *Amsterdam*."

Khatia frowned at the wall, her hand pausing on the small book.

"Is your mouth hanging? Do you look as if you have cocksucker's cramp?"

"Yummy! Talk about *my* mouth. No, it's not hanging open."

"I still want you to come with me."

Khatia shook her head.

"I know this is sudden. I won't be home for another week, but if *Aunt* Estella doesn't mind, I want to come see you to talk you into this, okay?"

"Shoshonah, not this again. I thought you had finally decided that was a bad idea."

"It's my dream, Khatia. I want you to be a part of it. We've done our year, now I think we're ready. We *deserve* this. I know you don't agree; you don't think you deserve anything."

"I don't."

Shoshonah ignored her and continued.

"That's why I called you first. I was going to just surprise you and cart you away, but I want to be fair."

Khatia could not answer.

"Come on. You aren't really that fond of your auntie. Nor your job. Nor America in general—"

"I've never been unpatriotic."

"Okay, okay. Maybe that's me. Look, I've got to go. The line for the phone is pretty long. I'll call you when I get back to Vermont. In about a week or so, if I can get the flight I want. Love you."

"Yeah," Khatia said, and then realized as she heard Shoshonah hanging up, that those words had not been spoken in almost a year by anyone in her close acquaintance. Love was not in her family's everyday vocabulary, not even as a quotidian superlative: "I just *love* bread–pudding with cinnamon ice cream." Her father spoke of a *fondness* for certain foods, books, even people. Love was serious business, and required a weighing out of the potential recipient's merits and faults. Even in correspondence they signed their letters "Always."

She listened to the dial tone for a moment, hanging up just before the recorded operator's voice came on the line.

The town of Bloomfield, New Jersey harbored some lovely parks, and she walked through them in the evenings and on weekends. Her father had found her this situation, living with her "Aunt" Estella, the woman who had played match–maker to her father's parents back in the late Twenties. Perhaps he had thought this ancient woman could be a substitute mother.

Shoshonah knew Khatia well: she did *not* feel ties to much of anything. Only to Shoshonah. And to her family, but sometimes she felt only because decency required it. Loving them was a strained affair. Was she evil incarnate for this? Convenience had brought her here. Convenience and the need to save money. To pay off the student loans. To obtain her keep. Her father called Estella's house once a week. If Khatia was not home, he received a full report from the lady of the house. Porter sporadically wrote her letters and postcards from his college in Rhode Island. These she did not mind. She worried about him, but that was duty too; they had never been close, and she wasn't sure if she liked him. He enjoyed the carelessness of *hubris*, spending more time with his guitar than any one person or book. His thoughts would lose themselves in the music, in the concentration of one finger here, one there and one over there, to create harmony. She envied his simple acts of pleasure.

The summer night was pleasantly warm. She went back to the porch to await the August moon. Inside the house, the old lady snored; her bedroom window was on the porch. Khatia knew her lace curtains fluttered because of slight breezes lifting off the day's humidity, but she liked to imagine the old woman's breath lifted them the slight distance, curling the fan–like folds into the stale air. Nothing could possibly stir this town to life, especially not its coppery residents.

"You can choose any of the upstairs rooms, my dear," Aunt Estella had told her when she moved in as her companion. "And make all the noise you like. These walls and floors are as solid as the wax in my ears."

13

Khatia thought of suggesting an ear wax museum à la *The Fanman,* but didn't think the old lady would appreciate it.

She chose the largest room with the most sunlight. It had once been Estella's, and her parents' before that. Cracked window panes and peeling paint: the ambiance of a college co–op, except her only roommate was a geriatric. Khatia did nothing to repair these small details except to hang up a cotton batik spread depicting monkeys dancing in trees. Posters covered up most of the other cracks. The decorations were incongruous with the rest of the house. Its Queen Anne grandeur was lost in her post–dormitory touches. At any moment she chose, she could reach up, tear down the crumpled pictures, water–starved house plants, and leave without any trace of ever living there.

It was an odd mix of transience and stagnation, pervasive even in normal, daily activities. Every morning, she got on the train with all the other commuters, steeling themselves for the fifty–minute train ride to Manhattan. Did they also become submerged in a tide of despair as the alarm clock went off at five–thirty A.M. each day? Did they shudder when the shower water stung their skin with its initial blast? Did they sigh as they munched on a bagel and cream cheese, hoping for a seat next to a person who had a relationship with anti–perspirant, and who would not use their shoulder as a pillow? Did they feel the actual physical life being drained away, the color in their hairs, the suppleness of their calves, as a round–trip of one hundred minutes, five days a week left them exhausted and confused, hopeless for any kind of change? Overwhelming dread came over Khatia almost every-day of her life. And yet, as if paralyzed, she went through it all without hardly any complaints. Like a trooper. She did it because she had to.

Drinking her small bottle of red wine, she celebrated. For one whole year she had lived with this old woman in her decrepit house, dining with her, watching TV with her, driving her to the mall on the weekends. And for one whole year, she had been with the law firm of Putnam, Shelding, Crofford, Sythe, & Fong as a junior paralegal. For some reason, even though a year had passed, the higher–ups had not changed her subordinate title. She had proven her efficacy, yet in all the legal red tape, her "paperwork" was still not processed.

Tonight, she finally admitted to herself that she did not care. Maybe had never cared. Shoshonah's call only strengthened her resolve. As usual, Shoshonah gave her seedling thoughts a crack in the sidewalk, sunlight, and

14

droplets of rain from which to bloom.

How she had survived this long, she did not know. Before she left work each evening, she stood in the women's washroom, running her hands under the hot water, soaping them up five times. The sting of the anti–bacterial liquid soap was like a panacea on her paper cuts. She tried to rid her hands of the smell of old law books and files, a smell of bookworm decay. But the smell was like that of onions or garlic cloves or Shoshonah's fish, as permanent as the sky. She would get off the train, ride her bicycle or walk the mile and a half back to Estella's house, and try again, soaking her fingers in soapy water until the tips shriveled like fresh chestnut meat.

Hadn't she been one of the lucky ones? How many of her peers, one year after graduating from college, could present their salaries to the ubiquitous judges of achievement (often, these deities took the form of parental figures) and say they were earning an income in the low thirties? Who else had health, dental, and life insurance? Who else had a 401K plan?

One week. When she first arrived at the firm of Putnam, Shelding, Crofford, Sythe, & Fong, she thought for sure she would only last one week there. But she ignored this because she was good at ignoring. All that first day, she wanted to throw up and give in to the receptionist's "confidential" offer of Zoloft. The gray–haired senior paralegal, Miss Walker, had droned on and on about filings, cite–checking, billing...Khatia became paralyzed with the sudden predictability of her future. It was obvious in the flesh and bones of this woman before her. At some point, this woman had to have been young and vibrant. She had to have thought more would happen in her life.

Or perhaps not. Perhaps working in this law office, pouring over dusty books, databases, receiving barked orders from self–important lawyers was everything Miss Walker needed to forge ahead. Optional pleasures lay in the realms of past–times or hobbies, and in the bare essentials of sleeping, eating, and breathing, and these may not have given her the rush that work did. If one could claim contentment in *one* of life's facets, Khatia decided that person must hold the key to self–fulfillment. Rationalizing: this came out of ignorance.

Listening to Miss Walker, following her around the firm's multi–level maze of offices, cubicles, and supply rooms, Khatia's body made itself aware

15

to her. Her control top pantyhose pinched at her stomach. Wearing them was like wearing a jockstrap: they were useless for her, since she was not fat. But they were the only ones without a run she could find in her drawer that morning. She wanted to scratch her crotch, loosen her collar, sit without crossing her legs.

"What am I doing, what am I doing?" she had murmured to herself in the ladies room on the second day. Hopelessness seemed to thrive in this place of money and deals. She felt sad for these people, even the lawyers. They took pleasure in their possessions, in their skills of oration and manipulation. But they did not belong outside of these walls, forty stories in the air. They did not belong on the banks of a river, sipping the water, spreading mud over their naked ankles just for sheer sensuality. She did not belong with them. Yet, she stayed.

Who was she to judge?

"What do you want?" Shoshonah had asked her this question many times while they were in college, as they lay naked, wrapped in blankets and sleeping bags under the bridge of their school's picturesque lake where no one else dared to go because of the legendary ghosts of suicided students. Khatia would often answer, "A kiss," or "World peace." But one time, perhaps they had been drinking wine, she answered selfishly: "I want to be recognized. I want the respect of strangers. I know I can get respect from my family and friends. But a bias always lies there: You all love me because you have to. Of course you would be proud of me, no matter what piddling job I get. I want to figure out where I belong. If it's worth all this."

Shoshonah did not bother to ask what "it" was. She nodded, and Khatia watched the wheels in her mind turning, probably wondering where she fit in Khatia's abstractions. "How are you going to get those things?" she finally asked.

Khatia shrugged, keeping her shoulders up and stiff. "I don't know. I don't know. I don't know."

In the law library, in the file room, in the lunch room, she looked at her supervisor almost everyday, and Khatia would sniff for signs of life: bird calls, dirty jokes, spring flowers. Nothing. Just White Shoulders, moth balls, and coffee breath. Khatia stayed away from coffee, not grown up enough to enjoy its bitter taste. She had avoided that addiction in college. About once a month, she would treat herself to a mocha with lots of whipped cream, anticipating the sleepless, jittery hours to follow as if she were committing some deplorable sin. She stopped herself once after exiting a café with her drink, the heat from the paper cup burning through her gloves to the skin of her fingertips. So, this was it forever: reckless abandon awaited in the matter of caffienated foods. She pondered the sky as she stood outside the café, looking forward to its darkening, that time when she could close her eyes, and there was no difference between what she saw behind her lids, and what she saw in front of her body.

If the Real World meant recirculated air vents and fluorescent lighting, it was not for her, and she was not for it.

Yet, she stayed.

It was partly Shoshonah's doing.

Fifteen months before, she and Shoshonah had graduated from college. Their parents had met for the first time, none of them suspecting that their daughters were actually lovers and had been for almost two years.

They met during their freshman year in the spring, playing on the lacrosse team. Most of her young life, Khatia was a loner, reading a book during recesses and lunch hours, usually on French art or history. Something about her kept most other children away. Girls liked to gossip and flirt, but Khatia could not bring herself to join in these sorts of activities. Snobbishness to a degree, but mostly fear made her avoid them as they stood around the monkey bars, tossing their blond hair, casting glances in the direction of the boys playing kickball. She would watch them until her gaze blurred, and they became no more than a pointillist painting.

In high school, she stayed in the ceramics studio, throwing bowls and mugs on the wheel. The glazes and slips she preferred were aquas, deep blues, and pale whites. Most of these she gave away to people she admired. They usually did not know where the gifts came from. Her mother was the school librarian, and Khatia would slip her big ring of keys out of her purse at night, sneak away down the road on her ten–speed, and prowl around the private school while the boarding students in the residence halls slept. She could leave the bowl or mug in a gym locker or on a person's homeroom desk. Her only friend, more of an acquaintance, was a girl named Bianca, the daughter of her mother's good friend, Meredith. They did not go to the same high school, since Khatia and her brother could go to the private school for free. "Faculty brats," Bianca called them. "Townie," Khatia would reply. The girls rarely saw each other, unless their mothers were doing lunch and brought the daughters along. They would gossip politely, be good for their mothers, and wish to be somewhere else.

The only place that offered comfort for her in large groups was team play. Because she was small, Khatia was the coxswain for her high school rowing team. In this environment, she could pretend to be a social animal. Along with the others, she swore as they jogged at least two miles a day, did fifty crunches without stopping, and rowed innumerable miles. She used her voice—that's why they needed her; she could be loud, yelling in the rhythm of "Stroke! Stroke! Stroke!"

She joined in the back–slapping, elbow ribbing, getting tossed into the lake. Good, clean fun. They called her Kat; everyone had nicknames. Somehow, hers did not stick. They knew when it was time to leave her alone, when she stared out over the lake, watching the sky turn crimson–orange, the color of fishermen's nets.

Four African–American students attended the Milford Academy. They stuck together. So did the nine or so Asian students. Once, a teammate said Khatia was mysterious because she was "Oriental." Khatia had tried to laugh the comment off, but instead she felt shame for being such an obvious weirdo. An anomaly. The others were distinct because they could blend. Most people did not even know she was Asian; they always guessed Italian or Spanish, something olive and tawny, yet of European descent. As soon as they found out she was a quarter Chinese, they seemed to be relieved: That's why you're such an odd bird. She longed to be like the other girls: unmoody, laughing, full of simple truth. But she was not like them at all.

Her college was all women, but that did not mean much to Khatia. In college, she decided, she would recreate herself, and headed straight for team–play. She did not make the rowing team in the fall, so she tried lacrosse in the spring, keeping to herself in the meantime. Her roommate told others that Khatia was immature. She spent most of her spare time at the library; it reminded her of her mother.

The lacrosse coach put her on the team—barely. Her awkward, knobbed knees cranked her across the playing field, and even though her running was not a pretty sight, the coach must have found beauty in her furrowed determination, in the fact that she did not get loudly mad when things did not go her way.

Shoshonah played forward, and she was a star, recruited by the college because of her prowess in field hockey, basketball, and lacrosse. She struck a remarkable figure, an Amazon with slender legs and a zaftig profile. Her nipples protruded visibly through the material of the thickest athletic bra, and she wore her long blond hair in a thick braid. Her mother was a New York Jew, her father a Vermont gentleman–dairy farmer of mixed Nordic descent, and they had met at Tufts. She often laughed, called to her team–mates in a high–pitched voice, the adrenaline of practice turning her into a ruthless yet cheerful banshee. She was what was called a born leader, and even Khatia felt her pull.

"Come on, Quigles!" Shoshonah would yell as Khatia lunged gracelessly about after the opposition. "Get out of your head!"

Simple words, but they made Khatia feel light as air, as if her knees were not weighing her down. "What," she would call back. "And get into yours?"

Khatia found herself laughing high, actually reveling in being an odd– duck.

They were roommates the next year, and after two months, Shoshonah revealed she was gay. Khatia spent a lot of time at the library again, twisting her repulsion and fear around and around as she twisted her hair around her finger. No wonder Shoshonah's best friend from home, Lauren, was always there on the weekends, or Shosh at her college. Khatia would return at midnight when the library closed. They slept in bunk beds, Khatia on top. She would lie awake in bed, trying not to move too much.

The passage of time, as it often does, took away most of Khatia's initial shock and aversion. They continued as if everything were okay, and it was. Khatia aspired to be a liberalist; socialism appealed to her. She relaxed, and life clipped along. They were monogamous in friendship. Being close to someone was new to her. Shoshonah was curious; she asked Khatia questions about being Chinese, and Khatia found she could not answer them. They enrolled in a Classical Chinese Poetry class, reading Li Po to each other. Shouting phrases like, "Cranes on the wind—Mountains reach the sky!" in unison during lacrosse practice.

They did not know people envied them.

The next year, when Khatia was a junior, her father announced he was leaving the family. Her mother beat him to it, dying of cancer that winter.

One balmy night, in the spring, Khatia picked a fight with Shoshonah: Shosh had recently broken off her affair with Lauren, deciding she wanted to see other women, play the field for a while. Morose Khatia: her mother had been dead less than two months. She hated carefree people, was sure she was the only person on the planet cognizant of futility.

The night was hot; she should leave, go for a walk, but she was too irritated to open the door of their room.

As she sat on her bunk, she crossed her arms over her chest, picked a topic out of the air for the way it sounded, and said "I don't have any friends."

"You have me," Shoshonah said, laughing.

"One friend."

"You have Nutmeg and Floog and Cork and Tricia."

"We just play on the same team, that's why. They're nice to everyone." She thought of something else. "And they're all women."

"Well," Shoshonah said, and Khatia could hear her rolling her eyes. "We go to a women's college. And you don't seem to like to go off campus very much. I always tell you we could go to a party in Amherst or at Hampshire, but you just like to stay in the dorm and get drunk on the weekends like the rest of us."

That was the truth. She couldn't remember the last time she had been off campus. Maybe it was two weeks ago when she went to the shopping center across the street to cash her work–study paycheck, but that did not really count since the college owned a good portion of the center's shares.

If only someone would take a piece of her misery. Maybe then she would feel the world lift away and forget about her.

"Those people are all your friends anyway. You knew them first. Besides, they make me feel a little uncomfortable."

"Why?"

Khatia shrugged. "You know."

"What are you talking about?"

20

Khatia swung her legs over the side of her mattress and jumped to the floor. Shoshonah was busy drawing doodles on her Spanish homework. She looked up.

"I just don't want your queer friends hanging around our room all the time," Khatia said. "They're your friends, not mine, and when I see all of you together, and think about the things you like to do, it makes me a little nauseated."

Shoshonah stared, frozen, as if Khatia had suddenly developed a giant boil on her nose.

Nothing had lifted off Khatia's head as she had hoped.

Shoshonah stood up, unfolding her legs and arms like a gift–wrapped present. Khatia knew she could be crushed and she closed her eyes, searching for apologetic words. But they had flown away, hidden behind the corners, and now laughed mockingly at her. This is not my fault, she thought. This is what grief does. Grief uses you, so I use grief.

Shoshonah took Khatia's hand and put it on something soft and firm. Then she put something warm and slightly moist on Khatia's lips. For a moment, she thought it was a stewed grape, unbearably sweet, almost ready to burst from its skin. She realized it was Shoshonah's mouth. Khatia opened her eyes. Shoshonah held Khatia's hand to her breast. She closed her eyes again.

Making love with a woman was like shaving her legs without soap. She did not know how else to describe it. Sexy. Dangerous. Mildly painful. A burning smell. She was surprised to discover that Shoshonah's insides did not smell like her own. Whoever said lesbian love was like licking a mirror was very wrong: Shoshonah's body was nothing like her own. She had seen it naked a million times, but never had she *seen* it. Somehow, she had known she could love this woman, as good as a sister.

Khatia toasted the moon finally, as her mind filled with images from each subset of her existence, tumbling into a frenzied dance of characters: a three–year old version of her brother Porter held hands with a boat–bound, imagined version of Shoshonah. A faded, brown and white photo–image of Estella from the 1920's did the Charleston through the cubicles of the law office. Khatia raked her fingers through her hair, imagining the people in her head

21

were lice, and she could catch them under her fingernails, scrape them away into the trash bin. She gave into the images, extracting one participant from the other, arranging them in their proper places.

Well, well.

She tossed back the last of the wine, pretending to her imaginary, sophisticated self that she liked the sour taste.

Chapter Two

Occasionally, Khatia pretended she was someone else. For her twenty–first birthday, Porter gave her a sketch pad. It was a last minute gift; he handed it to her in a plastic WalMart bag, the receipt floating around inside. She used the book to draw designs for ceramics. She wrote down interesting word definitions from the dictionary and immediately forgot them. Once she wrote, "I try to separate my love for Shoshonah and my attraction to men. I keep telling myself, you love the person, not the sex, the *person*, not the sex. In general, it's okay for a woman to love another woman, but is it okay for *me* to love a woman?" The book turned into a sort of journal, filled with her woes.

Telling her father or brother about Shoshonah did not occur to her, until Shoshonah brought up the fact that her own parents thought she was straight. Khatia's family did not speak of such things.

Their relationship was real so long as they stayed in the protective shell of their campus. To their families, they were merely close friends. She could not tell anyone. Shoshonah, on the other hand, talked to anything, people, rocks, birds, and all their teammates knew of them as a couple. But it went as far as that and no further. At first, Khatia told herself, "This is an experiment." She would always be Shoshonah's friend.

They had graduated together from the small women's college nestled in a town that straddled a state route. Their families met for the first time, sharing an awkward graduation lunch full of silences and stuttered words. The recently widowed professor Quigley on one side of the table and the owners of a burgeoning Vermont ice cream shop on the other. What could they have in common? Only that which they did not know: their daughters were in love.

Shoshonah's brothers were masculine versions of their younger sister. She knew all four of them were in steady heterosexual relationships, and that none of them knew about their sister's preference for women. Neither did her parents. They probably suspected. How could they not? Shoshonah, a beautiful young woman who never spoke to them about dating men, who hardly left her college campus except to sit in the café across the street and drink mochas while doing her homework with her roommate, who spent *all* her time with that roommate, another woman.

For the first time, as she sat at the luncheon table and listened to Shoshonah's father describe the process of authenticating his own version of Rocky Road(Pebbly Path), Khatia surprised herself with the wish that Shoshonah were a man. How odd, she thought. What had happened to the experiment of loving a woman? The savory jeopardy? When had they become so serious? Shoshonah had broken up with her first girlfriend to date other women. Instead, she fell immediately into another steady relationship. The experiment was over for both of them.

After the lunch, her father and Porter went back to their hotel to wait for Khatia. The Carters were ready to leave immediately, but they respectfully waited for Shoshonah at the student union so the young women could say their last good–byes in the room they shared. As they sat together for the final time, Khatia closed her eyes. Her stockings, like a hairshirt, rubbing against the bare mattress. Red–orange bursts of colors faded in and out behind her lids like sunsets. Sadness became physical, not in the way of crying and mourning. Not in the gut–wrenchings a death brought on. She could watch this pain, separate from herself, yet tied by some faint thread, barely tugging at her. Something whispered, *Let it all go.*

The room was bare of everything except their last suitcases and the furniture that belonged in it. Finally, Khatia thought. After this whole, long day we can hold hands. Outside, the campus was like a ghost town. Most students and their families had left already. The college was architecturally lovely, classically New England: brick buildings laced with ivy. Old, old trees—oaks, hemlocks, birch.

Don't go.

"What?" Khatia broke the silence.Shoshonah looked up from her lap where Khatia's hand rested in hers.

"I didn't say anything."

"Oh. I thought you said, 'Don't go.'"

She smiled. "You're starting to read my mind."

24

"Uh–oh," Khatia said. "Are we going to be able to communicate telepathically? Shit."

"You won't be able to get me out of your head," she whispered in a witchy voice. "Ever!"

"Then you won't be able to get rid of me, either."

"Well, damn."

They fell silent again. Khatia rubbed her thumb on Shoshonah's finger, worrying.

"Khatia, I want to tell you something." Shoshonah gently removed her hand as she always did when Khatia's habit started to chafe it.

"I've finally made a decision."

"What kind of decision?"

"About what I'm going to do after I go home."

Khatia waited, alarmed, suddenly picturing them together in New York. But they had agreed—

"I've always kind of regretted that we didn't go abroad for our junior year."

Khatia nodded.

"I mean, our year together was great, and who knows where we'd be if we hadn't gotten together, but I really think we should do some traveling before it's too late. I mean, *really* too late."

"Such urgency. 'Before it's too late.'"

Shoshonah looked out the window at the dying daylight. Khatia traced her profile with her eyes, wanting to remember her friend's outline at that moment. Later, she would lie in her girlhood bed at home, and she would redraw it.

"I'm going to do it," Shoshonah said. Her body stiffened a little as she spoke, the way she stiffened when a lacrosse stick flew towards her body. Embattled, perched on combat.

Khatia answered, "So go." She cracked the knuckles of her fingers. "There's nothing to stop you now. You don't want to come with me to

New York City, and we've already agreed that would be the best thing."
She sighed and could not help mumbling, "It's not as if you *couldn't* try to
get a job teaching chemistry in that private school that offered you a position as their basketball coach *in addition to*—"

"That's just something I thought I wanted," Shoshonah replied, hearing
her. "To work with ungracious children for a pittance in a city with an
exorbitant cost of living index. Can you imagine? It would be like working
in some office job." She said it as if she had said, "It would be like working
in a pile of baby shit."

"Thank you very much."

"Khatia."

"Look, Shosh. You're going to leave in ten minutes. Let's not fight,
okay? Let's just promise we'll write to each other, and miss each other, and
be as faithful as we can be. Does that sound good?"

"I want you to come with me."

"To Vermont?"

"No," she said in a voice one used with a developmentally deficient child.
"To Amsterdam."

"Amsterdam."

"Yes. That's where I want to go."

"To Amsterdam," Khatia murmured. Looking up at the blank wall, she
asked, "Why Amsterdam? You want to get legally stoned?"

"It's not legal there, you fool." She nudged Khatia's shoulder. "It's just
de–regulated. And no, that's not why I want to go there. I could just as
easily get stoned here."

"Then why?" Khatia looked at Shoshonah's face, flushed and beautiful.
She actually seemed embarrassed.

"I've never told anyone this," she said. "So, you have to promise not to
tell, okay?"

"No, you can't trust me. Am I the one who tells everyone we're lovers?"
Shoshonah did not notice her sarcasm. Khatia forced herself to bite back
any other words.

26

"Even though my hometown is a pretty cool place, I mean, you know, *liberal,* there aren't a lot of lesbians that are out. At least, when I was in high school I wasn't aware of them. So when I was first attracted to other girls, I thought I was totally abnormal. And I really didn't have anyone to turn to, except for maybe Ms. Richards, my gym teacher." Shoshonah chuckled. "She had short hair so everyone said she was a dyke."

Khatia waited.

"Anyway, I was at the library one night, researching a term paper. I was taking a break, looking at magazines, and I saw this article in *National Geographic* on Amsterdam." She paused and looked at Khatia sideways.

"Well, I don't know if this is true or not, but I got it stuck in my head that sex changes were done fairly easily, legally I mean, and without people laughing at you I guess, in Amsterdam. I became completely obsessed with the idea that that's what was wrong with me: I had been born the wrong sex!"

Khatia waited.

"I went home from the library and thought about it all night, about how I *had* to get to Amsterdam somehow. That was my first experience with insomnia too."

"They do those operations here you know."

"Yeah, they do. But that really isn't the point."

"So, what is?"

Shoshonah did not answer right away as she struggled to find the words, her lips working over them silently.

"It's hard to explain. I was fifteen! I guess it was my romantic, adolescent notion of going to Europe, like Daisy Miller, and becoming...transformed."

"Literally," she said. But she understood. She used to dream about going to Paris, meeting a French boy, purring perfect, witty French sentences through pouty, glossy lips to him in the Louvre, cooing facts to him about the Venus de Milo, Mona Lisa, Winged Victory.

Shoshonah lay back on the bed. "I know better now; I don't want a penis." Khatia felt a shiver between her shoulder blades as she remembered her thoughts from lunch. She realized she did not want Shoshonah to have a penis either. If she had one, she would just be another one of the Carter

27

boys and not Shoshonah, a lovely, sort of androgynous being.

"I'm glad." Khatia put her arms around her, and they settled easily into each other. "There are enough penises in the world."

"Come with me, Khatia," she said into her neck.

"I can't," she replied without thinking.

"Yes you can. We could get jobs teaching English."

"Everyone there already speaks English."

"We could get jobs waitressing or being au pairs. Anything! I don't care. I want you there with me."

"Shosh, I have to pay off my loans—"

"Lame!" she pulled away from Khatia. "Lame excuse."

"We agreed to separate!"

"I change my mind."

"You change your mind." Khatia threw up her hands and then buried her face in them, concentrating on the feel of her sharp elbow bones digging into the tops of her thigh muscles. "That's just fabulous."

"Why do we need to separate? Why? Give me one good reason."

Khatia could think of a thousand reasons, all good, but at the moment, sensibility was not in her grasp. Resisting Shoshonah's dramatic enthusiasm proved difficult: *Let us discourse, let us discord, let us argue, let us brave the storm of grown–up possibilities.*

"Khatia," she said in a calm but urgent voice: hurry, hurry, push, push, push. "No matter what I want for us, I think you need this."

Khatia stood up and paced. She often paced when feeling confused or ornery. Going for walks was often just a long pace for her.

"*I* need this. What? I need to go to Europe? What for? To *find* myself? To cliché?"

"Well, yeah, sort of. You've never really liked yourself. I mean, most people I know who put themselves down are actually arrogant bastards looking for some strokes. But when you're mean to yourself you are *mean*."

Khatia stopped pacing and looked at her.

"Well," she said. "Thank you, Ms. Al–Anon."

"Come on, Khatia."

"No, you're the one who needs Twelve Step. Wanting me to go to Amsterdam with you so you can co–depend on me. Don't you have the balls to go by yourself? Didn't we talk months ago about it being good and healthy for us to have time apart?"

Shoshonah did not answer. Her shoulders were slumped. Khatia almost felt relief; this exasperation was familiar: Shoshonah's emotions equaled an angel/devil jack–in–the–box, lit–up and wicked, a mixture of delight and unpredictability. And then the dark mood. Khatia nervously kept turning her friend's crank, waiting to see which face would pop up next. Like hawks, they had always been that way together, circling and circling.

Someone knocked at the door.

"Shosh, you about ready?" It was Alex, Shoshonah's gorgeous brother who made his living as a model, the youngest of the boys and a year older than his sister.

"Yeah," she answered. "I'll be downstairs in two minutes."

"Okay." They heard him walk off.

Shoshonah stood up and stretched. Her belly was exposed for a minute, tight and muscular. She put on her coat.

"You may be right," she said quietly,."About me wanting to co–depend on you. And I may be selfish in wanting you to go with me. But I am going to go to Amsterdam when I get enough money saved, and I wanted you to know that I want you with me. I've been thinking about it for a long time, and I don't think—honestly, I don't—that we need separation. And I do think this trip would be good for you."

"Good for me like good for Daisy Miller?" Khatia risked looking at Shoshonah's mouth. It smiled.

"Yeah, Khatia. Maybe you'll get consumption."

"Consumed by what?"

They laughed. And then they kissed. One last, long kiss.

29

"Call me, okay?" She brushed Khatia's hair away from her cheek.

"Okay."

After she was gone, Khatia sat down on the bed and cried. Big ripping sobs.

They saw each other one more time that summer, after Khatia had moved to the house in Bloomfield. Aunt Estella raised her eyebrows when Shoshonah said she would stay in Khatia's room instead of one of the other bedrooms.

Two months later, Shoshonah had left her family in Vermont. Her indignant mother phoned Khatia, demanding an explanation: Shoshonah was in Alaska, working on fishing boats and canning factories. Khatia could not tell them anything. She was just as surprised.

Shoshonah wrote to her after a week had gone by. She had turned down a job offer with Teach for America in Los Angeles. "I simply could not be tied down for two years. I'm giving myself a year, Khatia, to get most of my loans paid off. Then I'm headed for Europe. I'll be around to collect you next summer. Get ready."

And now it was all coming true.

Chapter Three

Sunlight has not yet poured into the room, yet John Porter Quigley is already awake. He blinks for a while to moisten his eyeballs, fixing his gaze first on one ceiling fixture, then another, his eyes traveling around the corners of the familiar room. He chose those scrolled flutings when the contractors built the house nearly thirty years ago in the New Hampshire countryside. At the time Annie protested that they were too fanciful for the farmhouse–look they were trying to achieve, but he insisted. He sketched out the dimensions himself for the man, the Italianate feathers and leaves. He wanted cherubs, but the price was too heady.

Today, his daughter will come home.

He turns to the clock, sees that it reads four twenty–two. For a man of his age, sleeplessness is normal. He goes to bed at ten, wakes up at twelve, reads for an hour, and then falls asleep again, usually until dawn, just as the light is breaking through the pale shade, illuminating it into a warm, eggy yellow. As it has since his Army days, the sun enables him to swing his legs over the side of the bed, put on his running shoes, and jog the two and three–quarter miles from his front door to the base of the fork in the road. One tine goes up the small hill, and the other keeps going on the flat, past the Rolands' orchard. He takes neither one, although he used to, turns back and across the road, careful to stay away from the convex curb leading into snow gutters, dead leaves, and animal feces.

Late August. Breaking, swelling air that sometimes turns to rain. The sun rises early, although it starts to taper off at this time of year. Something subtle, but he would notice. Perhaps that is why he wakes in darkness this morning. Perhaps his body is not adjusted to the change of light just yet.

After jogging, he usually takes a shower, puts on regular clothes, and takes coffee, a banana, and a scone into his study. At the present, he is working on a proposal. Five years ago, he was the director–in–residence of a student exchange program between his school and a government–run program in

Russia. Annie went with him, taking a sabbatical from the Academy. He hopes to go again, and although the Russian board of directors has more than assured him that he is their favorite candidate, he still must go through the formalities: writing essays, sending references, interviewing. He is almost sixty–five; they should know his capabilities by now.

He gets out of bed and puts on his shorts and shoes. Scratches at the scar burned across his flat pectoral muscles. Any cars on the road will see him because of all the reflective material the manufacturers put on athletic gear these days. He shines like a piece of aluminum foil when halogen lights hit the stripe on his tanktops, the triangles on his shorts, the almost ineffectual juliennes on the heels and toes of his high performance runner's shoes. No one should reasonably hit him.

As he gets into his clothes, he coughs, feeling the give of nylon mesh around the stiffness of the sewn–on reflectors.

Outside, nothing stirs except a heavy breeze. It causes him to bite at the insides of his cheeks, scraping downwards until his teeth clop dully together as if coated by some candied enamel. He stretches and then runs down the gravel drive, familiar with every dip and rise, pushing forward with assurance despite the darkness.

The air stays laden and does not cool anything, except for the crevices of him. He feels relief in the wings of his nostrils, between his first and second finger, and the fold of his earlobe against his head. His muscles are hard, but his skin has turned supple like a woman's.

The road lies unmysteriously before him, protected in the curve of trees, which apex into a pinpoint tunnel, both light and dark. He runs towards that point, trying to decide if white dominates black in his vision. The trees are ostrich feathers on a lady's hat overhead, the wings of Catholic angels, closing like horns, building a tunnel with no connecting rafters, held up despite gravity and the laws of physics, laws he used to understand, but has long ceased to care about.

He knows his daughter will be there some time soon. She has not called or written. She hardly ever does, unless he has called first. Usually, she would call before coming home, but this time she will not. She will walk up the drive, or perhaps take a taxi. She will have her bags with her, and an explanation for the impudence of her actions. Long ago, she learned how to talk at a slant, to say what needed to be communicated without any revela-

32

tions. Perhaps he instructed her in this through example, behavior adopted from his military days. Most likely, she absorbed it unconsciously from her mother, a certain reticence passed through the placenta twenty–four years ago.

He returns home, panting more than usual. He must pause at the kitchen door. Lifting one leg up onto the first step, he feels the energy that he needed before, trapped somewhere in the doorjamb he leans against. The sky is beginning to lighten into that blue of dawn, still dark, yet distinguishable in its lack of an element important to the day.

Because he is her father, and it is his duty, he has taught Khatia what to be.

Chapter Four

"Happy to see me?"

"Of course."

Shoshonah looked out the window and then back at Khatia. She smiled wide as she reached over to nuzzle Khatia's ear. She had been there for three days, but still needed the reassurances of Khatia, demanding kind words.

"I missed you. Do you know how much?"

Khatia rolled her eyes to the ceiling. "As much as the sun and moon and stars?"

"My, but you're astronomical."

"And you're my mariner's compass." She fluttered her eyelashes.

Shoshonah curled against her body, wrapping her heavy limbs around Khatia's small ones. Her muscles were more defined from all the hard, manual labor she had become accustomed to on the high seas. The food provided on the ship was hardy and spare compared to the rich, greasy college dining hall food.

"Oh you," Shoshonah said, her eyes moving everywhere on Khatia's face.

Khatia did not answer, breathing in the warm air of afternoon. In two hours, she would borrow Aunt Estella's antiquated Jaguar to take Shoshonah to the train station so she could go back to Vermont and begin preparations for her big trip.

Their big trip? Shoshonah talked about it as if Khatia were going as well. She tempted Khatia with the promise of art museums, cathedrals almost older than Christianity, and freedom. Her words were like a bout with tunnel vision, the only truthful image.

How much had they really missed each other? Was love measured in what a person gave you? What did Shoshonah really give her, what did she give Shoshonah, and how much of it?

"Tell me more about fishing."

Shoshonah spread her body on the bed into a heavy arrow.

"Out of Bristol Bay I worked on a gill netting boat. The fish get caught in this nine hundred foot gill net, not really that big compared to some nets, if you think about it. Their gills get caught in the hole of the net so they can't move. Then we close it up and let them fall out on the deck of the boat. It's a sad way to go."

"Why? Do you club them the death or something?" Khatia rolled over on her side, one hand cupped under the curve of her own belly, its hot warmth against her cooled fingernails.

"No. It's salmon, and they need to keep swimming to live. They need to be moving or they die. Of course, getting trapped in the gill nets, they can't move. Most are already dead when they hit the deck."

Khatia nodded, listening to her hair scrape against the pillow.

"That *is* a sad way to go," she said.

Shoshonah's departure held itself in the future like an unreleased breath. Khatia waited patiently for it. Sinking into the old patterns was so easy. The initial two days of hugging, touching, and falling into each others' eyes again had descended blissfully upon them. They caught up on what could not be communicated in letters and five minute long–distance phone conversations, telling stories in elaborate dramatizations, finding spontaneous, pertinent tangents from one story to the next. Shoshonah liked to use her arms when relating some of her Melvillian adventures. Pacing made Khatia feel in control of her words, her complaints having to do with the law office. She *had* missed this: sharing the frustration of her boring days puffed her up with satisfaction; not only could she tell Shoshonah what had happened when Miss Walker yelled at her, but also what she *would have* replied if she had thought of it in time. Deep down inside, Khatia knew she would never tell her boss off. Sharing imagined witticisms with Shoshonah was enough. As it had always been.

She was not used to talking since Shoshonah had left, and the words spilled forth in a smooth discord. Aunt Estella preferred a listener as a companion, and Khatia had grown accustomed to sitting mutely, sedately as she had always been until meeting Shoshonah. At work, the younger lawyers would ask her to listen to them so they could practice their oratory skills, and she would sit back, nodding and licking her lips: *Ah yes! Very good. Perhaps philanthropy is the word you are looking for, not perspicacity? No? Well, keep it. They sound similarly enough. It doesn't make much difference, you asshole.* She was not gregarious by nature, and Shoshonah always pushed her to share, share, share.

"Tell me again how much you missed me," Shoshonah said.

"Shoshonah," Khatia said with a small laugh, letting her irritation slip through just a little.

"Oh, come on, say it. Say it! Then, I promise, I'll be quiet."

"I missed you a lot."

"Only 'a lot?'"

"Come on."

"Okay, okay, I'll stop." Shoshonah closed her eyes, sighing into Khatia's hair. "No more separation. No more separation. But you *did* miss me. You did."

Chapter Five

Absence makes the heart grow fonder. Out of sight, out of mind.

Fourteen years ago.

"Which one do you think is true, Mommy?" Khatia once asked her mother as a child in the kitchen after school. She held up a mimeographed sheet to her. Mr. Winkelman, her fifth grade teacher, had assigned the students an essay. They were to choose one of the sayings and write why it was more true than the other one.

Khatia's mother tilted he chin down, blinking at the sheet for a while as she mixed some dough for bread or a pie crust.

"Hmmm…" she said. "Somewhere in between."

Khatia stared at the paper herself. Somewhere in between was not an option.

"What's that mean?" Khatia asked.

"It means that sometimes I think of people and I miss them, and sometimes I completely forget they exist."

"You don't ever remember?" Khatia asked.

Her mother shrugged in her accustomed, non–committal hunching. Her father said Annie Quigley held her posture in the shape of a question mark. It would have been funny if anybody laughed, but no one did, not even Khatia's father.

"Really, Mom," Khatia persisted, although she knew better than to expect a good answer. "How do you remember? Mr. Winkelman says our sense of smell is the best way we remember things."

Her mother shrugged again, but then her head went up. She looked out the kitchen window, the one where she kept her African violets. Porter was playing in front of their view on the gravel drive with a stick in the shape, more or less, of a pistol. He shot at imagined bad guys hundreds of yards off in the hay rolls.

"Whenever I smell sesame seed oil, I remember making wonton with my mother," Annie Quigley said. "She would sing an old song her *amah* taught her, about two silk worms who are in love." Her voice was far away, over the distance of three thousand miles and thirty–five years. A high soprano lifted into the space above Khatia, and she looked up at her mother's mouth. It was small and pursed. Khatia had inherited those lips, which she hated; they were hard for putting on a nice, thick coat of lipstick. She always had to build them up with her mother's lip–liner when she played dress up. She wanted lips like Bianca's, full and wide. Her hair too: long, blond Barbie doll hair.

But now she heard her mother's mouth instead of seeing it. The song filled the air, as if it were the only sound being produced in the world at that moment. The notes rose and fell in a strange staccato of rhythms, at once cacophonous and sweet. It was operatic jazz. Her father liked to listen to jazz in the car. At home, they listened to classical music. Khatia did not care about music very much. She did not understand why it sometimes made people cry in movies. Khatia cried when she did not get something she wanted, or when she fell down and hurt herself. She had seen Porter cry a lot, and once she saw a real grown–up cry, just standing there on the side-walk in Boston. Khatia had stared and stared, but her mother told her not to look, to keep walking, to keep her eyes averted, to pretend not to see; the lady was drunk or crazy, and probably slept on a doorstep. Khatia remem-bered her mouth, wide open and black, no pinkness at all. She couldn't remember the sound, just the tears and the black hollow of her mouth.

But now she heard a sweet song. There were no words to her mother's song, only sounds and gibberish. Khatia watched, wanting to remember the song forever, to be able to sing it too.

It ended abruptly. Annie still gazed out the window, her lips parted. Her eyes stayed wide–open. This was her usual look: surprise. You've startled your mother again, was another of John Quigley's favorite sayings.

"Can you teach that song to me, Mom?" Khatia asked in vain, she knew.

Her mother shook her head. "I can't."

"Is it a Chinese song?"

She nodded.

Khatia wanted to ask more questions. She knew very little about her mother's life before Khatia, about her mother's parents except that her grandma was white like their father, and her grandfather was Chinese.

What happened to the silk worms? What had her grandmother's wonton tasted like? Were they like the ones in that restaurant in Cambridge? *What was an amah?* Bianca's mom always said Annie was Milford's oriental–expert–in–residence, to which Annie shook her head and waved her hands as if fanning a terrible fart away. "I don't know anything, Meredith," she would say, reddening in blotches all over her already strangely tinged skin. Was that true? Was Annie an expert in something besides dusty, crumbling books at the snobby high school down the road? She would not know. Not even fourteen years later.

Excessive questioning in the Quigley household was considered rude. Unless they had company, which they rarely did, questions did not really have a place. If one wished, one could volunteer information. This was something she knew inherently now, although she forgot how she had learned it. The telling of a story, however, was seen as near bragging, and, therefore, conversations in Khatia's home were rather limited.

Still, Khatia sensed that her mother wanted to tell. And Khatia wanted to ask. She looked up at her mother, wishing she had never started this—what had seemed innocent discourse. Getting something she did not know she wanted—but sensed she needed—frightened her in to a state of embarrassment and surliness.

Annie looked down at her daughter, smiling, her eyebrows turning down the way most people's mouths turned down in sadness. Her eyes were bright, as if they were moist. She was always complaining about how dry they were, and could only wear her contact lenses for five hours a day. She lay in her dark bedroom for at least one hour each afternoon whether she slept or not.

"Mom?" Khatia said and emboldened herself for the moment. "When will we go to San Francisco and see your mom?"

Annie Quigley looked away from her eldest, her mouth set in a line.

Olivia Boler

"Go wash up," she said. "And you can help me mash the bananas for the bread."

Chapter Six

"We used to make banana bread together." She told Shoshonah this after her mother died. "I wish we had made wonton."

But Milford, New Hampshire was a town imbued with Americana—apple pie, not Chinese soup dumplings. She could feel it as she passed through its streets on the way to her father's house, the house in which she had grown up.

"Mom, have you read Li Po?" Khatia asked her mother one time when she was home for Spring Break.

"Who?" her mother said.

"Never mind."

"Miss Waters actually took the news rather well." Khatia twisted a tissue around and around between her fingers, feeling the tension in the frail paper cloth, the slight loosening of fibers that would soon become a tear. "I mean, she knew I couldn't stay there forever."

Outside, the interior lights of the house fell in slanting rectangles on the ground. She could see the spot where Porter, at about age five, used to claim he was going to dig a hole to China and shake hands with all their relatives. This was after he became cognizant of the fact his mother was half–Chinese, when his teacher had told him that he had roots not only in Europe, but in a *foreign* country as well.

"What kind of name is Chew, anyway?" he asked his mother one day, grumpy and tired from school work or a fight with other boys in the playground. He forever had bruises and bandaids as a result of boyhood skirmishes.

Porter, her quirky, elfin brother. He would stand under the largest oak on their property holding a yellow plastic shovel from his beach bucket, and Khatia would say to him in a snotty voice, "Well, how are you gonna get

41

around all the roots, dumbass?" Porter would ignore her; they usually ignored one another. He would practice his greetings: "Hello, my mother is Annie Chew Quigley. Do you know the Chews? You do? Yes, I'd like some tea, thank you." Or, he would sing, spinning around the yard until their father forbid it: "My grandma is married to a Chinaman in San Francisco!"

Grandmother: grandma. Grandfather: Chinaman.

Her father stood next to the opposite counter in the kitchen with his dour look. He had been stirring milk into his evening tea for the past few minutes as Khatia told him she was going to Amsterdam with Shoshonah. She watched him, trying not to focus on the way he stood, legs supporting his weight equally, his left hand hanging loosely at his side. Only the night–light above the stove was on. Being in the darkness with her father made her uncomfortable, and she walked over to the light switch, the fluorescent glare illuminating their faces. Her father looked pale, and the hollows of his cheek bones curved into recesses, giving the illusion of mud smears, a warrior's paint.

"Amsterdam," he finally said, shocking her with his usual quiet, gruff tone.

"Yes," she said.

"A fine city. I was there twenty–six, maybe twenty–seven years ago. Maybe longer. Your mother enjoyed it as well."

"Mom went with you?"

"Of course, of course. We'd been to Western Europe a couple of times before you and your brother were born. Your mother had a sort of parochial love affair with European cities. The libraries of the great institutions of learning. She had a gift for speaking the local *patois*. Would pick it up wherever we went."

"So do you," she said, crossing her arms over her chest.

"It's my job. What I get paid for, as they say. Speaking of, how do you expect to finance this escapade?"

She had been waiting for this, knew that they would eventually come to the money question. She wiggled. "I've saved up." How could she not, living in the most boring place in the world with the most boring living

42

situation? She was used to getting by without a lot of money. She could live off canned beans if necessary.

She thought her father might say something like "Don't think I'm going to help you out." But he merely nodded. She was not really sure how much money he had. It was not something she could ask, but she imagined he made a decent living as a tenured professor. He kept up this large house all by himself. He had not offered her an allowance since she graduated; the checks simply stopped coming in the mail. Not that she needed them. Finding her the Bloomfield situation had been his token of generosity, his show of paternal care: low rent, no utility bills. She accepted what she could get; they never touched each other, except for the occasional pat on the back or a shoulder squeeze. He was not a hesitant man.

"Well, I think it's a fine idea, Khatia, although I wish you had thought of it before you settled down to a steady job. Will the firm take you back when you return?"

What would he say if he knew that she had already sold all her belongings or given them away? She only had her clothes, books, momentos, photo albums, and letters left. Everything she owned was in the bags and boxes she had put upstairs in her girlhood room. Shoshonah had given her a drawing by an Inuit man: a salmon done in the native style—black ink like a wood–cut, the patterns filled in with crimson pokeberry juice. The fish's eyes rolled upwards, seeking a mate and the light of the sun through the waters. *Let's not be salmon caught in gill nets*, Shoshonah had written on the back in pencil.

Khatia's shoulders hunched up, reminding her of her mother's quirk. She shoved them downward, trying to maintain the good posture of a polished young lady, what her father expected. More than anything, she wanted to scoot onto the edge of the sink and dangle her legs over the counter, curve her back into the worst possible bending, and feel the stretch it would cause. Once, when she was a little girl, he had caught her doing this. "Get down," he had said with trenchant calm, more effective than any spanking. The Quigley children had never experienced corporeal punishment.

"I don't know when I'll be coming back," she said.

He answered with silence, which meant, Explain.

"Shoshonah and I plan to get jobs over there. I know it won't be anything permanent most likely, but I'd like to give it a try. I mean, I think it'll be fun to find a job, explore the countries..." She felt her words stumbling, as they usually did in his presence. He continued to look at her, his eyebrows shaped like small fans of boar's hair curling over his eyes.

She took a breath before speaking again, feeling her fingertips turn the shade of cornflowers.

"I've never been anywhere, Dad." She hesitated. "Not even to San Francisco."

His eyebrows lowered even more, and she realized her mistake. But then, she had known she was going to make it. She almost always made a *faux pas* with him, even though she tried not to. Porter was more of the trouble maker, if there had been one in her family. She waited, watching for emotions in her father's countenance, flexing her hands against the edge of the sink.

"Yes," he said. "I suppose you have led a rather circumscribed life, and I'm sorry for it, Khatia. Your mother and I were much too busy with our careers, but you have had some irreplaceable experiences."

Irreplaceable experiences: the White Mountains where her family went in the summers. They had a small cabin in the woods with no television. Books filled their hours; books, swimming, hiking, and fishing. All he had to offer his children sizzled like baking soda on her tongue, alive with consolidation: They visited his mother occasionally in Connecticut; Khatia did not know her very well, nor her Aunt Gretchen. Often, they went into Boston since it was so close, and into New York City at least four times a year to attend the opera, ballet, visit the Met, the MOMA, and do their Christmas shopping. Her childhood had not been lacking in culture and variety. She bowed her head to show him her gratitude, what she could not express in words to him, this master of languages.

"Well," she said. "Why not add to those experiences? I mean, I'd *like* to add to them. I'm going to add to them." She felt caught in the rhythmic repetition of the declension: I add, I added, I will add, I am adding.

She expected him to resist her reasons for going, yet he was not really saying no. Not that she needed his permission. She was twenty–three years old, an adult, "an individle" as the Scarecrow sang, who had been making independent decisions for a long, long time. Letting him know her intentions was merely a courtesy, but she felt like a servant asking the master's permission. Doing her duty. She always figured he had learned duty while serving in Korea, and simply expected it of any kind of subordinate, especially his children. Sure, she could do what Shoshonah had done, take off without a word until she got there. But the right thing, the right thing. The filial thing...It was a part of her and would not go away.

Her eyes traveled over the outside of his body, fixing on nothing in particular, but more focused on the cabinets behind him. Did light emanate from his body? An aura? They stood no more than seven or eight feet apart, but between them was an expanse of a canyon. Khatia had learned many years ago, when she had tried once, not to construct a bridge, not to try to come across. *Read me a story, Daddy.* The bridge had gone vertical— it was a wall. She told herself she was pretending: I don't really need his approval. I should just go, and forget about all the duty. Let Porter do it. Let him be the one, the son, the sun, the grateful child, the ideal offspring. I want to be released.

A salmon in a gill net.

Silence stretched and her thoughts rushed forward to puncture the suffocation of her mind. Informing her father of her plans should be easy, right? She didn't need his permission, right?. To tell him before she left was to do what was only decent and kind, not like the impulsiveness of Shoshonah— oh god, crazy Shoshonah—she was doing her duty, her filial duty, right? It should be easy. But nothing was ever easy between them.

Really, going abroad was not a big deal for a young woman in her position.

Yet, she noticed, he was not really saying no.

"Actually," she said on impulse. "They were very understanding at the firm. Miss Walker even took me out for lunch. She said I had a lot of potential and shouldn't give up the idea of law school."

Her father's eyebrows went up. She had goofed again.

"I mean, I never said I was going to give it up, especially I wouldn't say that to Miss *Walker*. We never talk about personal stuff. But I guess maybe she thought I was since I'm going to Europe and all."

She stopped talking. Her father turned to his mug of tea. Sipped it. She

45

was sure it must be cold by now.

"I—I think I'll go up to bed now. I'm pretty tired from the train..." She let her voice go. She remained leaning against the sink. He continued to sip his tea. Never gulping, not even after a long run. "Well," she tried again. "Good night, Dad." ,

He still did not answer. She began to slide her feet towards the living room; she would have to pass him if she went up the kitchen stairs.

"We'll talk more tomorrow," he said as she reached the doorway.

She caught her breath, relieved he had answered. "Of course."

She walked quickly out of the room and up the stairs to the bathroom. When she came out to go to her bedroom, she peeked down the stairs. Careful of the board that creaked, her toes splayed out, feeling for it, supporting her suspended weight until she was sure no sound would betray her.

The light from the kitchen threw her father's shadow into the darkened living room. The shape of his head and body were elongated into the grotesque of a wood goblin. She went back to her room with the image of his shadow–hands worrying his shadow–mug like a talisman.

Town was about three miles down the road, an easy ride on her rusty old ten–speed bicycle she had used since middle school. Her father had to go to work and took the car. All her bike needed was some air in the tires. She thrust on the tire pump with gusto, puffing up the rubber, giving tension. She coasted down the road, pedaling harder on the slight ups. Sweat broke out in a thin film on her back.

The town of Milford had all the basics of any small, rural New England village: post office, convenience store, consignment shop, diner, gas station, drug store, feed store, church, church, church, bar, bar, package store, town hall. A "new" shopping center, though now it had been thirteen years since its christening, was along the main highway a quarter mile away. It had a supermarket, Taco Bell, McDonald's, stationery store, clothing stores, book stores, hardware stores, department store, T.J. Maxx: everything town had except bigger and more modern. It did lack a movie theater. Since he was sixteen, Porter had worked for Milford's one movie theater in town. She passed it on her way to the post office. Its old marquis was crumbling around the edges. She imagined the building had possessed an urban beauty when it was first erected, a sort of testament to a small town trying to claim sophistication for itself.

She left her bicycle unlocked against a tree and went into the small, stone building with the American flag outside. Three mailboxes flanked the door, looking like eager, smiling blue monsters waiting to swallow correspondence.

Past the wall of personal post office boxes was the counter, and a young woman sat behind it. She bent over some sort of work, arranging something small into a pile with the side of her hand like bread crumbs about to be swept onto the floor. The woman had pale arms from being indoors all the time, and she wore the uniform of a United States postal worker.

"Bianca," Khatia said.

She looked up from her work.

"Khatia!" she said in slow surprise. "What are you doing here?"

She shrugged. "Visiting my dad."

"Pull up a stool," Bianca gestured. "No one's been in here all morning except people checking their boxes."

Khatia dragged the stool over from the self–service counter, wincing at the whine of its legs on the linoleum floor.

"Boy," Bianca said. "When's the last time you were home?"

Khatia squinted at the moldy ceiling. "Fourth of July."

Bianca nodded. "That sounds right. Old Man Corey was the Grand Marshal and he nearly had a stroke from the heat."

"What else is new? He's been Grand Marshal since high school, and he's not exactly in his prime anymore."

"Yeah, really," she replied with a derisive sigh. She pushed back the pale bangs from her forehead, messing with whatever was in front of her.

Khatia peered over the counter to see what Bianca had. A pile of tiny multi–colored beads sat in a small plastic cup. She strung them on a long needle and thread.

"My hobby," Bianca explained. "I've been taking a class at the Craft Store in Mont Vernon. I thought maybe I could start myself a little business. You know, sell the stuff to boutiques and go to craft fairs and stuff. I made these earrings." She thrust out her ear towards Khatia. Blue and black beads strung into triangles with five beaded strands of varying length hanging symmetrically from them.

"Very nice," Khatia said. "Very native. Like what vendors sell on the college campuses."

"Exactly."

"What else have you been up to?"Bianca shrugged. She had a way of looking over Khatia's shoulder when she began to speak and then quickly looking back at Khatia's eyes. Over and back. Over and back. "Working. Nothing. Billy and me went to Granby for an interview. He might become the manager of a Pizza Hut there. Pretty impressive, huh?"

Khatia knew Bianca was not being disingenuous. For her, the sun rose and set with her boyfriend who had recently graduated with a degree in hotel management.

"Yes," Khatia answered. "That is. Would you like living in Granby?"

"Well, you know what they say: 'Love lives in a tar–paper shack.'"

Khatia smiled. "*They* say that?"

"They do say that."

"Well, well."

Bianca shrugged again.

"Is Porter home too?"

Khatia shook her head. "He went back to Rhode Island a week ago. School started."

"Oh." Bianca's eyes flicked away. "So. Just a little visit with your dad, eh?"

"Just a little visit."

Bianca nodded. "Well. Say hi."

"I will."

They were silent for a few moments in which Khatia studied the posters of commemorative stamps and instructions for overseas parcels. She would need to learn about overseas parcels.

"Granby isn't exactly a town of tar–paper shacks," Khatia said. "It's a lot like Milford."

"I guess," Bianca said. "I mean, I've never really been anywhere anyway, so I guess wherever I go I can make home. I just want to get married soon. I mean, I love Meredith, but after twenty–four years, I think we've had enough of each other."

Khatia played with her cuticles. "How *is* your mom?"

"Good. You should go say hi to her."

Khatia looked up. "I'd like to," she said, meaning it but dreading it too. Meredith almost always wept when she talked to Khatia, even if they did not talk about Annie.

"Oh, but I forgot. She went to Braintree to see Aunt Rosalie. She won't be back until Thursday. You'll be back in Jersey by then, right?"

Khatia smiled, glad for the opener.

"Actually, I'm not going back there."

"What?"

"I quit my job and moved out of the house."

Bianca's mouth dropped open in sociable surprise. "No shit? You coming back to live with your dad in Milford?"

"No. I'm going to Europe with my college friend."

"Europe!" Bianca said, but with little gusto. Nothing seemed to excite her very much. Her intense concentration on the beadwork was the most focused Khatia had seen her years. "You crazy cat. What are you doing that for? You got such a good job, how could you give it up?"

Khatia almost said, "I couldn't take the boredom anymore, and I felt as if my brain were being ground into polenta," but then she looked around the post office. The tick of the wall clock became the rhythm of her heartbeat, the rhythm of her friend's heartbeat, the rhythm of her hometown's glide through the world.

49

"I just—want to. You know? I've never been there, and, you know. While I'm young."

"So they say," Bianca said.

"They do say?"

"Yeah."

Khatia looked at her, and they held each other's gaze, remembering what they had been. Once, they had been equals in everything, except Bianca was smarter. She never tried in school, but Khatia did. And so they balanced. Khatia went to college, and Bianca pledged to defend the Constitution of the United States of America, taking her seat at the counter of the Milford post office. Even physically they teetered on opposite edges, blond and brunette for one thing, peeping at each other since childhood from behind their mother's skirts for another. Their mothers: the women who so much wanted their daughters to be friends, just as they were friends.

"While *I'm* young, I'm going to be in love. And while I'm old too. You going on this trip with that Shoshone woman?"

"Shoshonah," Khatia said with the patience of a matador. "Yes. We're going to Amsterdam. She has some…loose connections there."

"Will you be gone long?"

Khatia shrugged, feeling a cramp in her shoulders. "If it works out, I guess. I'm in no hurry to get back here."

"What about law school?"

"What about it?"

"I thought you were going to save the rainforests and spotted bunnies."

"Owls. Spotted owls. Well, I'd still like to do that. But not by going to law school."

Bianca nodded. "I see," she said. The bell on the door jingled, and a customer came in.

Khatia breathed out. "Guess I'll let you go back to work."

"Okay," Bianca said. "Thanks for stopping by, Khatia. When are you leaving?"

"In three days."

Bianca nodded. "Well, give me a call before then. We'll get a cup of coffee or something."

"I will," Khatia lied as she waved from the door and slipped outside.

She wrote a note to Meredith, a woman she liked very much. When she was a child, Khatia called her Mom because Bianca called her by her first name. Khatia found this habit somewhat perverse and sinful, and she wanted to make up for Bianca's thoughtless offense to the morés of their culture. Meredith was from Brooklyn and called Khatia "Kiddo." Khatia loved to be hugged by her, this young, motherly woman who had breast–fed her daughter until Bianca was two and a half. She envied their closeness, considered calling her own mother "Annie," but knew that would never be acceptable.

She sent the note out, and tried to imagine what Bianca would think when she saw it in the mail. As a defender of the Constitution she was bound to deliver mail to people without thinking about the people—too much. What would she think about Khatia's note? Would she shake her head? Say to herself, "Fool."

Love lives in a tar–paper shack.

Chapter Seven

They stared wide–eyed as the sofa came through the large, open window, wrapped in a belt. It waved seemingly in mid–air like a half–grown rhinoceros being loaded onto a cargo steamer bound for a zoo.

Shoshonah hooted as if she were playing in a championship basketball game and her team had come from behind to tie it up in the last remaining seconds. She clapped her hands as the men standing by the window caught the sofa and swung it carefully to the floor, their hands protected by heavy leather gloves. Their t–shirts were stained with sweat under the armpits, smelling of sidewalks and cigarette boxes. One man made to take his shirt off a few minutes before, due to the heat and their labor, but his co–worker, an older man, objected, glancing at the young women who watched them communicating in Dutch. These men were skinny, and Khatia wondered how they could lift heavy objects with so little bulk on their bodies. Perhaps they did not eat enough beef or drink enough milk as children. Yet, here they were, moving furniture for a living, buoyed by the safety harnesses they strapped around the vulnerable small of their backs. The belts were signs of professionalism—skinny or not, they were careful of their spines. They knew what was important.

And everything important to Khatia was in her backpack. She could have been a walking advertisement for a student travel agency, for minimalism. The progression of her adult life had become a pattern of letting physical objects go, first in college, then at Aunt Estella's, now here in Amsterdam. With ease, she could have slipped into a Buddhist nunnery, shaving all her hair, giving up the rest of her worldly possessions, and grasping tranquillity. But that was not the real her. Somewhere, she belonged in *things*. Two summers ago, she had the job of packing some of her mother's belonging that her father had missed in one of the hall closets: hair combs, record albums, a box of junk jewelry, old scrapbooks in which she kept clippings from newspapers and magazines that interested her. Khatia, respecting her mother in death, did not peek inside any of these things. But she did think to herself, and rather irreverently, "So much crap."

"Excuse me," one of the movers said, indicating her backpack with his eyebrows. Khatia hastened over to the offending object, kicking it out of the way with her booted foot. She went back to Shoshonah's side, embarrassed that the man had acknowledged her presence.

"It used to belong to my mom," she explained to Shoshonah, although she did not know why she was explaining. "We went on a lot of backpacking trips in the White Mountains when I was a kid, going to the cabin...My mom gave it to me when I went to college because she was getting a new one. It feels like a family heirloom or something." She sighed. "Using it for urban excursions just doesn't seem—natural."

Shoshonah grabbed her by the shoulders and gave her a big kiss on the lips. Khatia turned red. She glanced over at the movers, but they were too busy unhooking the heavy straps from the belly of the couch.

"I can't believe we're here!" Shoshonah squeezed Khatia in an ursine embrace. "Do you see what the arrival of the couch symbolizes? We've come home. We're here to stay, and there's nothing the bastards can do about it."

"Except for the bastards we owe money," Khatia mumbled, thinking about rent and food and bills. Who would give them work to do? No work permits, foreigners—*American* foreigners at that. Didn't Europeans have some sort of disdain for their Yankee cousins? Maybe that was just the French. There were sure to find out soon enough. She could picture them in rags on the streets of Amsterdam, hocking their passports for a hot meal.

"Hush up with that talk. You promised," Shoshonah said.

"Okay, okay. I'm just really scared, is all. Am I allowed?"

"Sure. Just remember: you have supper duty tonight."

Khatia closed her eyes and tried to picture heavenly light.

Shoshonah hung her arms on Khatia's shoulders like a healthy vine. Excited and happy, she had no time for any of Khatia's doom.

"This place is great. Isn't it great?" She breathed in and out. Fortune of all fortunes had come Shosh's way. She had rediscovered an old acquaintance from the ski resort where she used to work during the college's long winter breaks, a woman from the Netherlands whose parents happened to have two apartments in Amsterdam, which was not allowed since housing was so scarce. They had kept the extra for their daughter, but since she decided to travel around the world for a few years, they needed people to stay in their second apartment. As long as they could keep up with the rent, Khatia and Shoshonah could be there for a very long time.

"Yeah. We're really lucky those other people were moving out just when we wanted to move in." Another foreign couple from Spain, were done with their adventures in the Dutch port and had moved out only a few days before.

"We have a lot to do," Shosh began counting off on her fingers. "Buy groceries, light bulbs, get bicycles—"

"Find jobs," Khatia interrupted.

"No problem. We'll go to cafés and restaurants tomorrow and look for work."

"Good. I need to start getting money soon."

Shoshonah was on the edge of good–natured exasperation. She was not the kind of person who appeared to be down for long, probably because she had worked every summer since she was twelve in her father's ice cream store. Selling homemade ice cream to people was like selling rainbows and dreams–come–true. Customers were happy to receive a scoop of sin and heaven on a cone. They beamed their rays of gratitude back at the little girl behind the counter. How could Shosh *not* be a happy person? Except when she talked about some of the other women she had dated. Then her voice would lower from its normal, high–pitched chirping, the words, if she spoke, drawn out, tied without raveling to the thread of past affairs. Everyone has her secret life, Khatia realized without wonder; but it only made her sigh. At one time, making this realization was all she thought she would need to understand what made some people cruel.

"Relax, will you?" Shoshonah said. "You need to get over your jet lag. Get settled in. We have enough money to give us some breathing room."

"Shoshonah, we've been in Europe for two weeks now! I've had plenty of time to 'get over my jet lag' while we've been gallivanting around." They had been to London, Brussels, and Rotterdam before arriving in Amsterdam, staying in youth hostels, exploring monuments and pubs, wandering the streets in a safe, adventurous dream–state.

Khatia crossed her arms and walked closer to the window where the men were fitting the glass back into the frame. She wanted to get closer, to look at the water in the canal down below. The movers paid no attention to her. Their smell tasted like warm milk in her mouth.

A long time ago, she had held a boy's penis in her hand. Her last year in high school, a boy asked her out on a date. He took her to his dorm room on the private high school's campus, sneaking her in through the chimney of the sitting room, the boy waiting on the hearth with a plastic bag of her. clean clothes. They lay together on his bed and kissed for what seemed like hours, tongues sliding over teeth that clamped down in damp nips, while something pointy prodded her thighs and stomach through the crotch of his pants. She heard the zipper and waited.

"It's okay," he had said, his voice hoarse from dehydration. "I'm circumcised."

She thought this was a strange thing to say, and, confused for a moment, though he was making an obscure, inside joke about geometry. But they were in English together. Was their something sexy about math she did not know? She held it—him— gently in her hand and he rocked forwards and backwards. How could she know the difference? Erect, they probably all looked pretty much the same, circumcised or not. As a little girl, she peeked into a book of nude photographsin the art section of a Boston bookstore. Black men turned a bronzy brown by the film's color, well dressed in suits with their penises hanging out, hugely elephantine and cocoa.

Whenever she saw an attractive man, she wanted to ask him, "Circumcised?" But she never would. She did not talk to men, unless she had to, and usually saying such a word would not be amusing. The lawyers would not have thought it amusing.

She moved away from the workers, back towards Shoshonah. She could see the canal later.

Penises—what ugly parts of the male anatomy, like a cosmic joke on men for having beautiful arms and control of most of the world's societies and customs for the last five thousand years. How men coveted those fleshy lumps of skin, naming them fondly. She tried not to look at the movers' arms as they puttied the edges of the window, the muscles under their skin slipping in and out of use as they moved. She turned stared at a wall, mixed up. Why was she so hot? She hoped they didn't notice. Her thoughts were probably all over her face. She distrusted the world, sure that everyone had the gift of mind–reading except her.

Shoshonah was being quiet, but Khatia forgot why. After all, a year had passed, and she could not read every sign with clarity.

Shoshonah took her hand. "Let's be nice to each other. It took a long time for you to decide to come with me. I'm not going to let you talk yourself into regretting your decision." She gave Khatia a light kiss on the cheek. "You've made me so happy by coming here," she said. "Let's have *fun*."

Khatia turned and smiled, promising herself she would behave. She picked up a flower one of the old tenants had left on the coffee table for them. It was fresh and young, a yellow tulip. The petals fit together perfectly, and when she pulled them apart a little, she could see the indentations of their intrinsic resting spots.

"I'll try. I don't know if I know how to have fun."

"What did you do while I was gone?" Shoshonah asked.

Khatia shrugged. "You know. The usual. Watched TV. Hung out with Aunt Estella."

Shoshonah rolled her eyes to heaven and kept them there.

"Kha—tee—ya!" she growled.

After the movers left, they decided to go find bicycles and explore their new neighborhood. As they headed for Utrechtsedwartstraat, where used bikes could be bought but perhaps not registered since their serial numbers were often filed off, they linked arms. To the world, were they lovers, sisters, or good friends? Were they of any interest to anyone? The city breathed friendship. It breathed respite from appraisal. There bodies melted together, keeping each other up and forward–moving. Their steps fell in sync, and she counted the beat they made: one, two, three, four. One, two, three, four. Khatia was not used to this freedom on sidewalks with Shoshonah. But no one was around to care.

The weather was turning milder, their landlady had told them. Khatia rolled down the sleeves of her shirt as they assessed the bicycles displayed,

56

feeling a chill coming on.

"I like this one," Shoshonah said about a little one speed. "It speaks to me."

Shoshonah wants to be so deep sometimes, Khatia thought, and smiled.

"Oh, really? What does it say?"

"It says, 'Remember when you were a little girl, and you lived in Truro during the summers and you rode a bike like me? And you would go to the shore in the morning and come home when dusk fell, and you would put seashells and sand dollars in the old, ratty basket just like I have. Remember that was the only time in your life you ever found whole sand dollars?'"

"Really?" Khatia asked. "That was the only time?"

Shoshonah traced her fingers on the basket. The handlebar sat in her other hand comfortably as if it already belonged to her.

"Yes." Her voice was distant, belonging to the thousands of miles between the them of now and the yesterday of Cape Cod. "The only time. 'And remember that little girl you played with who lived around the corner from you? Her mother was beautiful, but she had the fattest hips in creation—'"

"Creation?"

"Creation. It was the weirdest thing! A slender torso, normal legs up to her knees, but hips from the Mesozoic. I always wondered if she had tried to lose weight and it just melted into her thighs. And she had a handsome father, that little girl, but he scared me."

"Why?"

"The day I met them, we were both playing on the shore. The girl brought me to her parents to introduce us. As I said hello, her father told me I got sand on his blanket and to move. It was so rude, in a way. My parents would never act that way towards a child they had just met. They're a little more protective of a kid's dignity." Shoshonah frowned, holding back words. Khatia did not press her, but she wondered if all girls who went to single-sex colleges harbored some fear of men, some need to be away from them and their mysteries, for a while. "I decided he was probably rude to his wife like that, and that's why her hips were so enormous."

"Because her husband was rude to her?"

Khatia watched her friend, waiting for the punchline, saw something new in her face. She realized that Shoshonah had been in love with that man's wife. A childhood crush, unsoured.

Shoshonah rubbed the handle of the bicycle, her voices getting low and trailing. "He could have been a lot nicer to me."

Khatia reached across the bicycle and squeezed Shoshonah's shoulder. Shoshonah looked up, responding to the fragile touch, the soft offering of understanding and camaraderie Khatia was often so reluctant to give. She reached up to her shoulder, awkwardly lacing her athletic fingers in between Khatia's slender ones. A tranquil moment, an offering of things to come: The twilight cut across the low, ancient buildings of a canal town, destined to someday sink into the quagmire of its own conception. They were a pair of lovers gazing across the meager distance of a foot or so, love and desire for unity pushing them towards the edge of small and large questions. The world was wreathed in a purple aura, and warm breezes licked at their faces.

With a crash, the bicycle between them toppled over, the pedals scraping Khatia's shins.

Shoshonah grinned down at the bike, as if she had never been melancholy one instant in her life. A path wend through her memory, littered with sand dollars.

"I have a really good feeling about this," she said, picking up the bicycle.

This? Khatia wondered. What this? She looked at her leg, dabbing at the shredded membranes, peeling them away as if they were the skin of an onion.

"Me too," she said.

September, Amsterdam

Dear Bianca,

Well, it's been a week, and we've been exploring the city. Old is a good word for it, and kind of seedy. But that's what we came here for! Certainly not for quaint and puritanical. I could have

58

stayed in Bloomfield for that. Sorry I am only sending a post card right now. I hope you got my others from Haarlem and Brussels. Here's my address, so write soon, postal chick. Give my regards to your mother.

Khatia

Mom and Dad,

We're here! I am so happy. Tell Alex that it's just as he said it would be. Our landlady is great, and she says she is definitely going to drop in on you guys in Vermont next year, so beware! It's only been five days, and I already have a job offer from this hotel, but I'm still looking around for something a bit more bohemian, if you know what I mean. Don't swoon, we're doing fine. I love it here, I've come home, but I miss and love you all too.

XXXOOO—Shoshie

Porter,

Hey there, little brother. How's school? Well, here we are in the city with more canals than Venice. According to a man who started talking to us in a coffeehouse one night, our apartment is in one of the choicest neighborhoods, and we're very lucky to have a view of the water. I don't know what your long–distance writing skills are like, but I hope you write back to the address below. Maybe you can come visit me for winter break because I don't think I'll be making enough money to come home for Christmas. I think I have a job even though it's only been about a week since we got here. But, don't tell Dad, okay? I'm going to write to him myself. Thanks for your discretion.

Khatia

Chapter Eight

I know you're not supposed to admit stuff like this, but when I was a little kid, I was in love with my sister, sort of. At least, I had a deep appreciation of her, and a firm belief one day, we were to be married and run away from our parents.

Recently, I found out that's not all together a crazy idea: In the old Chinese tradition, a boy grew up with a girl, often his cousin, who was his caretaker and playmate. She was usually a few years older than he, and when he became a teenager, they married, and she was his number one wife. She got to boss the number two and number three wife around, plus all the concubines. Her offspring ruled the nest. So, you see, if Khatia were my cousin, and we were in China a hundred years ago, it would be kosher.

Of course, I'm too American and too much of a womanist to have more than one wife and, after kissing my roommate at Sigma Chi's Oktoberfest last night, I can also safely say that I am straight and that I will not join a fraternity. This morning was a little awkward, but he was too drunk to remember much of anything, and he was kissing a fair amount of people besides me. Personally, I think Stu is in for a lifetime of denial regarding his homosexual tendencies, but that is his problem, and I'll leave it at that.

I suppose I should clarify being "too American." Well, faulting my parents might seem simultaneously justified(*they* raised me) and unfair(this *is* America, and they want me to succeed in this culture), but that's really a moot point. I'm taking a Chinese History class because I want to know what Mom never talked about: What is being Chinese like? What have I missed, and what can I get back? Maybe she couldn't tell me; she was only half, raised in America herself, and maybe her mom Americanized her too. I'm going to find out though. What it's like to be Chinese that is. I'm going to Feel Chinese. Why not?

Or maybe I should just study Taoism.

I don't know my mother's parents. They might as well be dead. Maybe I'll find them someday. If I do a PhD in cross–cultural anthropology. A white woman and a Chinese man married in the 50's? Practically unheard of. Miscegenation is generally a big no–no. It would be a bad–ass study, to be sure.

My sister wrote to me from Amsterdam. I have decided I'm going to be a better correspondent. Communication is the key to happy relationships, according to Professor Reichmann, my psych instructor. Khatia is quiet, like Mom, but sort of a passive rebel. She would give if I asked. At least she writes back. I wish my dad would talk more, but then again, I don't. If he changed in any way, I'd probably have a heart attack. I mean, he talks about Mom sometimes, but it's stuff like, "Oh, your mother used to keep the coffee beans on the second shelf, not the first." My sister is young, so maybe there's something salvageable there.

She doesn't look like our mother at all. I do. My face is all warped and twisted like hers. I am very much into genetics even though I haven't taken a class in the sciences yet. Next semester. I can't decide if I want to be in a band, become a doctor, or study Chinese History. I fucking love taking classes. I just wish I could stop going to them after two weeks and start another one. It's hard to keep track. It's hard to keep track.

Another thing I'd like to know more, about is my dad's time in Korea. He's got this gnarly scar on his chest, and I can hardly bear to look at it, but it is so fascinating. When I was a kid, sometimes I heard him moaning in his sleep, and it was not in ecstasy. Mom would shush at him, like at us kids, and it would get quiet again. I just remembered that the other day when we rented on of those Oliver Stone/Vietnam Hell movies. Memory can be such a pain in the ass sometimes. It has a mind of its own.

Dad gave us a scare before Mom died, saying he was going to leave the family. Of course, he was all calm about it, but *I* flipped at least. I punched a hole in the boys bathroom wall at school. Had to paint lockers for two weekends for that one. I don't know what Khatia thought. She had the comfy cushion of one hundred miles to keep her from facing Mom and Dad everyday, knowing that they weren't really together, but still living in the same house. I think back to that time every now and then trying to figure out what set him off? Why did he decide that, and why then? Nothing comes up, nothing that I recognize. I come from a family of runaways: Khatia running off to Amsterdam—well, she's never really been with us to begin with. When she's being really quiet, she gets a look on her face, it's like a cross between a nun and a serial killer. I don't know what to make of Dad though. He pisses me off, but I have some deep pathos (Professor Reichmann's words) over Mom. Who knows what will trigger people. Who knows.

There's no glue in this family.

When I marry, it'll be forever, and we'll talk talk talk all the time.

Chapter Nine

The little office was on Lauriergracht, near a bookstore Shoshonah liked called the English Bookshop. Inside, a young man named Ulrike, just into the publishing business, fumbled through piles of papers, touching the sides of his eyeglasses as if to make sure they were really on his face, the phone tucked painfully between his ear and shoulder. Khatia watched him for a moment from the doorway, one foot in and one foot out. She glanced back at the street where the comfortable trolley had let her off.

He needed help with office things—stuffing envelopes, typing up orders in English, running courier errands on her one-speed bicycle. Too bad she did not speak Dutch because he could have used a translator. She knew she was lucky. Almost any person he grabbed off the street could do the job ten times better than she could. Almost all Dutch people, especially in Amsterdam, could speak three or four languages. At least she had semi-decent French, and a bit of Spanish. But Ulrike took her because of two things: she was cheap, under-the-table labor; and he fell in love with her voice.

Their meeting was like a country song. She and Shoshonah were in a bar that offered cheap food from four until seven in the evening. Khatia ordered drinks at the bar while Shoshonah scored a booth. She said: "Two Heinekens, please."

A man standing next to her howled. "What a great voice!" He was tall, an Ichabod Crane type, with an Adam's Apple a person could hang his bath-robe on, and tiny, round spectacles.

Khatia smiled cautiously—completing ignoring the insane populace of Amsterdam was hard for her; she did not want to hurt their feelings—and went back to Shoshonah with the beers.

He followed.

"What?" Khatia said, trying to be snotty and rude as he sat down with them, uninvited.

He was blunt. "I need someone to do voice recordings for laboratory tapes," he said to her.

It was the weekend. The crazies were out. Khatia glanced at Shoshonah as she held her hand on the table of their booth to get this guy off her back. To show him she was *not interested*. She remembered a woman in college who was so proud of the fact that when a sleazy guy would not leave her alone she would tell him, "Honey, I'm a lesbian," as if it were the most clever, devastating line known to womankind. Some men got the hint. Some men got turned on, challenged: A beautiful, delicate woman could be a *lesbian?* Oh, she must be a *fem.* Well, all she needed was a little encouragement. Khatia could not remember if that woman really was a lesbian or not, but somehow, she found such a line offensive, smacking of some sort of *ism*.

As it turned out, Ulrike was at the bar with his wife, Frithe, a quiet, smiling woman with a long nose and dry, brown hair. Harmless people. Youngish, struggling to make something work in a place where original was mundane. They appealed to Khatia, to her sense of the underdog: Try hard, get stomped. Try harder, maybe you'll get to do a little stomping.

Khatia kept watching him from the sanctuary of the open door of the office, like a bug in a magnifying box. She could close the lid now and walk away, find that coffeehouse where Shoshonah was applying for work.

"You have to give me a regular job too," Khatia had told Ulrike in the bar. Boldness welled up into those vocal chords that seemed to mesmerize him. "I can't just live by freelancing." He had nodded vigorously. Yes, yes. Urgent, platonic desire: He would do anything for her voice, and he needed an assistant besides. Being brave to a docile, kind person was easy enough. He was pushy, but mild. Ruthless would never be his epithet. Hard–working, determined. Sincere. Hypnotized by something she had never thought about: her voice. The words that came out of it. The tone. The volume. It had not received compliments before this.

He looked up from the phone and saw her standing there.

"Ach," he said. "Khatia! Come in, come in! Your desk is there. I will show you everything in a moment." He returned to the phone, mumbling away, half in English, half in some other language. She peered around his body into the narrow room to the place he had gestured, but saw nothing.

65

Outside, the street. Inside, a narrow room. A pull, invisible persuasion, and she stepped onto the worn, wood floor, shutting the door which tinkled as it closed.

"Good, huh?"

Khatia gnawed on a chicken bone, her teeth grasping for bits of clinging meat. She had learned to suck out the marrow from her mother.

"What?" she grunted, glancing at Shoshonah.

"Everything," Shoshonah said. "Wait a minute. You've got something there..." She reached over the kitchenette table, pointing at Khatia's mouth.

"Where?"

Shoshonah pointed to her own face. "There. Wait, let me."

Getting up from the table, she pushed away her chair. It clattered, falling over. Shoshonah leaned over and licked the corner of Khatia's mouth, pushing the morsel of meat in with her tongue. Khatia did not resist, her hand reaching for Shoshonah's breasts, her nipples already knotting, and the diamonds they had seen earlier that day in a jeweler's display case strayed across Khatia's memory as her nails grazed Shoshonah.

"Thanks," she said when Shoshonah released her.

Shoshonah picked up her chair and sat down again. She smoothed her napkin over her thighs.

"My pleasure," she said, bread shredding between her teeth.

Had they found paradise? Kept at home, passion flourished like a hot–house flower, breathing in damp, warm carbon dioxide, and giving back life–rich oxygen. They were two sides of balance with their fingers joined, locking them into a warm, amniotic bathtub.

But Khatia would remember. Remember to worry. Remember that perfection and happiness were merely constructs of those who rationalized.

At those moments, she would pedal her bicycle furiously down the twisty, cobblestone alleys, getting away from her life. If she could just choose her own body before her soul was born to the earth. And peel it off, starting over.

Her body. It careened toward a velocity, playing catch–up. It left behind the main, intense gridwork of the canals at the center of the city that fanned away from the Amstel like the fluting on a semi–circular grate. She could not get lost as long as the water was there surrounding her, floating into the grand Het Ij. She longed to be lost. Where could she go to get lost? Already, it seemed, she had been everywhere within the city limits, although she knew this could not be true. Museums, parks, bars, clubs, coffee houses, shops. All she wanted was diversion from herself, the near perfect comfort of her new life.

It couldn't last anyway. Something would come up. Something always came up.

Her muscles were taut, her calves straining up and down in propulsion, her skirt flying out behind her. She was a pretty strong woman, but deceivingly slender. Even when she was simply the coxswain, her teammates did not believe she could do it, have the strength in her lungs to challenge them, urge them on. Harmony in sweat: *that* was rowing.

Her bicycle whizzed by the Snooker Sociëteit, a place Shoshonah wanted to explore when she saw it in their guidebook because it was something she knew nothing about. The building was sooty and a little dank, but Khatia was getting better at being less discerning. She was not a jock, not like Shoshonah who was the Most Valuable Player in college because of her prowess on the basketball court, on the lacrosse field, in the swimming pool. Shoshonah took good, clean fun to another dimension. As captain of each team, she led their teams to Nationals for the first time in ten years. Surprisingly, competition did not factor into Shoshonah's way of thinking, as she had once said in an interview for an article in *Sports Illustrated* on women's colleges sports: "I want to have as much fun as possible, challenge myself to play at my full potential. I gauge the success of a tournament or meet on how much I am enjoying myself. That does not necessarily mean I have to win. I know it's not sportsmanly, but I'm not your average athlete. I'm just a big kid at heart."

Khatia had two copies of that article. One she kept folded in her journal. The other was still intact in the magazine, sitting with her books in her room in Milford. How wonderful it would be, she thought, to be able to see

67

yourself clearly, and give yourself a definition. She and Shoshonah were two halves of one(weren't they?), and if Shoshonah loved herself, that should suffice for both of them. Shoshonah's family had tradition—they observed Chanukah and Passover, called each other Mushuganah. Khatia believed in relics: if she could touch Shoshonah's world, maybe she too could feel whole.

A small park lay ahead, and the wheels of the old, black bicycle squealed against the back pressure of her heels. Lanes of brown gravel, some paved over for wheelchairs, she guessed, lay before her. Surrounding buildings, skinny and high, though not as tall as most of the buildings in Amsterdam were, to avoid the heavy property taxes of the 1600's, shrouded the park. Sunlight dappled the grass as it slipped between the buildings, turning the aging afternoon into a blanket of spotted, glittering wonder. A bird twittered and then was silent. After a moment, another answered from a different direction. Calling to each other, they waited for the insects to swarm in dusk.

Standing on the pedals of her bike, bracing her hands on the handles, she balanced, taking in the square of blue sky and the trees, wondering at the contrast of shade, squinting her eyes to see what the great ones saw to put on canvas. Van Gogh had seen the world in waves; that was evident from his paintings she visited in the museum named after him. In a face, streams of smoking colors made up the skin, the hair, the collar around the neck. In a field, large, tidal strokes turned wheat into hay–gold tsunamis, bordered in their own twilight black from the blue–green hills of watery mounds. Smoke curling out of a country cottage, given solidity in gray, black, and lavender, each thickly twining around the other. Amorphites of the tangible: an idea on cloth, easily struck out by more paint layered on top.

She touched her cheek, clean of make–up, a tickling film of perspiration caught in the transparent fur on her face. Like the smoke, could she too be painted away, prevented from becoming?

Behind her, the sinking city spread, beckoning her back into its simple maze, but she did not turn around to let her eyes trap her into going back, for the moment.

An old man sat on one of the park benches, a book in hand and a bag of bread crumbs in the other. For a fairly warm day, he was all bundled up in a corduroy coat, felt hat, and scarf, one of those older gentlemen who sit on park benches all day, with a large, cartilaginous nose and lots of spidery gray hair growing out of the edges of his spotted, red ears. Khatia watched him and leaned on her bicycle, as he softly sprinkled crumbs on the pavement in front of him. Her eyes blurred, his form wavering, and she imagined clouds billowing out of his body, the brown herringbone of his coat, the crimson scarf securing his invisible neck. He was not looking at his bread crumb hand, too engrossed in his book. Occasionally, large, pigeon–like birds would swoop down from the trees and peck at the ground, but they did not stay for long, making passes in the air, a large bell–shaped swoop back into the branches.

For the first time since she had left her family and the Carters in Logan Airport with Shoshonah by her side, Khatia experienced homesickness, a burst of multi–sensory pain. Ears, throat, the muscles in her calves: her body hit the consciousness of knowing, of realizing that she was in a foreign country, all alone, not ties or connections of any kind to reel her in. She went through life completely alone with no obvious agenda. The monstrous significance of the moment might have knocked her over in a faint or tears or something dramatic, had it not been for the source of her epiphany: the old man saw her watching, and smiled.

His croaky voice called out something in Dutch, and she shook her head apologetically with a cowed smile. He paused, frowned, and she cursed herself for forgetting her crummy Dutch/English pocket–sized dictionary.

"I'm American," she said, aware of an obnoxious, nasally twang she did not usually notice in her voice. Her new job made her self–conscious. Compared to the Germanic sounding Dutch, she sounded like Fran Drescher.

"Ah!" he said, the frowning wrinkles melting into understanding ones. "Yes, of course. I speak English myself. How are you?"

"Oh, fine." Her toe scraped the gravel, and her eyes shifted just to the left of his hat. She could see a couple of young boys with shaved heads on skateboards carrying a homemade ramp, their t–shirts displaying the names of popular American rock bands.

"Are you a student?"

"No, I'm just a tourist, sort of."

"How delightful." His words were slow and precise. "How do you enjoy Amsterdam?"

"It's a beautiful city." She prayed he would not ask her if she was sampling drugs with wild, American abandon at all the coffee houses, as some elderlies were wont to do. Her grandmother Quigley had no qualms about utilizing the convenience of her advanced age as an excuse for being a real bitch sometimes; boy, could that lady make a person squirm.

The man's lips were curled in, as if he were constantly chewing on them. He seemed to have a few teeth, glowing a dull brown as he chuckled. Khatia realized he had the look slightly retarded people are born with, big child-like eyes, an enlarged, bulbous forehead, and a receding chin. Other than that, he did not appear deficient; his eyes held the gravity of intelligence.

"Come here, Miss, and help me feed the birds."

Khatia hesitated. Normally, she would make up a polite excuse and get out of there as quickly as possible without causing a ruckus. Nothing, she thought, was "normally" anymore. When had anything been normal? Smiling, raking her fingers through her hair, she walked her bike over to his bench and laid it in the grass, sitting down on the edge of the corner. He handed her the bag, and she breathed shallowly through her mouth, in case he smelled, she realized, and then felt slight shame at her shallowness. She spread the crumbs, feeling their aridity in her moist fingers, shaking her hand when they stuck. The old man smiled at her, his eyes squinted in bunches of skin as he softly nodded, and chuckled a rolling sound like river water over smooth rocks.

"Where are you from in America?"

"Uh...near Boston."

"Ah, Massachusetts?"

"No, New Hampshire?" A lot of Europeans, she discovered, were unfamiliar with the names of the States, except for New York, California, Texas, and Hawaii.

"New Hampshire. Of course. Dartmouth College." He jabbed upwards at the sky with a shiny, pointed finger.

"Yes, that's right." She smiled and bobbed her head for a while, lost in an internal rhythm. A voice in her head said, "uh–huh, uh–huh, uh–huh, uh–huh." *Shut up!* she told it, and her head stopped bobbing. The old man, oblivious, looked at the ground thoughtfully.

She continued to spread crumbs, thinking of something to say. Here was Dutch History, sitting by her side, and she was too stupid to think of anything to say. She shook the bag of crumbs with an involuntary lurch, and half of them spilled like enlarged, rejected confetti.

"Ha—have you lived in Amsterdam all your life?" she said to cover up her tweakiness.

"No, not all. I actually grew up in Australia because of the war."

"Australia! Really?"

"Yes, near Perth. But I had to leave as soon as I could," he waved his finger at her. "Could not abide the heat."

"I bet." She looked down at the ground, thinking about hot deserts. She could detect a difference in his voice now, different than Ulrike and other natives she had met. Her feet kicked at the ground in a rhythm, sending up puffs of gravel dust.

"I always liked it cold. When I turned sixteen, I moved to Norway and worked for many years on the boats. I met my wife, had children. I have fourteen grandchildren! Imagine, it all started with me."

"That's a good way to look at it."

He chuckled. "I am tiresome, no?"

"Oh, no! No, no, no, no, no, no, no. No, no. Not at all. Please, tell me more."

"I would like to hear *your* story. Young people are so much more interesting than old ones. They have such vibrancy." He jabbed his finger gently her way. "You have that, you know. Vibrancy."

"Oh, well, thank you." She did not like receiving compliments, never believed them for a minute. "I'm rather boring, really."

"No. You are strong."

How odd a connection that was. Did strength cancel out dullness?

"It's interesting that you bring that up, because I think a lot of people are looking for sources of strength these days. All the old ideas seemed to be used up, and I don't think we know how to go on." She got excited, using her hands to conduct her rushing thoughts. "You were able to start a life so

71

young."

"Ha!" he roiled. "When does one 'start a life?' Are we debating an abortion issue? To become an *adult*, perhaps that is what you mean."

"An adult. Yes. I guess I do mean that. I'm twenty–three, and I can't seem to figure out what to do with myself."

"You have the energy. You travel. You will find it. Nothing can be gained by staying still." His shaky hand gestured over the space above her own hand, and he patted the air. "You will find it. *Then* —you can stay still." He pursed his shriveled lips and shook his head, gazing to the side of her. "I left Perth, and I found it here. People have been saying the ideas are dried up for thousands of years, and look where we are today?" He spread his arms out in front of him. "My second daughter contacts me from Queensland by E–mail. Even I, an old man, take advantage of forward motion."

Forward motion. She smiled to herself, peering into the bread crumb bag which seemed to extend endlessly. She saw herself in the recent past, as if through a funnel, sitting still in a law library doing someone else's research for which she cared nothing.

"But," said the old man, pointing in the air again, "you must set a goal. Even if you cannot yet name it, you must set a goal. Do you have one?"

Panic sped up her heart a little, and her eyes darted around inside the files of her head for a goal. Maybe an old one, like finishing college. No, she had done that already. A goal. They talked about them all the time at work, in school. A goal, like in lacrosse: an achievement. Points scored. "Goals," her father said, a word strung through with other words she had stopped listening to, although she did not think he knew it. She still looked at him when he spoke, as he expected her to do.

"I guess my goal is to find a goal," she said to the old man. Having said it, she waited for him to rebuke her: *That's not a goal; that's an excuse. A cop–out.*

She waited with a cringe, but instead he said, "That is excellent! Yes, that is exactly what you must do. Take a step each day at a time, and enjoy each step as you take it, no matter how hard it may seem. Remember Dylan Thomas: 'Though they go mad they shall be sane,/ Though they sink through the sea they shall rise again.'"

72

"I love Dylan Thomas," she sighed.

He held up his book with a picture of the poet on the cover.

"He was a drunken philanderer, but he had occasional insight," the old man said. "*His* goal was to be the best poet he could be, doing what he loved."

"What's your goal?"

His eyes opened widely, and a soft "ahhh" flew out of his lips, leaving a dusty trail of infinitesimal spit bubbles in the air. "Which one? A person is allowed to have more than one goal in his life. Do you not know this?"

"I guess I forgot. It's been so hard to figure out *one*."

"My first goal was to leave Australia and make a fortune in the Old World. Well, I did not quite make a fortune, but I am comfortable, and I was able to help all my children with anything they needed, beyond the age of sixteen, like my own experience. Thinking beyond myself helped me to work harder with the big ones—having a family, finding a nice house to live in. Others," he waved his hand again, "one day at one time, as you Americans say. I saved enough money to buy my own boat and a bit of land for sheep. Wool sweaters. Each day, I said to myself, 'This money I earn today is my goal.' If I tried to achieve anything faster than that, it would become too big for me to see, and I would get tired and frustrated. You understand?"

"I think so."

"Good, good. Little baby goals," he said, enunciating carefully. "I do not mean be lazy. Do not pick aims that are unimportant to you. But do not forget to lose the fun." His mouth screwed up a little, and he thumped the book cover. "Sometimes, I think he forgot the fun. But, yes, he did have insight."

"Occasionally," she said, amused by his quasi–New Age philosophy. She was lucky to be such a simpleton, aiming to please, or else she probably would never have listened to the man's enthusiastic, saccharine advice. Guilt immediately flooded over her. She was *not* so simple, and his advice *was* a bit saccharine. But was she so jaded? How could a person her age be cynical and idealistic at the same time? She felt as high–strung as a stallion about to be gelded. "Breathe," she told herself, and began to silently count to a thousand in French: *Trois cent deux, Trois cent trois, trois cent quatre…*

Silence grew comfortable. The old man smiled at her thoughtfully, but she was deep in her own rumination.

"You have a love, yes?" he said.

"What?" she asked, startled. "Oh, you mean, am I seeing someone?"

He chuckled. "Your terminology: 'Seeing someone.' Yes, I suppose being in love is seeing a person's soul with the eye of your heart, and his body with the eye of your brain. But you do more than see with love, do you not think so? You become one and the same. Seeing the person you love is seeing yourself."

"So, you know you aren't in love if you don't feel you are with yourself?" she said. She did not want to think about that right now.

"Why don't you go home and tell him you love him?"

She stared at the crumpled paper bag in her hands, finally empty. His kind of assumptions made her embarrassed, although she was accustomed to people making them. Responsibility for his ignorance lay on her shoulders. She thought about the power she had to take that blindness away; what might he say? Nothing, probably; this was Amsterdam.

He blinked at her, chuckling away. "Go on, go on. You are very new. Everything will be all right," and this time, his soft, smooth old man hand connected with the tight, thin layer of the skin of hers. The touch was not repulsive, as she first thought it might be. To be touched by a complete stranger in a pleasant way did not happen very often. Her eyes blurred again, and she saw the whorls of his loose skin become waves.

She looked at his face, childlike with grooves and lines. She thought, I owe him a reason.

"My situation is very simple to explain. It's all the emotional stuff that gets complicated. You've been really nice. Thank you."

He waved his finger at her again.

"You will see. It only gets complicated to make it interesting. That does not mean it has to be sad too. Do not be sad on purpose. That will just rob you of what should be yours, so easily." He paused. "Forty–two years I was married to Kristin, God rest her soul. They were not complicated years. Just lucid."

Lucid.

She stood, ready to go, and picked up her bicycle.

"Come again, young lady, come again. I am always here." He leaned forward. "I will provide the bread crumbs."

The wheels of her rickety bike seemed to barely touch the asphalt as she glided towards home. She would cook a wondrous supper of sautéed chicken and marinated artichokes, serving it up with polenta and salad.

Mulling over her afternoon, she decided not to see the old man again, as he had invited. To be touched by a complete stranger in a pleasant way did not happen very often, and she did not want to spoil the memory. Sometimes, getting to know a person was the worse thing to do.

She parked her bicycle in the rack and clambered up the old, wooden steps, two at a time. It was about five o'clock, and Shoshonah would probably be lolling on the couch reading, absorbing a story to think about while she worked the night away at the hotel as a maid, the job she had finally settled for.

"Shoshonah! Shoshonah, I'm home!"

The apartment was quiet. Khatia saw the impression of a recent body left on the cushions of the couch. A blanket tossed aside at one end, dangled onto the floor, abandoned. She looked in the bedroom. The kitchen. The bathroom.

She looked on the coffee table for a note or a sign of departure.

No note. And nobody to return her greeting.

Chapter Ten

Change.

That day. That day she met the old man in the park. Shoshonah did not return until three in the morning. Khatia had waited for her in the dark.

"Oh god!" Shoshonah had yelled drunkenly into Khatia's startled face. She had been dreaming deeply about riding a horse into a lake, rubbing its tender belly, her hand tracing the way to where the men had snipped—"I remembered our phone number but I forgot to call you!"

Khatia decided not to ask her if her words had been a little mixed up. She wanted to believe they were. Some people, she did not mind if they forgot her in desultory mirth. But alone with one friend in a strange country, she was ready to be remembered.

An almost undetectable alteration was born that day. The first day of wondering what her hours would be like. The day before, Shoshonah had caressed her body into a shuddering of muscles, slippery juices, and hot skin.

Two changes: one, her job gave her days validity. Two, Shoshonah's presence altered. She was the same as she ever was, but a piece seemed lost.

Thanksgiving occupied the thoughts of those in America, and two months had gone by. They still cuddled. They watched TV. They went to the market. Passion in fruits and vegetables, not in the meat of their own bodies.

An evening alone. Shoshonah at work, the night shift at the hotel. Khatia went to the kitchen to rummage around for some of Shoshonah's snickerdoodles. For some reason, Shoshonah had taken to baking in vast quantities: breakfast muffins, madeleines, apple cookies, raspberry tortes, German chocolate cake, banana bread, challah. Anything she could think of or remember the recipe to would be on the kitchen table when Khatia got home from the office, steam rising like peyote spirits off its new formed body.

The kitchen was a constant mess, as much of the house was. Shoshonah seemed to have a high tolerance for dust and disarray, claiming that cleaning did not interest her at home, since she had to do it all night at work. Cleaning became Khatia's tacit duty, although she realized that she had a high tolerance for dirt as well. She did not remember their dorm room being this messy, but then again those close quarters did not really allow for high volumes of disorder. Khatia stood in the middle of the room, bored and alone, and *Anna Karenina* was not holding her attention at the moment. Shoshonah was at work, she reminded herself; she would work all night and probably go out with her new friends to the lesbian bar, Chez Manfred.

Those papers on the dining table: she should stack them, sort out the bills. Perhaps, even pay them. Satisfied with herself for having found a project, she picked up a cookie from the plate and poured more milk. Cookies and bills. The evening stretched out. She shuffled over to the Formica table and slouched in one of the kitchen chairs, pushing the papers around with her pinky. The pile was high; even an old classified section with potential jobs circled lay at the bottom on top of a plate of stale, buttered bread. Khatia wrinkled her nose and began sorting. An old letter from her brother that still needed to be answered lay squashed and wrinkled amid the phone bill and a flyer from a gym Shoshonah was thinking about joining. Khatia took up the letter between her greasy, crumby fingers.

> Dear Khatia,
>
> I got your postcard. Amsterdam seems pretty bizarre. I know it's supposed to be the drug capitol of the Western World, but what else in there in that place? You aren't a druggie, are you? I think Dad is convinced that you are. Ever since you left he has been calling me more and more. Three times a week sometimes! It's driving my roommates bonkers. All Dad and I ever do on the phone is sit there through long silences. I don't know what his deal is. It's so strange because I can't believe we lived in the same house for eighteen years. I sort of hinted about that last night when he called, and he said it was okay back *then* because I was not a "fully formed and function-

ing human being." I wonder what the hell *that's* supposed to mean. Actually, I think it's the most I've ever gotten out of him. I always wanted to ask you what you think about the old guy. It's not something we ever really talk about. Not that we really talk anyway. But I thought about what he said for a long time. You know, I always felt like I was really *ready* as a kid, that I knew everything in the world that I needed to know in order to get along in this world. I always kind of felt like I didn't need anyone. I still feel that way to some degree. Unless I'm in Organic Chemistry class. Then I don't know my ass from my armpit! Ha ha. Didn't know your little brother was so crass, did you now? Well, I'd better go. The band has a gig this weekend at some junior high sockhop, and we have to practice. I'm getting twenty–five dollars, so I'll be able to make gas money for October break.

—Porter

P.S. Do you ever feel as if you know everything? I guess not or you wouldn't be in Amsterdam.

Khatia blinked at the page, running her eyes over the P.S. again and again. *Do you ever feel as if you know everything?* The words began to blur, and she stopped listening to their distinct sounds in her head, letting that blur as well. Her arm rested on the table, and she put her head on it. Even when she felt the layers of skin, fat, and muscle falling asleep, she stayed that way, not opening her eyes.

Days fell into routine. She went to work. She came home. She did a little shopping if necessary. Then she returned home again to read or watch TV. Their reception was poor, annoying to the eyes. TV snow fell on almost all the images, obscuring them in a white noise winter–wonderland. Watching American TV shows dubbed in Dutch made her a little angry. Why couldn't the Dutch make up their own dumb sitcoms? Shoshonah claimed to watch those shows all day, sometimes at a friend's apartment.

She had numerous friends hooked on soap operas like *Santa Barbara*. Sometimes Khatia would arrive home to Shoshonah on the phone with one of those friends, hashing over the days happenings in imaginary, sunny California.

Making language tapes with Ulrike gave her something to do. It embarrassed her, but secretly she enjoyed it:

"Jim likes basketball, football, and tennis."

"Susan likes tennis, soccer, and water–skiing."

"Robert likes baseball, soccer, and Frisbee."

"Hello. What is your name?"

"My name is Jane. What is your name?"

"My name is George. Nice to meet you!"

"The pleasure is mine!"

Her wages manifested through various forms of labor. Making tapes for language textbooks was one form, and probably the most glamorous. On taping days, Khatia could be sure of long hours. Long hours of verbal repetitions. Long hours of sitting in the small sound booth Ulrike had constructed in the attic of his house. Attics made her nervous, but in Ulrike's home she tried to pretend she was simply high in the atmosphere. Sitting on a small stool with a backrest that only went up to the middle of her spine caused her to hunch over, rounded like her mother had rounded her own body in a question mark. Her ears sweated—imagine that—encased in vinyl earphones, heavy on her head, reminding her of language labs in high school, the indignity of sitting in front of an old–fashioned reel–to–reel machine, those unattractive earphones, like Marvin the Martian, mussing up one's hair, and the droning of voices. She remembered that best—that beehive murmuring of students repeating after the tape in Spanish, French, German, Italian. Occasionally she turned down the volume of her own machine, simply to listen to the comforting proof of warm, viscerated bodies nearby.

"Your voice," Ulrike told her over and over. "Is a godsend."

Khatia abashedly curled her hands around her ears like fleshy seashells, listening to the hum of her breathing, trying to hear what he heard. The attention, the pressure were too great. Yet, she believed in him and in his enthusiasm.

Since they started work so early in the mornings, Khatia usually arrived sleepy and quiet, speaking only when necessary. Her voice was deeper in the early hours, throaty. During those first days, Ulrike would watch her voice with the fascination a grafter watches his Bing cherry tree grow: his discovery, his creation. He could even tell if she had been drinking or smoking cigarettes the night before.

"Your tone is perfect for Mr. Charles. He wants American voices instead of British ones, and you have the perfect standard pronunciation of middle America. The slight New England trace is infinitesimal, and I'm sure he'll agree with me that it adds charm. Really, American English is so in vogue, he'll probably beg to use us for all fifteen chapters."

"Fifteen chapters of *this* stuff?" Khatia held up the script, understanding how Ionesco could find absurdity in the words and create theater around them.

"Be grateful," chided Ulrike. "Most tapes require bilingual speakers. We are hiring someone else to do the translations."

They had only done one project so far, as Ulrike waited to hear from Mr. Charles, draw up the contracts. Sometimes she would work with another person, usually a man, another random American in Amsterdam, looking for a good time and some extra cash. Ulrike did his best, but he usually shook his head after the other person left, making sad comments like, "He was all right, but he told me he is from Tennessee. I do not know if we'll be able to use his tape...Did you notice that twinge?"

"You mean twang?"

"Yes," Ulrike said. "Perhaps you are right. His voice is not for us. I wish Cree were still here. He is my American associate. He has a beautiful American voice: masculine, yet not over–bearing. I can play his tape for you." He looked through his file of high density cassette tapes until he found the right one. A young man's voice played over the speakers. Khatia did not find it all that extraordinary, although he seemed like a friendly, tall person. She did not know why she thought this, but it seemed right.

Ulrike exhaled. "Maybe someday he will be back. Another traveler like you." He put his hand on her shoulder consolingly. "I will get someone worthy of you, Khatia."

That night, Cree's voice worked itself into her dreams. "Going to Hong Kong?" it said, and then laughed. She had the dream more than once, her dream eyes shut tight, seeing nothing and only hearing.

She heard the voice at work occasionally, but she often heard voices in her head and even welcomed them to keep her from falling asleep. They were usually her voice yelling, "Don't you DARE fall asleep."

Work instigated a breaking down of her body into parts. They did so to protect themselves, one from the other. If an angry writer yelled at her on the phone because the galley copies of his book were completely out of sequence, and then implied that she must be incompetent, her ears would hear but her heart would not feel. If Ulrike had her typing up any kind of mindless letter—a rejection, a proposal, a thank you note her fingers would dance over the keyboard in activity, but her mind would be thinking about food, or Shoshonah, or nothing at all. Sometimes, she wrote letters in her head to everyone she knew, liked, or disliked.

Two things saved the job from becoming as insufferable as the law office. The first thing was the audio tapes she made. The second was Ulrike himself.

Ulrike liked early mornings. Starting work early meant ending the day early and going home to his wife and child. As the days grew shorter, the small office seemed to hunch in dimness during the mornings, keeping itself warm.

One day, Khatia bent over the fax machine, trying to clear a paper jam.

"Damn," she mumbled, but Ulrike was on the phone and did not hear her. His desk faced the one window, built into the door, and he could watch the streetcars go by. He hardly ever did, always on the phone or the computer. Khatia's little *escritoire* stood behind his large desk. He let her turn it around so she too could look out the window. Before that, all she had to contemplate was a mildly shredded poster of a windmill.

Ulrike rambled on in some language she did not recognize. He seemed to know twenty languages, and their distinctions were beginning to blend, even the ones she thought were familiar.

"Ach!" he finally spat, banging the phone on its cradle. He cursed for a while in a variety of sounds and languages. "Ach" was his version of "damn."

81

"What is it?" she asked because he seemed to want her to.

"My contact in Brussels. He does not think he can meet me there anymore. His ex–girlfriend just showed up again and told him she will be having his child at the time of the conference. They are getting married and going to Switzerland for their honeymoon. Nothing I could say would persuade him."

"Wow," Khatia said, standing up straight. "That's really responsible of him though. I mean, to marry her and all."

"Ach," Ulrike waved his hand in disgust. "Marriage is a passé institution. Frithe and I only did it because we were not sober. Either was the priest who married us." He shook his finger at Khatia. "But we are lucky we can joke about it. And it is good for business with the Brits. If you ever marry Shoshonah, make sure it is for the right reasons."

Khatia felt something in her abdomen jump, and she said quickly, "Oh, if I ever get married, I'm sure it'll be to a man."

"What?" Ulrike started. He sat down in his chair. "What do you mean? You would deny your true nature?"

"No!" She laughed, and tugged at the jammed paper. Her true nature? She knew she still liked men, perhaps(was this wrong?) preferred them. Ah, disloyal, wicked girl! The taboo of her feelings. The taboo of this conversation. She glanced up at him, knowing he thought she was a wolf in sheep's clothing. "That's not it at all. My true nature, whatever the fuck that is, tells me if I were to marry, it would be to a man."

"But Shoshonah is your lover now. Do you not envision the future with her?"

"I—" Khatia stopped, squinting at a water stain on the wall. Ulrike, gender–neuter creature, adviser, boss, the only man in her life whom she could talk to without squirming; he scrutinized her, confused. They really did not know each other very well, despite their candid fronts. She looked at him shyly, willing to step into an unexplored cave. "I can barely envision five minutes from now."

He shook his head.

"But what is that?" he asked.

"Forget it."

"You are a confident young woman, Khatia."

She laughed. "Gee, Ulrike. I wish someone had told me that sooner. Now that I know, I suddenly feel confidence oozing through my veins." She furrowed her brow and shrugged her shoulders and asked in mock–wonder, "Why didn't I feel this invincible before?"

He looked at her soberly.

"So, you prefer men as well as women?"

She smiled, tired. The corners of her eyes were red, and her skin was flushed, the way it got when she was drunk. Shoshonah often called her Tomatohead. She sat down in front of her desk, giving up on the fax machine.

"That's a very good question," she said. "I'm beginning to think I prefer nothing at all. But I know that can't be right."

"To prefer nothing is to need a change."

She laughed, an awful sound, the sound a cat makes when getting hit by a car. "Coming to *Amsterdam* was a pretty big step, Ulrike! My whole environment? Leaving my birthplace? Where I come from? I think I'm running out of things to change." She frowned at her hands, the fingers loosely clasped, interlaced.

They did not look at each other for a while, fiddling with this or that on their desks. The intense focus of their work moments before had vanished.

"Do you ever wonder if you've made a wrong turn?"

He frowned at her hands as well, as if she had asked a trick question and held the answer on her palms.

"I do not understand," he said.

She shrugged, tasting her tongue for the first time that day, repulsed by what was there, a slicked–down film like the underside of mud.

"Forget it," she said, waving her hands and smiling at him. Everything is okay, see? she wanted to say.

They were quiet for a while. Outside, people moved around in the early afternoon, doing what people do then on sidewalks, eating, walking, pretending they do not mind having nothing else to occupy their fingers and minds.

"You should come to Brussels with me. Instead of Vlad." He nodded his head. "Yes. I will close the office that week anyway. This way you can still earn money and take a trip."

She waited for the balance to shift because he knew now. He knew. He knew she liked men too. But the balance did not shift: they were the same, and the earth kept turning in its journey around the sun.

She bought burritos–to–go at Shoshonah's favorite taco stand(hashish available in the basement) and two chocolate milkshakes. The wind stirred up the rain, and she had left her hat at the office. What did it matter that her hair and clothes were soaked? Shoshonah would be home, and they would celebrate Khatia's first business trip into the world of textbook publishing.

She bashed up the stairs, forgetting to be mindful of the downstairs neighbor, an old woman who had lived there since childhood, and who called them "little hyacinths," when she was not cursing them in Flemish or Dutch for all their "stomping about." Khatia didn't care, eager to find Shoshonah luxuriating on the couch before heading off to work.

"Hello?" she called.

No one answered, but she could hear soft laughter, and what sounded like the murmur of an uninterrupted conversation.

Which was exactly what she found when she reached the top of the stairs.

Curled up on the couch, heads close together. Deep in conversation. Two women, one large and blond, her body dominating the surrounding space like a bright lightbulb. The other one, smaller and long, aware of that light, basking in it. Khatia's eyes shifted to the mantle behind their heads. She seemed to see it for the first time, noticing a long, spidery crack from the cornice to the floor in the cement filling that used to be a fireplace. She noticed how deep the crack was, how riveted the damage, and her eyes did not want to pull away.

She cleared her throat without thinking, softly, ladylike. The others apparently had not felt her hovering on the landing.

Shoshonah pulled her concentrated gaze away from her companion.

"Hey, luv. This is Mina. Mina, Khatia."

The woman turned around and stood up. She had dyed red hair cut in a bob. She held a metal purse, a miniature lunchbox that matched the color of her knee–high boots. She leaned over and kissed the air near Khatia's cheek.

"How do you do?" said Mina.

"How do you do?" replied Khatia in a toneless voice as if she were recording tapes for Ulrike.

"What've you got there?" Shoshonah asked as Mina burrowed back into the couch pillows.

"Oh." Khatia remembered with effort. "Some food. Just some food—for us. If I knew you had company—" They hadn't had any guests up to their apartment before. At least, Khatia had never invited anyone. Who did she know to invite except Ulrike?

"Please, do not worry," said Mina, her accent filling her mouth like a fuzzy chick. "I am not hungry."

"Hm," was all Khatia could manage to say. She could not remember if her parents had ever taught her manners or the appropriate things to say, but she was pretty sure they had. She could not remember them now either.

"I ran into her while I was getting some coffee, and we've just been talking all afternoon," Shoshonah laughed.

Khatia remembered to smile. She even nodded.

Silence; she used it to imagine the ticking of a clock. The one on the mantle was broken, placed there only for show.

"I will go now," Mina said after a moment, hesitation in her voice. She looked to Shoshonah for a command.

"Oh, you should just hang around and we'll go to work together," Shoshonah said.

"Ah," Mina began to say. She glanced at the bag of rattling food as Khatia put it on the coffee table. "Thank you, but I must get my clothes from home. I'll see you soon anyway."

"Oh, all right," Shoshonah sounded disappointed. She stood up with Mina. "See you then, darling. It was really cool to run into you."

Darling? Khatia thought. She watched them peck on the lips.

"Ciao!" Mina said, waving to Khatia as if from a great distance.

"Right," Khatia said.

They listened to Mina's boots clomp down the stairs and the door open and close.

Shoshonah fell back onto the couch. She pointed her chin at the paper bag, crumpled from Khatia's hands with greasy spots on its sides.

"Mmmm. Smells good. Burritos? Man, I love those things. Could you get some plates from the kitchen? Oh, and get me a beer too."

Khatia walked into the kitchen. "So, she works with you?" she called back into the main room.

"Yeah. She lives with her parents and works. She quit school when she was fifteen, but she totally reads. Doesn't she seem cool?"

Khatia returned with dishes and utensils. She sat down next to her on the couch, feeling the novel warmth of Mina's butt radiating out of the cushions. She pretended the sensation away, imagined no sensation at all. Her thoughts grasped unconsciously at the past as a truth, totemic.

"Sure, I guess."

Shoshonah laughed, wrapping her arms around Khatia's neck, rocking back and forth. "Don't get all chartreuse."

Khatia sighed out the stiffness in her body. "Qui? *Moi*? Never." She glanced at Shoshonah's tanned arms around her, resting on her sternum. Momentary, fleeting.

Towers of paper piles leaned precariously on desks, filing cabinets, any surface that could be spared. The fax machine whirred all day, and the phone constantly rang. Messengers delivered packages and envelopes, demanding a signature on their beat–up clipboards, then careening off on their bicycles in haste. Ulrike raked his hands through his hair every two minutes, and by the end of the day it would stand on ends in a prickly, greasy mass. Khatia ran around the tiny office, diving to answer the phone, although it was not her job because who could predict what language the caller would speak? She shuffled through papers when Ulrike requested a search for a "very important scrap of information," typing up his scribbled letters, sometimes in languages she did not understand. Her fingers bungled everything, her mind on a pair of silver boots, tramping up her stairs. Using the international keyboard on the computer gave her a sense of power and blindness, an apt reaction to the chaos in the office as she and Ulrike prepared for their approaching trip and the shut down of the office for a week.

Rain poured down on a city that welcomed the close of autumn into winter. The surface of the streets and sidewalks turned as liquid as the canals, puddle skins popping up and down as the drops broke their surfaces. The water levels rose, and Khatia longed to see the sea, the metallic foaming of stirred up water gods.

"Ach!" Ulrike fell back into his chair, his hands permanently clamped on his head. Khatia no longer became alarmed by his guttural exclamations. She continued to stuff envelopes, her imagination its own boss as it gave her visions of Shoshonah asleep on a houseboat in the middle of the Pacific. In her mind's eye, the boat was like a large cradle, only big enough for Shoshonah and her pillow.

"This is no good. No good at all." Ulrike shook his head, sweating and aging before her very eyes. "The dike breaks, and we are flooded."

"What is it, Ulrike?" she said mildly.

"The messenger can not come here until five o'clock, and by then it will be too late. I must get these proofs to Mr. Charles immediately before he leaves for Monte Carlo."

"Is he in Amsterdam?"

"Yes, yes." Ulrike took his hands away from his head. His hair did not spring back so easily as when it was clean. "I would go myself, but I am waiting for an important call from my American contact." He glanced at Khatia next to the phone, started, doing a double take of her, as if she were a roadside attraction that had failed to shock him the first time. "Perhaps you could go."

In this rain? she wanted to protest. But she was not comfortable with questioning authority. Her mouth opened, her lip curling upwards a bit.

"I will give you my raincoat," he said.

She shook her head. "It's too big. I'll take my umbrella."

"Take mine," he said, hastening to get it out of the pail next to the door. "It is stronger than yours."

"Where does he live?" she asked, taking the umbrella by its large wooden crook.

Ulrike sifted through some papers on his desk for the hundredth time, frantic with nerves. "Koestraat. It is in the Red Light District, but you will be all right since it is day time right now."

Khatia looked out the window at the darkened sky. She had been to the Red Light District once with Shoshonah about a month ago when they went to a party Shoshonah had "heard about" from one of her co–workers. Her heart beat a little faster, and she could feel a slight strain in the skin of her forehead. The sensation reminded her of hair braided too tightly, tugging at the follicles until they tore, sending up chunks of epidermis. Her mother used to braid her hair and keep it that way for days until frail ends crept out of their binds, giving her a look of insanity.

Ulrike noticed her hesitation. "You are not frightened, are you Khatia?" he asked.

She turned to him, her boss. "No," she said. "Why would I be?"

She was a woman who had lived in the balmiest womb of modern civilization. From a tiny New England town to a tiny New England college, to another tiny New England town, Khatia could boast of experiences compact and without much fiction. Death and love, those experiences came to her doorstep, but they came in a tiny, New Englandish way, quiet and predictable. The cities of Boston and New York had shown her their pleasantest sides, their sides of commerce, prosperity, art, and charm. She always stuck by what was wholesome: her parents, her job. No one would ever describe Khatia as street smart, although one might call her painfully aware. Or perhaps wary. Living in the protective crook of American middle class society's arm had only made her more cognizant of how easily all that goodness could disappear.

But right now she needed to be outside. To leave intellectualizing by the wayside like an old, often–fingered memento. Hanging on to the past tired her.

Her watch told her it was ten forty–five in the morning, but the sky wanted time to pass quickly. Bring on the night.

The Red Light District was a place of night. She passed the women, men, and men dressed as women who floated the streets, their pimps. They were brazen ghosts, waiting for the next life. In the rain, they stood in doorways of shops whose sign's screamed SEX, ADULT BOOKS, ADULT TOYS, ADULT PROPHYLACTICS, LIVE GIRLS, LIVE MEN, FANTASY. The drug–dealers prowled about. She was used to the dealers of the coffeehouses, had watched the hashmen with their chalkboard prices, their discounts on cigarette wrappers. These Red Light salesmen sold a different kind of drugs, deadlier because their drugs damaged the body more quickly and efficiently in different areas—the brain, the nerves, the veins, lungs, spinal juices. And they destroyed those areas the body invents—memory, dreams, hopes, desires. They replaced those things with their own versions, pilfering ephemeral originals.

Even the puddles on the sidewalks glowed red: devils' piss.

She arrived at the apartment, a building that had been elegant at one time, but was now as used and broken as the men and women on the streets. Its façade was painted over and over, observable through the rips in the veneer. She entered through a rusted wrought iron fence leading down a small path to the front door.

A muffled, yelling voice answered her knock, the window's rectangle filled in by a wet piece of particle board, wet because of some strange leak in the roof of the tiny stoop. A man opened the door. He was middle–aged, and at one time he had possessed the space around him like a fire possesses the warmth it exudes. But his nose had grown into a blossoming snout, his eyes were bleared with broken capillaries, and his red hide made his blond–gray hair look dry and sickened, like dead grass. His soul wanted to leave that damaged sac of water, shrink into a little point of light, but he would not let it go just yet. He was the type who suffered common, daily, human fear.

"Ulrike sent me to give these to you," Khatia stated her business, looking around him with cheerful insouciance. Do not see what you do not want to see, and do not judge people by their misfortunes: everything in her upbringing, in her notion of right.

89

"Ulrike's girl," the man said after looking her up and down for a few moments. He was an Englishman. "Won't you come in?"

"Thank you, but I need to get back to the office," she said, smiling with what she hoped was frankness, bowing her head. He is a good person, she told herself. If I believe this, it will come true.

"I insist. Ulrike will not miss you," he said, walking away from the open door into the dimness and fried odor of his apartment. He pulled at her invisibly. It was the call of authority, a moral quandary. She did not want to jeopardize Ulrike's business, or her job, or this man's feelings. No embarrassment, no confrontation, no scandal. She remembered the time she got detention in junior high for chewing gum in English class. Her mother had picked her up after school crying. After a while, Khatia asked, "What's wrong, Mom?"

Her mother looked at her , her face wet.

"You have shamed me," she said.

She stepped over the threshold, out of the leaking, rainy roof of the open sky.

In the corner by the door, she leaned her umbrella with his. Down a moaning hall into the darkness of his chamber. She calmed her breathing, sure she would be able to know the day when something terrible would happen to her. Premonition came in waves. She had it the day her father informed her of the seriousness of her mother's sickness. It was a profound emptying of all things good, and that emptiness was too heavy for her to carry. But she did not feel it today.

She arrived in a backroom. Muddy light fell across the pink–faded oriental rug, bald in patches under the scratched up Formica table and chairs. Underneath it was some sort of mustard–patterned carpeting, flattening down by grease, hair, mucus, and time. All the furniture had a thick, barely disturbed layer of dust, and even its one living occupant seemed to exist under grimy powder; the plants did not suffer, she noticed, since they were plastic.

"A nightcap," he waved a dusty, sticky bottle at her chest. "Then it's back to work for you, my sweet little sugar cube." He turned his back on her as he poured the liquid into a mug on a table by the window, looked around in vain for another. He shrugged and tipped the bottle to his lips. "I like to suck on sugar cubes."

90

Khatia swung around to look back from where she had come, trying not to see too much of her surroundings, yet not wanting to look at his body, the only other living thing in the room. He gave off heat, drawing her eyes towards him.

"You're a writer, Mr. Charles?" she asked.

"Whatever," he mumbled. "I'm a fucking degenerate loser, is what I am. But I suppose you couldn't figure that out when you walked in, eh? I wrote poetry," he said into the yellowed window shade. "But then I had to make a choice between the drinking and the writing. Now I do textbooks to help finance that choice." He turned his head towards her without turning around. "You're the voice." She heard a buzzing like scraping wind near the bottle on the table.

She was confused for a moment, looking at the back of his quartered profile. "Oh, you mean for the tapes. Yes, that's me. I'm—"

"Talk to me. Talk to me in your voice."

She tried to laugh out loud, while on the inside, she whirled: *Polite. Good girl. Suburbs. College degree. Errand runner. The wrong side of the tracks. The home of Rembrandt. Van Gogh's waves, his smoke, his vision.* Goodness, wholesomeness, love of the ground, the puddles, life, drink. Love of a woman, a past that no longer matters.

Blinding her mind, Khatia forgot the question. She cleared her throat.

"That's good," he said.

"Put your mouth around me," he said.

He turned to her, the bottle in hand, his cock sticking out of his trousers, straight and mutilated. The end of it was swollen into a lavender shade, and Khatia thought how wrong that was, how it should have been red like his face.

Shoshonah had once joked that you could tell a lot about a person by looking at their genitals. Khatia blushed, remembering this thought, how, in the case of Mr. Charles, it was so true. Swimming upwards towards refracted light—her mind blank for the eternity of a nanosecond, quiet panic, the need for air.

The knocking of boots on stairs.

91

Olivia Boler

The sensation of muscles asleep. What color were muscles under the fat and skin?

Pock–marked gray. An ancient, sidewalk gray.

But that was not it at all. That color was outside. She had made a mistake by coming in again. All she wanted was for that color to be under her feet. Then she would have reached safety. The red neighborhood, its color, would not matter any longer if she could simply feel her feet on concrete.

She dropped the package with a breaking thud on the floor, backing away towards the hall.

"Suck me, sugar cube." As if he could care less.

"I have to go," she said.

"I would hate to report to Ulrike that you had been uncooperative," he asked. His words lapped at her, their reality, and she felt that pull more intensely even though he had seemed to break some tacit rule of fantasy. Yet, not at all. This was a neighborhood of fantasy, and with a dream coming true came compromise and payment: she had been wrong about his flame diminishing.

"Tell him whatever you want, Mr. Charles," she said, moving with the break. "My duties don't extend to blow jobs."

"What else do you and your pimp do all day? Send out faxes? Talk on the phone? Avoid touching? I find that hard to believe."

She reached the entrance to the hallway, turned, and strode to the door, a model on the runway, her face a marble carving, eyes oblique.

Outside, in the night rain of late morning. She walked quickly down the street towards the trolley stop. Her body wracked in small spasms. Self–reproach. Revulsion. Shame so acute she could have scrubbed her own body raw with a brillo pad if given the opportunity. She found a seat on the trolley and sat with her wet head against the window; she had left Ulrike's umbrella there.

The spasms turned to shaking, and then to quiet trembling. Her breath fogged up the window, proof that she was alive. Her stop came up faster than she had expected, and she missed it.

She got off at the next one and walked slowly back to the office, pausing

92

at the window of an antique store, staring rudely at the plates and silverware on display.

He was a man. She had stood up to a man. She had resisted the direction her knees had wanted to take.

Gradually, standing in front of that antique store, she became aware of her body: her knees, her skin, her eyes. She could be anyone. She could disappear: he had not even asked for her name. That potential anonymity: it aroused her more than anything else.

Chapter Eleven

John Porter Quigley holds the letter from his daughter in his right hand, the delicate airmail paper curving under the pressure of his fingers. His fingers are damp, leaving whorls of scaly prints on the pale blue sheaf.

He moves from room to room in his house, large and empty. His assistant, Dorinne, has been trying to convince him to sell it and move to the city. Too many memories, she tells him. Pain, she wants to say, but he understands. Get a plush little condo. Wouldn't she like that? he thinks. Perhaps then she'll receive an invitation or proposal. He has slept with her occasionally after cocktails and faculty picnics, off and on over the years.

In the kitchen, he contemplates the refrigerator for a moment. It's one of those large, restaurant models; he insisted on the best. No magnets or children's scrawlings marked with gold stars mar its exterior. Its well-kept, like an undoodled page. He cannot stand it when he catches his students doodling in seminars. He has a reputation, he knows for being a "hard ass," he believes that's the term they use, those students.

Opening a kitchen drawer, his fingers rumble around inside, searching. Paper clips, rechargeable batteries, emergency flashlight and first aid kit. Ah. There it is. He pulls out an ugly clay creature, the size of a half–dollar. Obviously, one of his children made this long ago. A gummy, dyed–green feather, tattered with age sits in a hardened globule of old glue. It must represent hair, he thinks. On the back , the same kind of glue squeezing behind it, is a small black magnet.

He puts his daughter's letter on the refrigerator, opened, fastening it there with the magnet. He lets his fingers trail along the edges of the paper, and then they move almost on their own to his shirt front, slipping between the buttons, and over the scar across his chest.

The nightmares have started again, at least once a week. He wakes from them quietly, his eyes open serenely to gaze at the blank darkness of the ceiling. The skin on his lower back is probably slick, but he does not move after the dream. He remembers when it started, right after he came home from Korea. As a young man, he had a different reaction to the dream, its invidious imagery making him crawl and limp to the toilet in order not to vomit on the floor.

In the dream, he can see only the face of a person whose skin smells like half–cooked brain. The person's brain *is* actually cooking, an eggy substance, oozing and congealing from the ears, nose, and mouth. The mouth: it grimaces, partly hidden in chiaroscuro. It rounds into a plaintive O, and the colors of brain become seeped in a swirling sorbet of pinkish crimson. *Forgive me. I do not understand.* The smell gets to him the most, the cigarette burning of knuckle hairs, wrinkling elbow skin, the sinew of knee joints. John Porter Quigley reaches out a skinless hand to the face, absolving it of sins. But as his palm connects with the cheek, the face dissolves, collapsing in on itself, giving in to melting, greasy streams. He is left with a tepid pool of jelly, running down his arms. His arms raise above his head, and the globules pour into his mouth. He turns to a wall, flips a light switch, and hears the screams of that mouth, as electricity runs up and down the circuits of the fleshy pulp.

In the beginning, the face was the prisoner in Seoul, the original: Sung Ko. Why must he know his name? After he married Annie, it became her face, the face of old, the face he fell in love with, the young face, the face he could not bear. And now. Now that she was gone, it was his daughter's face, her O screaming, *Forgive me, father, for I have given in, and this I promised I would never do.*

"Promised whom, my child?"

He looks up, realizes he has wandered into the downstairs guest room. He does not remember walking there. He sits at the writing desk, looks out the window facing the fecund land, his unused property. The room feels like a motel, the bed neatly made, everything dusted, some dried flowers in vases here and there. Magazines and books on the bedside table: *Architectural Digest*, Coleridge. His hands idle at the desk drawer. Inside is some paper. He takes out a sheet, carefully draws his fountain pen from his breast pocket, uncapping it, proud that it has never leaked.

Dear Khatia,

Enclosed is a check. If, for some reason, the check

95

should be missing from this envelope, please inform me immediately, and I will issue a stop–payment on it.

Your brother seems to be doing well in school. I talk to him occasionally on the telephone. He is spending a lot of time with that ensemble he calls "the Band," but appears to be getting his studies done satisfactorily. He sends his best regards.

I went to the Winter Festival with Dorinne. Some of the other faculty were present as well. Peter Marklov was giving a lecture and slide presentation on his recent trip to Kharkov. It was quite fascinating. Peter, as you remember, has an amusing repartee. Marvelous fellow.

My students are shaping up. Horrible accents. Dorinne will chaperon most of the lower divisions on a field trip to New York City later this month. If you are still considering graduate school, I suggest you talk to her about the options. She is a wondrous resource, and has been encouraging most of our students to apply as soon as possible.

I hope all is well. Take care, and call if you need anything.

Love,

Dad

He caps his pen, placing it on the table's surface. The ink on the paper stays glossy for a moment, then fades into drying. He blots it with another piece of paper just to be sure.

In his study, he writes out the check, finds an airmail stamp. On his desk sits a picture of his children leaning on the porch, their elbows digging into the railing, their poses identical. They seem shy of each other, awkward relatives, near strangers or distant cousins. They both have a thick glow to their skin, a golden hue of pound cake. Porter's hair is that dull orange–brown, confused genes. It matches his freckles. His eyes make him look

96

Slavic or insane. John Porter Quigley can not look at those eyes for too long. Khatia's hair is more ordinary, darker, a ruby aura coming through in highlights when the sun hits it. He has always associated her with the bark of a redwood tree. She has never seen one, and he has not told her about this.

He covers his eyes with his hands, leaning his own elbows into the blotter on his desk, blocking the view of their visages. He wants very badly to put the photo in a drawer, up high, or onto the burning logs in the fireplace. Such an act, he decides, is savage, and he is running out of the little ceremonies that save him from becoming inhuman.

Chapter Twelve

As the train rocked gently, speeding southwest to a place only three hours away but with a completely different language system, Khatia held her arms, watching countryside stream by. Van Gogh's countryside. The flower fields stretched raw and blank with scabs of ice on them here and there. The repetitiveness of the landscape began to wear her down, and she looked for the greenhouses, trying the peer inside them for the millisecond the train allowed. Pink, yellow, or white flowers? This was her game. Find the color. Determine the texture of the petals' skins, the graininess of the thickened, silky flesh near the stalk.

She shifted her legs, feeling the rub of her light wool trousers on the insides of her thighs. The pants were lined, but she detected the itch of the natural material through the shiny, inner acetate anyway.

A flower was like a man.

In her lifetime, not counting art and photos, Khatia had seen two penises in–the–flesh. One was of the boy in high school, the one whom she had visited in the dorm. The other was Mr. Charles'.

Within her arms, squashed against her chest, was a scrap of paper she found in her back pack. On it she wrote: "Todd. Mr. Charles." Strange: she could only remember the first name of one and the last name of the other. She did not bother to ask Ulrike for his name or look for his paper work. Knowing more about him would not make the offense against her any less great.

She told no one about the incident in the Red Light District. When she had returned to the office, Ulrike did not noticed anything wrong with her. Her nature demanded a display of normalcy. *Everything was just fine.*

Next to Mr. Charles' name, Khatia tried to draw a picture of a penis. The curvature was not right. She had little formal instructions in art, not since high school when her teacher suggested she stick to ceramics and leave drawing to those who had the talent to grasp the concept of depth perception. The comment had been devastating, but she had complied, obediently throwing pots and mugs, telling her mother, when she asked her daughter with concern why she failed Introduction to Drawing, that she had not turned in her final project. Such was the standard reply. Khatia was known as one of those quiet students who did not kiss up to teachers. She once overheard some women at the supermarket talking about a boy in the neighboring town of Mont Vernon, a quiet youth who "kept to himself," who had shot his whole family with his father's hunting rifle, then bled to death by chopping off his own hand with an ax. Khatia had bought a newspaper and found the story. Yes: the boy usually sat in the back of his class just as she did. He didn't have many friends and had always been quiet and well–behaved. Khatia had signed up to try out for the rowing team the next day.

The penis she drew looked like a two–dimensional snake being swallowed by a large flower. She had only seen a pocketing of Mr. Charles' scrotum, that meatball–skinned sac. She could not remember Todd's. Less hairy. The flower was a mutant tulip, and she let the stem grow out of it, into a dragon's head, fire–breathing nostrils of smoke. She cross–hatched without compunction.

Ulrike snored across from her, a closed–mouth snore. Two nights before, she had baby–sat his daughter so that he and Frithe could have a night on the town before their four day separation. Frithe and Ulrike complimented each other, both slightly unattractive people, unaware of their lacking physical beauty, making up for it with radiant good natures. They did not know nor care. Little Sofie did not care either, but then, what does a two year old care about? She would probably be a great beauty, Khatia thought, although she did snore like her father. Ulrike was the only person Khatia knew who preferred to ride backwards on trains.

He woke with a start, some dreamed bump making his legs kick out against her shins in a gigantic twitch. He stared about in bleary nearsightedness. Fumbling his hands along the seat, his fingers came to rest on his small eye-glasses, folded in his lap. After affixing them to his face, tucking a tiny amount of hair behind each ear for padding, he looked at her.

"I have to piss," he said in a grave voice.

Khatia pointed behind them.

"They're that way."

He followed the direction of her hand with his eyes.

"Right," he said, standing up.

She continued to look out the window, waiting for Brussels, and the end of this slight confinement.

Ulrike returned with a paper cup of coffee for himself. He handed her a tea. She swallowed the hot liquid, the teabag not yet having its full effect on the water. She folded the drawing and put it on the seat next to her with her book.

"This is a significant trip, Khatia. I went last year. That is how I met my American contact. You remember I have spoken of him, yes?"

She frowned at him, trying to remember. Ulrike had so many "contacts." The American contact. "What's his name again?"

"Cree."

"Right."

"I met him through a mutual friend, also in the business. Cree is not, but they were having a torrid affair."

"Torrid?"

"Is that not the right word?"

She shrugged, tired of coming up with definitions.

"Their romance was not serious, and I convinced him to come to Amsterdam with me and make tapes. I played one for you, do you not recall?"

"Of course," she said. The friendly, tall voice.

"I wish I could have convinced him to stay, but he missed his home in America."

"Where is that?"

"San Francisco."

"Oh." Khatia looked back out the window. Her breath stopped for a moment when they went into a tunnel. The blackness of the train spooked her, and she saw the reflection of her eyes in the glass.

100

When they came out into the brightness, she breathed again.

"My mother was from San Francisco," she said to the eyes.

"Cree tells me it is a wonderful city. The jewel of the United States."

"Well," she said with a smile. "I don't suppose *Cree* would lie."

"He would not," Ulrike said seriously.

Khatia cleared her throat. "Is he gay?"

Ulrike chuckled. "No. Although such is a common yet illogical conclusion. Cree said that people do not assume he is gay when he tells them where he is from, but they assume all his friends are."

"So the torrid affair was with a woman," Khatia said, feeling as if she should apologize to someone. The proprietary right she seemed to be privy to, to be able to make blasphemous remarks about gays, no matter how mild, simply because she was considered "gay," had not taken hold of her. Labels, in general, never had.

"His old lover? Yes. There are many women in the business now, Khatia. Frithe was very active, my partner in every facet, until we had Sofie," he hunched forward. "Perhaps this is the career for you as well."

Khatia sat up straighter. She vacillated between being honest and not wanting to hurt his feelings.

"Making tapes is...kind of fun," she said, giving in to herself.

He nodded. "But there is much more to this work than making tapes," he said.

"I know," she said, sighing.

They sat for a while, the train's forward motion carrying them through silence. Khatia slipped the paper into her backpack, she would put it in her journal later, and reached for the book she had borrowed from Frithe's bookcase. Ulrike watched the scenery, gulping his coffee, his Adam's apple and throat muscles working conspicuously like weights in a glass elevator.

"Look!" he said, tapping suddenly on the window with his protruding knuckles. Khatia looked out the window, her eyes following the sound of the rapping. Outside, a field lay in full flower, a mass of yellow against the bleak, coffee–brown of the earth.

Surprising how conventional a convention could be. Publishing houses, type–setters, illustrators, agents, book–binders, software sales. All had booths in the main convention hall of the hotel, their displays and give–aways of pens or plastic mugs garishly decorated in neon colors with the intent of drawing potential clients their way. People drifted from booth to booth, discoursing in various languages, laughing at private moments, networking with energy. Khatia had never seen so many people in business suits smiling. She attended a few of the workshops held in the smaller conference rooms. Almost all of the talks were given in French, still considered the international language by those who spoke it, and she could follow along tolerably. Being semi–versed in a language excited her. She eavesdropped on other people's conversations, learning the terminology of textbook publishing but not really understanding: anything in French sounded like creamy food and steamy breath.

Impressive were those people who could switch from one language to another such as Ulrike. These people were abundant in Brussels, the center of European economics and commerce, of coming together.

Ulrike did not have a booth, but on their last day there he was going to do a presentation in one of the conference rooms, and Khatia would assist him, punching the button of the slide projector on his signal. He loved having her there. A small fish in a mammoth ocean, having an assistant made him a bigger contender.

"Last year, Khatia, I did everything wrong," he told her. "I only had one suit, one tie, and one shirt. I carried an inexpensive, vinyl attaché. Everyone knew I worked alone, that my wife could not even assist me anymore because of the baby."

"They held that against you?" she asked. "I would think they would admire you for working on your own."

He shook his head. "Small businesses have some clout because of their integrity, and the employees usually work harder than those at the large corporations. But they are unstable. I was too eager to demonstrate my enthusiasm last year, but my energy was wasted; I had no one with me so that I could display my authority."

"No one to back you up to show you're in charge," she said, nodding.

She smiled. "It's a good thing Frithe bought you that stylish leather soft–sided briefcase too."

"Yes," he said seriously. "And now I have two suits and a shirt and tie for each day as well."

Khatia ducked her head into her program booklet to smile more widely.

"But the most important improvement is you, Khatia. You—what did you say?—You back me up. That is why you are important, Khatia. You back me up."

He patted her hand briskly. Someone called to him, and he was carried away on the networking tide, his new poise and affected aloofness that had replaced the old eagerness intact. Khatia trailed after him slowly, running her tongue thickly along the roof of her mouth, trying to swallow her breath. Her heart beat faster.

Where was Shoshonah, right at this moment?

After three days of workshops and speeches, she was ready to kill something slowly and with her hands. She needed a break from the talk of perfect–bound laboratory books and intonation tapes. She needed to get away from the pushing crowds, wafting colognes, and, especially Ulrike. Her shyness, she supposed that was the conventional word for it, was painfully evident in the throngs of all these people. She could not smile, stumble about in her awful French, and look interested any longer. Still, speaking it was invigoration; she wanted more, but she wanted out.

"Ulrike," she said the next morning. "I am playing hooky today."

He paused in the doorway of his hotel room, a little puddle of cologne evaporating in his left palm.

"I have never heard of that game," he said.

"It means that I'm going to go do some stuff on my own," she said, waving her hands in a circle in the direction she believed was the center of the city.

"Oh! I see," he clapped his hands together and then slapped his cheeks. "You do not want to go to the workshops today?"

103

She tried not to stare at his ostrich–like throat as he rubbed the strongly smelling moisture into his neck. "If you don't mind. I didn't want to just sneak off without telling you. But I don't think I can handle another day of this. Besides, tomorrow is your big presentation, and if I take today off, I'll be fresh for tomorrow."

Ulrike's eyes glazed a little behind the shiny glass of his spectacles. Their presentation tomorrow was to be the crowning achievement of his young career.

"Yes," he said, his mind far away: Khatia clicking the little button of the slide machine, her recorded voice rolling over the amazed audience in proper, American English as they gazed at images of tastefully rendered language textbooks pages. "Play the hooky. Here." He handed her some Belgian francs. "I'll see you tonight. We have dinner with that professor, Bernard Tasselhoff, remember?"

"I'll be back before then," she assured. He nodded, knowing it. How he counted on her: the knowledge surged through her, and she felt a heat similar to that she had experienced the day the movers brought the couch. She turned away from him, striding down the hall, waiting for the sound of his door to shut, waiting for him to stop watching her retreating back. Waiting, waiting, waiting…

Chapter Thirteen

The bell tower clock struck eleven thirty, and Khatia stretched as she sat on a park bench. The city of Brussels was empty of tourists, and although no snow fell, a bitter wind swept through, whistling against the sides of buildings. Khatia could feel it through her body, actually taste it with the pores of her skin. It sucked the moisture out of her cells, except for her nose and eyes. It caused those parts to water like crazy. More than one stranger had asked her if she were okay. She was not sure what to answer.

"Ce sont les larmes du vent, simplement," she would say to the kindly person, and smile to prove her hardiness: "It's just tears from the wind."

In a *tabac*, she bought a pack of cigarettes, a Danish kind that came in an elegant, blue box. She had read in *Newsweek* that the younger one started smoking, the harder it became to quit. So the statistics said. She figured she was old enough, strong enough, to quit when the time came, if she let the time come. Juliene, one of Shoshonah's friends from Chez Manfred, encouraged her to pick up the habit.

"You are sexy when you are smoking," Juliene cooed into Khatia's ear, letting her moist lips graze her lobe. "Have another. Come on, smoke with me. One should never smoke alone."

Shoshonah seemed amused by Juliene's apparent infatuation with Khatia, screaming out her banshee scream across the crowded bar every time she saw the woman salivating over her lover. But she frowned when Khatia smoked. Everyone smoked, even Shoshonah. Just socially. Just with drinks. Khatia did not drink very much. Someone had to keep a level head. Someone had to carry Shoshonah home if she needed it. Khatia might as well smoke, getting a small spin in her head from the first cigarette which tapered off during the second.

"You enjoy it too much," Shoshonah said to her. That was all. But pointing it out was enough; it bugged her. Everything about Khatia seemed to

105

bug her these days. She was always with her hotel friends or at Chez Manfred or with pouty–lipped, faux–redheaded Mina, and they rarely saw one another anymore.

Something about smoking did fascinate her. She had always noticed people who smoked, how sexy they were, and dangerous. She seemed to fade into safety as they took their lives in hand, sacrificing each breath to wreath themselves in instantaneous beauty. By inhaling, she could be noticed through the smoke, revered by others as she revered them.

The bench was next to the one landmark she knew of in Brussels, a fountain of *le petit pisseur,* a small stone boy with a stream of water coming out of his little penis. Legend had it that during World War II, a little boy had saved Brussels by pissing on an undetonated bomb dropped by a German airplane. He deactivated the bomb permanently. Khatia gazed at the little boy, posing picturesquely, as she practiced her French inhale, blowing the smoke out of her mouth and up her nostrils like a confused dragon. Someone should take her picture here with the fountain in black and white film. Since it was winter, the stream coming out of the little boy's member was turned off, and only feathery stains of rust ran down his legs like lovely garlands.

The clock struck twelve, and Khatia looked off in the direction of its chimes. She got up from the bench and, like a lemming, followed the intermittent stream of people on the sidewalk. Her legs were icy cold against the material of her jeans. She should have brought long–underwear. Christmas decorations hung from every street lamp, and garlanded all the shop windows. When had holiday and good cheer come to the world? She must have been asleep. Or at least inside a hotel's convention rooms.

She arrived in the ancient town square, through a maze of crooked and narrow medieval cobblestoned streets and close–rising buildings of stone and tile. The windows of apartments above stores remained tightly shut against the wind, their warped, bottle–like panes giving the impression of waving water. She stood in the center of the square and looked up at the city hall's clock. The granite walls were sooty with age, and the aqua–green copper steeple rose bleakly against gray clouds. She looked up at it, head back, feeling the stretch in the front of her neck, letting her mouth hang open, saying "Wha—? Wha—?" softly to herself. "See how you can't say the 't' when you look up?" Porter had said to her as a child. They would giggle, saying "Wha—?" to each other, looking into the blossoming branches of the apple trees around their house, pretending to be half–wits.

No one paid her any mind. She looked around the square, picturing it in the past when horse–drawn carriages had rattled over the large, marble cobbles, transporting dukes and princesses to important rendez–vous. She imagined the space packed with bodies in order to watch a beheading or hanging; punishment was diversion like television or the Internet today.

If only it were summer. Summer, when all the cafés had umbrellas, tables, and chairs set out in front of their doors, women in flower–print dresses, men with slicked back hair. Love in the air.

Love was in the air right then. Couples walked mittened hand in mittened hand. Older pairs with netted bags full of embryonic, winter fruits and vegetables.

She settled on a pub for its plum purple trim around the windows. The sign above the door read *Le Primereau*. She tossed her cigarette in the gutter, ignoring her conscience(after all, she had thought she'd someday practice in Greenpeace's law department) and walked over. Inside was warm and elegant. Chairs covered in brown, crushed velvet. A fire blazing in the fireplace—with no grill. If her mother were alive, she would ask where the smoke detector was.

If her mother were alive.

Europeans did not like loud, intrusive chatter in restaurants, although in bars it was a different story. But in the middle of the day, in the middle of a work week, all was quiet and slightly gray. The other customers whispered to each other in low tones. Khatia smiled to herself. She was alone. She had always been alone, confusing it with loneliness. Still, the difference was not completely clear to her.

She pulled out a little notepad from her backpack. Ulrike made her carry the paper, in case he was suddenly inspired with a new scheme, so that she could write stuff down while he dictated. She saw other publishers doing that with their assistants, the young women and men writing furiously while their bosses shouted orders over their shoulders, running as if their life depended on attending the next workshop. So far, she had written:

1.) pick up carton of cigarettes

2.) wear green tie to dinner

3.) call Frithe

"I feel like a Kelly girl," she told him. "Like I should be in the ladies lounge with all the other secretaries and geisha girls doing our nails, while you smoke cigars and drink brandies with the other big time Babbitts in the billiards room."

He had looked at her with a frown, and then smiled patiently. "Are you trying to confuse me with your crazy American humor again?" From the bar, she ordered a Heineken and went to a little table near the window. Staring at Ulrike's list, she wished she had her journal, but she had left it on the floor of her closet back in Amsterdam. She drummed her fingers on the table, lighting another cigarette, although the back of her tongue tasted like a burnt plastic straw.

A man and woman leaving the restaurant talked as they passed her table. She heard the woman say, "Solitude," as they disappeared out the door, clasping her hand around the inside of his crooked elbow.

Solitude.

I'll pretend, she wrote on a fresh page, that I am someone else. Let me cliché: I'll pretend that I am a poet. An intellectual from America, come to find words for fresh poetry, in Belgium. I wear black, because that is what poets do. I wear heavy, telephone-pole scaling boots, to scare strangers, make them think I will kick the ever-loving shit out of them if they piss me off. I meet people and make them fall in love with me, although I do not fall back. Men and women, I don't care, as long as they can deal with me talking poetry in my sleep. I'll pretend I keep a journal, write my poetry with my new words, drink scalding cup after cup of coffee, smoke Pall Malls, let my hair get greasy, never smile, never run out of money, get fat, become bulimic, shoot heroin, contract a venereal disease, put a deadhead sticker on my scooter, do it all wrong.

I'll pretend I like solitude. That it does not matter to me if another person never talks to me again. My body needs no nourishment. My soul needs the words. It needs a dictionary. But every other part of me can live with nothing else. That's where I want to be, pretend.

She looked up from the page and realized her nose was running. She swiped at it. The pen had pressed down heavily on the cheap paper, almost ripping it. What would a handwriting specialist say?

Perhaps he would say, "Nothing extraordinary happens to those who are

108

alone."

She scrawled her reply: The familiarity of the past holds us, masks the solitude. We are alone surrounded. Fungus, clinging to a rotting tree.

She ripped out the pages of writing and the blank ones below it until the impression of the words disappeared, and folded them into the pocket of her jeans. Later, she would tape them into her journal along with her sketch of Mr. Charles.

Khatia grasped the bridge of her nose between two fingers, pinching, squeezing her eyes shut.

"Oh, Shoshonah," she whispered to herself. "What are we doing to each other?"

She opened her eyes and looked around, noticing what everyone else in the bar was drinking. Expensive German beers never even heard of in America, and spritzy drinks with lemon wedges on the glass. She caught the bartender's attention, pointing at one of the drinks. He nodded, fixing one for her and bringing it to her table.

She sipped it, tasting the usual alcohol burn at the back of her throat. A clearing of her taste buds so that the greasy tobacco of her cigarette stood out in full relief on her tongue and inner cheeks.

"Parlo italiano?" a swarthy young man in a black, floor length leather overcoat stood next to her. His eyes held aloof earnestness. He had been sitting at the bar. Everything about him was unlit: hair, eyes, stubble. The archetype of the tall, dark stranger.

"Non," she answered, stubborn. "Je ne suis pas italienne."

"Espagnole?"

"Non."

"Portugaise?"

"Non."

"Mais, quoi?"

"Je suis américaine."

"Mais duquelle origine?" he said, a little impatient.

"Ma mère était une moitié chinoise," she said with a sigh.

"Ah," he said. "American. Yes, I have done business with the British, so I know a little English."

"C'est bien," she said, and waited for him to lose interest.

"I am Benoit," he said.

"Khatia," she offered. "Enchantée, alors."

"How much Chinese are you?" he asked. Not a question people usually asked her. She often forgot that she was Chinese at all. She looked this man up and down. The expansiveness of his coat, the stretched, expensive skin of cows or lambs or goats comforted her.

"A quarter. My mother was half–Chinese."

"And your father?"

"Mostly German with some English, I think."

He looked a little puzzled. "Tu te sembles italienne. I know Italian very well."

"Oh," she said. "I know a little French and a little Spanish."

"Pas de chinois?"

"No."

"Why not?"

She shook her head, drumming her fingers on the side of the glass, counting a rhythm: one, two three, four, five. Five, four, three, two, one. One, two, three, four, five...

"I don't know," she said. Strangers, she thought. We talk to strangers in bars. That's what they are for when one is alone.

"But that is a big part of you," he gestured towards her chest, towards her heart, where origins were kept. "It is your culture."

She laughed. "Not really. Not for me anyway. My brother is more interested in that sort of thing. He's in college right now, finding himself through undergraduate seminars. I think he's taking one on Asian History. He doesn't look like me at all." She changed the subject. "You've never been to the States?"

"No," he said.

She looked into her empty glass.

"Let me get you another," Benoit said, signaling the bartender with his up–pointed finger. Smooth, manicured fingernails, she noticed. He gestured to the seat across from her and she nodded her assent. She watched him fold himself into the chair.

He ordered a drink for both of them called a madrigal: beer and grenadine. She said thanks, sipping it as they sat in silence for a while. He offered her a cigarette out of his silver case.

"What is your business? The one you do with the British," she finally asked, exhaling the smoke with poised expertise.

"Finance," he said, and no more. She nodded.

"What are you doing here in Brussels?" he asked.

"Business," she replied and raised an eyebrow. He smiled, and she almost felt they had made some sort of connection reaching beyond their apparent foreignness.

"Khatia," he breathed around the phonetics of her name. "Would you like to have something to eat?"

His apartment was small, in the turret of an ancient building. The furniture was black and chrome—modular and Bauhaus. An anomaly in its fifteenth century surroundings. She sat on the leather couch trying to remember how many cigarettes she had smoked that afternoon. They ate canned corn with sliced tomatoes and tuna doused in vinaigrette, smearing the whole thing on baguettes. Anything went with baguettes.

"My family owns this vineyard," Benoit said as he poured wine into her glass, "I trust it will be satisfactory."

Khatia looked in her glass, watching for her eyes as she had done on Aunt Estella's porch a few months ago. "Wine is a bitter drink," she said.

"This whole concept of you being Chinese without being Chinese," Benoit said, lighting her cigarette with his crystal coffee table lighter. "It is not right."

Khatia did not know what to say. Her brain felt muddled, perhaps from the wine, or perhaps from her companion's obsessive pushing.

"Why didn't your mother teach you Chinese?"

"Why would I need to know it?"

"Why would you not? Language informs our culture, our identities. Words connect ideas and expression, give meaning to chaos. Without communication, we are less than animals. Even animals have signatures. They piss on the ground that is theirs."

She put her wine glass on his coffee table, pushing aside their dishes. He was obviously one of those fatuous dilettantes she had avoided in college who sat around the student union over watery *espressi* arguing endlessly over the finer points of Derrida and Foucault. "I'm an American. One language."

"But I know of America. You are not composed merely of Anglo–Saxons."

"You yourself thought I was Italian," she said, not able to hide the defensiveness in her voice, a defensiveness she could not explain. "What's more important: my origins or what I look like?" She balked inwardly at her words; something was on the verge of breaking, but whatever it had been, she lost it as Benoit continued.

"You can not just adopt a culture to suit your will. Some facets of human nature are inborn, instinctual."

"You sound like one of those advocates for the bell curve."

"*Pardon?*" he asked.

She drew in the smoke. One day of smoking. In her mind, she could see the pink, spongy matter of her lungs turn to cheesy pizza. Health to decay.

"It is shameful that you do not have an identity."

"*Pardon?*" Her turn.

"Your parents should have told you about yourself."

She almost laughed but opted for dignity.

"Maybe I should leave."

Her words were like heavy coins falling into an empty sink, ringing and clanking loudly in her ears.

She searched his eyes for a split second and found the innocent carnality she was looking for. This is what she had come for, what she knew would happen the moment he sat at her table. She thought about his leather overcoat, now hanging next to her old, cracked leather jacket on hooks by the front door. How comfortable and right their coats must look together. When he took his coat off she saw he wore a nice button–down shirt and jeans. And he was naked under his clothes. And warm. Alive. With her.

"This is not about betrayal," she said softly, her chin lowered and her eyes on the edge of the glinting chrome. Shoshonah. Ulrike. Ulrike. Ulrike would never betray Frithe or his daughter. What was she looking for? "I have this problem, you see, of falling in love with people if I spend even a little amount of time with them. I mean, if they show a sign of liking me. There's no in between. Just love. Fondness confused with lust." She looked at his blank face; the only recognizable emotion was the heat in his eyes. "Do you know that ?"

"Je comprends pas," he said.

Shoshonah, she thought. And Mina. Shoshonah, Mina, Ulrike, Frithe, Father, Porter...And who else? She thought about letters on paper, entries made in journal. Nothing, not even penned recordings, kept the world stagnant. Khatia knew where this week off had been leading. She could not talk to anyone. She could not share and perhaps Shoshonah had finally given in to Khatia's taciturnity.

My guide, she thought, is a little known spaniel. Or a mermaid. It's a fairy tale and a warped looking glass. Finally, it is absurdity.

Benoit would not understand.

Khatia leaned towards Benoit. She took his face into her hands, the stub of her cigarette still burning between her fingers. The smoke clouded his face, changing the color of his skin to a blue, his eyes becoming onyx. The only real brilliance was that of her cigarette burning, the cherry's redness mixed with dead, sticky ash.

"I need to make a phone call," she said.

"You have another engagement?"

113

"I can cancel."

His bedroom was hidden by a curtained partition behind his desk.

They lay on the small bed together, staring up into the ceiling. Halogen track lights marched up and down his ceiling in the dark. She wished for candle light. Fluorescent and neon were always too harsh.

The blankets sighed as he turned towards her. His hand came to rest on her thigh, his arm across her belly. She stared up. She wanted to breathe through her nose, but it whistled. His fingers were tracing feathery circles on her hip. She tried to remain supple under his touch.

The fingers were firmer now, pressing, pressing the same circles. She realized he was drawing her towards him. She remained limp. The fingers molded into a cup, then a grip around the jutting bone. He was anchored. He slid the small space of inches to her. Hotness which turned to condensation formed on her neck. His tongue whipped out in tiny pricks of wind.

She turned her lips towards his. His tongue like his fingers, soft, soft, circling, catching her upper lip, drawing away from it in a tickle, coming back to the corners of her mouth, leaving her mouth for her right ear. Again, barely touching her so that her back arched towards phantoms. Immobilized. Back to her mouth so that her eyes could actually open, she could have free will, barely.

His hand slipped under her blouse, the fingers moving delicately up her stomach, over her bra. He touched the pebble of her nipple through the satin cloth. It burned, hurting a little. If he took her clothes off now she would lose the heat. His mouth came down, sucking her through the material, a flash of wet tongue encircling. His head like a child's on her chest. The maternal instinct aroused. This was familiar; this she knew. A tongue was a tongue, man or woman's. His body still rested next to her, but he was above her, supported by his other arm. She wanted that other arm, wanted those fingers to join the others.

His power was in sensation. Quivers, heat, wetness. Her bra was unhooked. So that's where his other hand was. His tongue on her eyelids, sealing them.

"Les yeux bruns," he whispered in her ear. "*Khatia.*" His voice, guttural,

114

sounded like Ulrike's, how she imagined his would sound in this kind of darkness—hoarsely.

She sat up, startling him.

"I don't know if I can do this," she said.

He nuzzled her neck. "T'es frigide?"

"Frigide?" she repeated. "No." She laughed. "No. No. Just a little loopy, I think."

She looked away, out the window. The silence between them saturating, the solid world melting a little, leaving them dripping in its dew.

"Attends!" Benoit said suddenly. "T'es vierge!" he breathed.

She looked down at her hands. A tear fell into her palm. "Define virgin," she said.

She could feel his hand on her hair, stroking softly. A prized China doll.

"It happens sometimes," she said. "Twenty–three years old, but it does happen."

She looked into his face, and the smoldering in his eyes was gone, replaced by a strange sadness. Would he tell his coworkers about the bizarre American Virgin he met one Thursday afternoon in Le Primereau? Would he brag how he had de–flowered her?

"Benoit," she said. "End it."

———————————

During the cab ride, she sat on the edge of her seat. The windows of shops were dark; no one was out on the streets this late. Only a dozing clerk rested his head on the counter in the lobby of the hotel as she passed through

In the bathtub of her room, she sat. There was no shower, but she had managed to rig the handheld device on the soap dish so that the water fell on her head which hung down between her knees. She tasted the tar on her tongue and watched through her slitted eyes the blood as it washed away from between the V of her legs, sliding over the white porcelain and down the drain.

115

Chapter Fourteen

Basically, their presentation had not gone well. All the slides had been put into the projector backwards and half the room's stereo speakers did not function. Afterwards, Ulrike collapsed from the devastation like an abandoned marionette. He insisted they go home on an earlier train. He needed a longer weekend. He needed his wife and baby to comfort him. The earlier successes of the week died by the wayside like roadkill next to this seemingly major disaster. Khatia let him sleep backwards on the ride home clutching a new book like a teddy bear. He needed women, but he did not need her. They separated with few words at the train station, each heading in a different direction.

As the trolley bore her from the train station towards her flat, Khatia thought, Strange hour. Few people rode during mid–afternoon; the rain kept them from moving around. She missed the people. Usually, she was glad to have a trolley all to herself.

A small membrane of skin and blood, barely the shade of a translucent bandaid, had been torn away inside of her. She had thought she was not a virgin—making love with Shoshonah counted. In the sub–culture she had entered by falling in love with a woman, same–sex sex counted. That act was a rite of passage of its own. The walls of muscles, both voluntary and involuntary had been stretched, rubbed, yielded. Yet, with a man, she had bled: an ubiquitous, constructed sacrifice of women to men and nature. A little hemoglobin. A dab of iron.

A rite of passage. An act culturally imbued with profound significance. The fact that living was a series of changes was hard for her to accept. Any kind of change rubbed her uncomfortably, like string–bikini underwear. How could she get used to something that, in her mind, was not supposed to happen, to fit that way, to "go?" She stared out the window of the trolley.

The world *did* look different.

"Funny," she said to the passing sidewalks. "But I feel a little sad." In a world that declared progress and change as good things, she could not help but notice she could never go back. She often yearned to go back, but not to her childhood or anything specific. To a feeling. Something she could not name, a fleeting moment of her fantasies, of her conceptions of happiness caught at her like a memory. An ice cube could become water and then an ice cube anew, but cooked meat could not be raw ever again.

"The rice is cooked," her mother used to say. Khatia wrote it on her hand with a pen; she would write that into her journal later when she got home. Remembering things her mother had said gave her trouble, and remembering them was even harder.

She was not sure if it was innocence that she had lost, as one was supposed to believe in this situation. What she had lost was a lie. A self–made, indulgent lie.

Shoshonah was not at the flat when she arrived. Khatia exhaled in relief. She was not supposed to be there yet, and perhaps Shoshonah was out getting special food for their dinner. A welcome home dinner. New lumps of guilt found their way to her stomach.

The rain had stopped, leaving the streets bare of garbage. Everything in the city seemed washed, turned a quarter of an inch. She threw open one of the windows flanking the large picture–window in the living room, the one the movers had to take out to get the couch in. Fresh air spilled into the room, wafting into the stuffiness. The place was a mess, naturally. Khatia breathed deeply of the oxygen richness, closing her eyes to the caresses of wind that turned her nose into a shining, freezing river stone.

In the kitchen, she found a letter from her father and one from Porter as well. She ripped open her father's envelope. Enclosed were a check and a short note reporting on the mudaneness of his life. A push for graduate school. Porter's letter berated her for not writing. *Where are you?* he wrote. He called her a womyn, said he was making friends with the feminists/ groupies who liked the Band's music because the lead singer was a woman with blue hair who sang about neglectful boyfriends and comforting womynists. He thought his sister, "the womyn's college alumna(the feminine form of alumnus, aren't you impressed, mi hermana, with my latent Latin?)," would appreciate that.

Laughing for the first time in two days, she read over his note. Perhaps

117

they were becoming closer. He had always been a non–person to her, a blob of life, less than the barn–cats they kept around for hunting mice. She did not even take advantage of the privileges of age when they were young and beat him up. When their parents had brought his infant body home, she had been surprised by his existent, but she realized now that this was only a mirror of her parents' reactions, a mixture of strain and relief. Khatia could not remember her mother getting fat or skinny with him. Simply, he was suddenly there, another life–form sleeping and crying in a room that used to be her mother's study.

She folded the letters and went to her room to put them with the others. She had a few from Porter and Bianca as well. One from Meredith with local town chitchat. Bianca had broken up with her boyfriend, although she did not report this in her own correspondence, written in a bubbly, eighth grade handwriting. Hearts for the dots on her i's.

Khatia kept letters in an old cracker box on the floor of the closet. A pile of laundry buried the box, its corners crushed slightly, heroically guarding the correspondence. Rescuing it, she stuffed the new letters in and held her breath against the human odor emanating from Shoshonah's dirty underwear and shirts. She knew she was supposed to adore this smell, not care, and see beyond it. But it annoyed her. Dropping the clothes, she turned to the desk where she had put her travel bag.

Her journal lay on the crate Shoshonah used as a bedside table. What was it doing there? She had just been thinking about her journal, thinking that it should be under Shoshonah's laundry, on the closet floor where she had left it carelessly. It was not as if she did not trust Shoshonah. Khatia usually carried it with her or kept it on the floor under the bed. Leaving it in the closet had been an oversight, but one she did not regret when remembering on the train. And yet, leaving it there was a mistake. She could see that now, as she could see the pattern of the last few weeks, of her life, adding up into a picture of connect–the–dots becoming recognizable. Yet, deliberate. Trust. Privacy. Journal. These were not words she thought about in the solidity of their encasement of letters and definitions. Yet, they were perhaps the most pervasive words in her world. Her journal on Shoshonah's crate: emblematic.

She went back to the front room and sat in front of the windows. The sky darkened as a cloud blocked out the already weak sun. The streets seemed bare of life, as if a nuclear winter had settled in and humanity ceased to thrive. Occasionally, a cyclist passed sedately by, body upright, basket full of groceries or a briefcase. She listened to the high–pitched, complaining engines of scooters tumbling down distant cobblestoned alleys. The world hid from her around the corner. Inside, her stomach yowled like a housebound dog with a distended bladder needing release. She reached in her jacket pocket—she still had not taken it off—and pulled out her box of cigarettes. Smoke instead of food. A cigarette instead of a glass of water. Replacing the essential minerals of her body with elements of addiction.

Down the street, through the haze, two people approached. She could see them from above, and they were that gray of distance, their limbs blending and dripping into the gray of the sidewalk and street. Their figures jittered, and Khatia thought of a line of Walt Whitman's: "We two boys together clinging." These people threw their arms out in wild gestures, paused to throw back their heads, their mouths, a smear of black, wide open, largely appreciating a small joke. Their knees knocked together and against each other. They linked arms, elbows into chained hooks. Connecting in every way, their faces came together in a kiss.

"Oh no," Khatia said out loud. Two small words, near mirror images of each other. What one should say, what *she* should say when looking out a window and seeing the immediate future clearly. The instant after discovery, she thought, had to be a lapse in time. All over the world, clocks would stop ticking, workers would pause in their fields, at their desks. Discovery was a shared experience, even if no one knew it.

The moment passed, and Khatia watched Shoshonah sink into the embrace of Mina, their arms wrapped around each others' heads in a way familiar to Khatia. Shoshonah had to bend forward a little—she was so tall—but not as far as she did with Khatia.

What did they look like when they kissed? In movies, couples made love to be watched. Khatia could not abandon that self–conscious restraint; as a child, she believed her family's life was on TV, strangers watching their goings–on as they watched *Star Trek* and *Bewitched*.

Wasn't this justice? She had "cheated," Shoshonah was "cheating." What right did she have to the falling out of her abdomen, to the bitterness of the cigarette, the bitterness she ate like a medicine—resisting yet hurrying its effects?

In the corner by the window, she turned on a lamp. The couple, still many feet away on the sidewalk—

Her coat was on. Money in her pocket. She hurried down the stairs, slipping out the door. They were far away, too caught up in their own moment to see her slide against the buildings in the opposite direction.

Chapter Fifteen

Caught in the middle of a day. She thought about finding the old man in the park, the admirer of Dylan, and started meandering that way, like a snake that has been hit by a car, swerving through the grass, dying and broken. This city harbored those with nothing better to do than try to leave themselves for a while.

Once at the dinner table, with a twitch of his mouth, her father gave her mother the advice of never living her life by absolutes. "For example," he said. "One may believe I am purely Caucasoid, but that is not absolute. You can not know. Right, Annie? Our *race* does not define us."

Khatia and Porter, children at the time, did not understand what he meant, but they did know that their mother smiled shyly as she clattered her fork on her plate, her lids lowered, revealing its tired creases, the eyeshadow caking like muddied snow in the skin's crevices. Her mother's eyes, always too dry, bulged forward a little as if they did not trust their position in her face. Khatia wanted to reach out with her little girl's fingernail and pick the collected powder away. She did not think her mother was a pretty woman, but she had an elegant dignity; she was a soft–spoken dowager in a middle–aged woman's body. Khatia wanted to help her keep that dignity, that potential command of a situation.

Their father hardly ever smiled around them, but then he was hardly ever around. Mother was always there for them, fetching cups of water in the middle of the night, reading them stories in bed, putting Mentholatum up their small nostrils in the winter to prevent nosebleeds in the stuffy house. She was softly restrained, smoothing back their hair instead of hugging them, giving them peeled orange wedges when what they wanted was a word: "Nice job on your spelling quiz. I'm so proud of you." Her compliments were backwards: "You may not be handsome Porter, but you're smart, and you'll make a lucky girl happy someday." "Khatia, did you finally lose some weight? Those jeans don't look as tight anymore."

Khatia wanted to get angry at her mother's lack of sensitivity, so obviously masking love. It had to, she thought. No other explanation could exist for such gentle cruelty. But she did not display outbursts as most teenagers, keeping them inside, sullenly watching her mother from the doorway of the kitchen or of the school library, wherever her mother was, hating her, wanting to protect her, thanking god that she had her own life, that she was not *that* woman.

"Read me a story, Daddy."

She remembered saying this with clarity, and she paused on the wet Dutch cobblestones. Where her mother had been, she could not recall, but there she was, a little girl, holding up a Charlie Brown and Snoopy picture book to her father. She was young enough to be brave. She sat in his lap, and he read the book, his voice low, almost a mumble. He read very fast, impatient for it to be over. She could tell he did not want to be doing this. She never asked him to read a story again.

Never live your life by absolutes.

She understood this now as she trudged through the streets of Amsterdam. Her love, what she had believed was her love, did not define her. The phrase ran through her head like a mantra, turned a quarter of an inch: *I live my life by absolutes. I live my life by absolutes.*

How pathetic.

Right and wrong. Black and white. They existed in the center of prismatic light, a light in which she was a believer.

The façade of Ulrike's office came into view. All around, the sky pressed down, a dumbbell of clouds dropped and pushed by a wind. The rain came down, pelunking in sheets. No choice but to run to the office, pull out her set of keys—She moved her hand to the doorknob. A light was on inside.

Ulrike sat at his desk. He looked up as she approached the glass window in the door. Her hand hovered over the knob and they looked at each other, both in surprise and expectation. He finally smiled, breaking the small moment, and her fingers twisted the handle.

"You haven't gone home?" she said.

He shook his head. "I could not just yet. Facing Frithe's questions would only sadden me more. It is better to find comfort by candlelight." He flitted his fingers, imitating a flame. "She will light candles for us tonight with dinner. It is our homecoming custom. I wanted to leave my paperwork here, but then I sat down and seemed glued to the chair, as you Americans say," he chuckled. Khatia remembered the lights in Benoit's apartment, her wish for candles. He had been kind to her, baffled by her strangeness.

"Is that your rolodex I see?" She pointed, meaning to tease him, but he was too oblivious to notice. "Can't leave business alone, eh?"

He looked at it as if it were a little green spaceman. "Yes, yes. I thought I would make a few phone calls. Let Frithe know we are back early. Now I might as well go home and surprise her before she and Sofie get in the car."

The phone rang, scaring both of them; Khatia's eyes widened. Ulrike gave a little yelp.

"Could you get that? I do not want to talk to anyone right now," he said.

"Why bother? The machine will get it," she said.

"I listened to our messages and disengaged it."

Khatia scooped up the receiver.

"Hello?" she said.

No one answered.

"Hello? Hello?"

"H–hello?" said a cautious voice.

"Yes?" she said impatiently. "May I help you? Do you need Ulrike?" This was why she never answered the phone. People who called usually spoke English, but there was the occasional monoglot who had the audacity not to know it.

"Is this Frithe?"

The voice was decidedly American and familiar. She tried to place it.

"Cree?" she said.

"Frithe?"

"Give me the phone," said Ulrike.

123

"No," Khatia said, looking at her boss. "This is Khatia. I work with Ulrike."

"Oh yeah! The voice," he said, laughing. She winced, Mr. Charles' raspy words clanking in her memory.

"Right," she said. "That's what Ulrike tells everyone, at least."

"Is it Cree?" Ulrike whispered.

"How did you know it what me?" Cree asked. "How did you know my name for that matter?"

"Oh," Khatia said, distracted by Ulrike's fingers wiggling under her nose for the phone. "Ulrike played a tape of you once. He talks about you a lot."

"Sure he does," Cree said. "All the man ever does is talk. Where are you from?"

"Khatia!" Ulrike hissed.

"New Hampshire. I'd better give you to Ulrike. He's turning twenty shades of indigo."

Cree laughed. "Well, maybe we'll meet someday."

"Nice talking to you," she shoved the receiver at Ulrike as he snatched it from her grasp.

"Cree? Yes, yes. You are using my phone card? No? Ah, well then."

Ulrike's urgency was obvious now: long distance phones calls from the U.S.A. were not peanuts.

"Yes, a very nice girl. Perhaps later. What? We were in Brussels, remember? Well, why did you not call Frithe?"

Khatia stopped listening. She sat in the chair opposite his desk, sifting her fingers through a pagoda of triplicate forms. Cree's voice was still friendly and tall, even more so because she could hear him laughing, a good–natured, infective kind of laugh like Shoshonah's. Khatia realized she did not have that kind of laugh. She was a person of the dark space in between emotions. Her state was one of indecision, of compromise, of doing the "right thing." Don't raise waves.

She looked at Ulrike as he babbled into the phone, punching at the air

124

with his hands for emphasis. Where were those feelings, that ambivalent confusion of embarrassed desire she had begun to feel yet avoided in Brussels? It had been that, but she had not wanted to give it a name, to gel it into existence. Perhaps Benoit *had* done something more for her than sex. She looked back at the floor: the connection of lust to kindness was her myth—making. Beyond it, she could see a friend in her boss, and that was all.

And so.

Shoshonah liked another woman and was acting on that attraction. For a whole year, Khatia had remained faithful to Shoshonah, or so she had told herself. What had she been doing in Bloomfield, New Jersey? Trying to recount those days was like remembering kindergarten: a fuzz, an amalgamation of one typical day, twenty–four hours compressed into one. Had her thoughts been filled with *Shoshonah, Shoshonah, when are you coming home?* Or was it more accurate to say they were filled with the blankness she felt now, the blankness she could not shake from that space behind her forehead, the one that said, *"Come here...Give in."*

She held her head, leaning on the chair's armrest. She was light–headed and slightly nauseated as if a gorilla pounded on her head with its heavy fist, looking for gold in her hair follicles. The last thing she had eaten was a *pain chocolat* early that morning, hardly a substantive food source. Wouldn't it be funny if what she mistook as desire were merely hunger?

"Yes, yes," Ulrike was saying. "Yes—ach!—yes. I will tell her. Of course, of course. Excellent. Well understood. See you soon." He hung up the phone.

"Is Cree coming to Amsterdam?" she asked, shifting so that she cradled her own cheek.

"Yes. He is coming here for a visit in two weeks. He had a birthday and his old uncle gave him a plane ticket, so he will be here for a visit. You will like him very much. We are like brothers."

She already knew she liked Cree just from their brief phone conversation. They would get along, she could tell. Gazing at the windmill poster she said, "I don't think I'll be meeting him."

"Why not?" Ulrike asked absently. His head bent over his agenda book.

Khatia did not answer. In the softest of breezes, a windmill's wings were

125

designed to move, to push energy into a harness for man's use.

"Ulrike?" she said.

"Yes," he mumbled.

"Did you know as little as I do when you were my age?"

"You know more than you think," he said, his voice muffled in the collar of his roll–neck sweater. "And how old do you think I am? I am only thirty–two."

"I know," she said, biting at a hangnail intently. "I just think I should be aware of more by now."

"For example?" he sat up in his chair, putting his pen aside and rubbing his eyes.

"What love is all about."

"Oh. That little matter of *love*," he laughed, looking at her. She took her finger away from her mouth, spitting out the bit of skin. Her finger throbbed a little where the flesh and nail met. "Was your specialization in college philosophy?"

"No. But I can tell yours was."

"Yes. And linguistics," he sighed. "You are a difficult young woman."

She shrugged, the lightness in her head receding and coming forth in waves. She concentrated on a hole in her jeans, sticking her sore finger inside, pressing it on her kneecap.

"You know what love is," he said softly, and she did not look up. "You even know what you want in life. It is buried in your mind, dormant like a bear. It wakes slowly, not in one vertiginous instant." He paused. "You have to tell Shoshonah what you want."

Did he know? *What* did he know? And what did it matter?

"But I'm not sure," she said.

Ulrike looked at her with a tenderness she had seen in his face when he looked at Sofie. Not lust. Attention.

"What happened to you in Brussels, Khatia?"

She shook her head, and a small laugh escaped her lips. "Half of everything."

"Sometimes, your responses are so Asian."

She squinted her eyes at him. "What does that mean?" He pressed his lips together. "I did a little business with the Japanese last year—" He said "the Japanese," as if he had done a little business with all of Japan "—they were quietly restrained, always on the edge of letting me know what they really thought."

"I don't understand you Europeans and your sweeping generalizations," she muttered, and they laughed at the irony.

"That in itself is a sweeping generalization, Khatia," he said.

"Duh," she replied.

He continued: "Americans have this idea about Europeans—"

She held up her hand to stop him. "I don't want to get into it right now, Ulrike."

They stared each other down for a moment.

"Well," he said. "What is next, Khatia?"

"I think it's time for me to go," she said. The lightness was replaced by a heaviness in her throat.

"Where?" he asked.

She laughed again, deciding on the spot, giving into a girlhood dream born from all those art history books she used to read. "I was thinking Paris. It's either that or back to New Hampshire, but I can't do that right now." She shook her head. "I would feel like a failure."

"I need you here, Khatia," Ulrike said quietly.

She looked into her lap again and watched the salt drops of water plunk onto her jeans.

"You'll find another voice, Ulrike. There's millions of them in this town." *And I don't belong here,* she wanted to add.

In his face was the sadness of loss. For the first time, he was paying attention to *her* and only her.

127

"You are more than just a voice, Khatia."

She nodded, not looking at him. "Maybe I'll make it to San Francisco, eventually," she said, trying for humor. "See the birthplace of my mother."

"You have never been there?"

"Never. My father never let us go. He wears the pants, you know?" She wiped at her nose. "At least, he has the money. But I'm a grown–up now. I can go where I please. I just don't have much money."

Ulrike took out a piece of paper. He flipped through the rolodex and began scribbling.

"Do you know anyone in Paris?" he asked.

"No," she said. A little drop of fear took away her tenuous resolve for a moment. She was insane, *loopy* to think she could do this, leave Shoshonah, leave the security she had found. *But it's not there anymore.* She was leaving nothing.

Ulrike handed her the paper.

"Some contacts in Paris. They have a boy Sofie's age. Maybe they'll need a nanny. I'll call them before you leave. And also, Cree's address and telephone number. He said you were nice." Ulrike's fingers slid away from the paper slowly. Underneath it was a check for double her last week's pay. "Perhaps you two will meet someday, as I have hoped. When you get to your mother's birthplace."

Khatia looked at the slips of paper. They both calmed and frightened her. Ulrike expected her to go now. A decision had been made. No turning back. No turning back.

"Thank you," she said. She did love him in a way, as she was beginning to love her brother. She put out her hand, and he took it. They remained clasped for a moment. Khatia thought of mad butterflies, circling around their heads, creatures of sun, creatures that looked for warmth in nectar, nourishment in flower ointment. She could not wait for Spring, for a time when she could write to Ulrike and tell him she was okay.

128

Chapter Sixteen

The apartment was quiet when she returned, but it was not empty. Khatia tossed her keys onto the coffee table, though usually she carefully hung them on a nail in the kitchen. The nails were there because she had found a toolbox under the sink, and thought it would be a good idea if they got into the habit of being organized. Shoshonah was always losing things.

"Hello?" Shoshonah called from the kitchen. Her voice cracked a little, sounded tentative and strange.

The light Khatia had left in the living room was off, replaced by the glaring light in the kitchen, which spilled through the doorway and splashed on the walls in parallelograms. Shoshonah sat at the kitchen table in her pajamas. Her eyes looked over Khatia, wide like a doe's, and her hands were clasped together. The only thing on the table was a small mountain of bread crumbs, not one speck out of place.

"You're back," she said. Khatia could not remember a time when Shoshonah looked and sounded more strained. Before a game, nervous energy took over her body, the desire to win, but it was also confident energy. Now, in the kitchen, in her flannels, she seemed on the verge of subdued hysteria.

Khatia nodded. She looked around the kitchen. It was clean. Sparkling. Shoshonah had been busy.

"So?" Shoshonah asked. "How was it?"

"It was good," Khatia nodded again. She tried to look Shoshonah in the eye, to act normal, but she couldn't. "I want to see more of Europe. Paris."

"Me too," Shoshonah said, letting her breath out. "We should do it, you know? Maybe after the New Year we'll have enough money. Get those Eurail passes and go. I really wanted to get to Barcelona—Hey, did you speak French in Belgium?"

129

"Of course."

"Great." Shoshonah's hands flew up, away from the table top. Her body moved a little out of the chair, but then she settled back, looking down at the pile of crumbs in front of her. "I cleaned the house," she said.

Khatia sat down in the opposite chair. Shoshonah's thumb plunged into the crumbs, and she twisted it around.

"I wanted to surprise you. I thought you would be home earlier and we could go out to dinner or something. Then I thought, well, we could go to Chez Manfred, but I got tired." She glanced up and smiled a little. "Juliene misses you. She asks about you every time we go in there."

We. Khatia crossed her legs, letting her arms crawl up the sleeves of her jacket to warm her cold hands.

"You go with people from work?" she asked.

Shoshonah began swirling the crumbs into patterns resembling broccoli florets with her fingers.

"Yeah. You know."

Khatia got up from her chair. She went to the bedroom. The laundry was gone, and the bed made. Her journal was now on the floor next to her side of the bed. She walked back to the kitchen. Shoshonah still swirled the crumbs.

"Ulrike and I took an earlier train back," Khatia said.

Shoshonah's fingers paused for a moment, then kept going.

"Oh?" she said.

Khatia leaned on the wall, resting her head on it. Realizing she smelled like a traveler, stale in the crackly shell of her clothes, she wanted very badly to take a bath.

The artwork on the table ceased as Shoshonah suddenly swept it onto the floor. Her hands fluttered again, looking for something to do. They found her hair and began twirling a piece of it, a pale, silvery section, dulled in the kitchen lights overhead.

"Oh," she said again.

Khatia looked at the floor.

"So," Shoshonah said and stopped. She was rarely at a lost for words, and Khatia felt somehow embarrassed for her. If only she could walk to her and pat her on the shoulder, hug her, say, "It's okay. We had to do this." But she couldn't. The backwards absolutes were a part of her, and such actions would be false.

They were silent for a while, and in that time, Khatia remembered that Shoshonah told her she had had sex with a man before. A youth, really. In high school, Shoshonah had been out–going and popular, crazy and fun, the complete opposite of Khatia. She had many friends, both boys and girls. Her best friend was a boy, and they had slept together so that Shoshonah could see if heterosexual sex would tempt her away from her desire for girls. They slept with each other more than once because the first time was not supposed to be so great. But Shoshonah's first time with a girl had been heavenly. Kissing Lauren, touching her body, had been a thrill. It was right, and she wanted to do it more. With her best friend, the boy, she just wanted to talk about things like movies, sports, and girls.

Shoshonah taught Khatia her art of lovemaking. They tumbled everywhere, grabbing and nipping, but Khatia always held something back, formalizing their lovemaking: We are going to have sex now, a thought that always preceded a kiss.

Her old anxieties seemed small now—that Shoshonah was a woman did not matter. That they were not in love did. Looking at her guilty friend, she realized that being with Benoit was more than just a rite of passage, more than just curiosity.

"Khatia," Shoshonah said, breaking the quiet.

"I know," Khatia said. "I know."

"I'm sorry," Shoshonah said and suddenly began weeping. Khatia watched her, fascinated. Shoshonah was not a person who cried. She was not. Her hair fell over her face like a veil, an acknowledgment of the act's rarity. "I'm so sorry," she said between high pitched snuffles. "I did the dishes and swept out the living room and got a feather duster from work—"

It was over very quickly. She flipped her hair back, her face red and wet. "I love you," she said. "I want to be with you. But I look at other women sometimes and—I can't help myself."

Outside the rain fell, and beautiful women and men existed, waiting to be loved.

"I love you too," Khatia said. "But, if you wanted this, you could have said something to me. Back in the States—"

"Back in the States, *this* is what I wanted," Shoshonah interrupted. "I—I thought about you all the time while I was in Alaska. I had the fantasy. We had such a good thing in college. I wanted to take you with me into a new environment, like Gertrude and Alice. And besides—" She stopped.

"Besides what?"

Shoshonah's voice softened. "There were other women. When I was in Alaska."

Khatia caught her breath, wondering why this should hurt at all when she could barely react to Mina.

"I didn't think they meant anything."

"How many?" The question seemed to come from someone else's mouth, a ticket–taker at a movie theater.

"Four," she said into her hands.

"Four."

"Khatia—"

"No," she said, holding up her hand and turning away. "Don't say anything. Don't say another goddamned thing."

Thinking back to that time, she remembered what it felt like to care. She wanted to shout at Shoshonah, "Well, I've slept with a man, and I liked it much better than I ever did with you! You said the first time was the worst, well, the second and third time in a row are the *best!*" But she knew this was not true. The words would merely fly through the air in untruths Shoshonah could not recognize, but only guess. The ambiguity of their meaning would be unfair. Shame: the fact that Khatia had the potential to be cruel was enough to keep her from doing it.

"Because, Khatia! Because." Shoshonah stood up, ignoring Khatia's protest. Below, they heard a tapping on their floor. It was the old woman downstairs, banging her broomstick on her ceiling, telling them to keep it down.

Shoshonah swallowed. She looked terrible, swollen.

"You seethe deep down, do you know that? I love you, but you have all those rules of what's okay and what's not. It's so cold."

Cold. Was she cold? That was a word fitting her mother, her father. The inheritance of ice.

"But then you have this way about you, of needing to know only good things," Shoshonah continued. "It's not that I wanted to hide the truth from you. I mean, I wanted to tell you *all* the time. But I kept remembering what you said: 'Let's just try to be faithful to each other.' And I tried so hard! But I want others and I want you too. And..." she twisted her hair around her finger until Khatia thought it might break. "I know I can't do that. I don't think you'd put up with it. But something about—about your *demeanor.* You demand to be protected from these *unpleasant things.* Just pretend like things don't happen that do! And I tried to get you out of it— I tried—but—I just gave in! I just—" Shoshonah could not go on. Her words came in cramped, choking gasps, competing with the constricting of her throat muscles. Khatia walked numbly to the sink and got a glass of water for her. Shoshonah sat down at the table and took the glass with trembling hands. It slipped a little and sloshed onto her legs.

Their breathing became synchronous. Physically, emotionally deadened. Numb Khatia. A quote by Marianne Moore ran through her head over and over, "Omissions are not accidents."

Shoshonah emitted a shuddering sigh, and Khatia touched her for the first time since her return, putting her hands on her head, stroking down her tangled, damaged hair.

"I only did what you wanted," Shoshonah said, her voice low with exhaustion.

Khatia nodded. "I know."

That night, Shoshonah offered to sleep on the couch. Probably Mina had been in their bed, and Khatia was reluctant to sleep in it, especially by herself. But then again, she had *seen* with her own two eyes Mina in the living room. She could only imagine her in the bedroom, and it was the more innocuous of her two choices.

Before she went to bed, she picked up her journal from the floor. If other eyes had been on its pages, she could not tell. But what did it really matter? For her, was the truth written on blank pages, recorded in flesh–bound words? "Romance languages." She took out the pieces of notebook paper from Brussels and taped them into her book, including the notes Ulrike had dictated.

"In college, Ulrike, that was my specialization." She whispered the words to the dark. What good did language do her, but make her feel inarticulate? Her parents had not taught her how to use words to her advantage, romantic or not, only to hide them. Mask pain by masking meaning. Forget its origins and it will go away, replaced by a nothing more comforting than anything tactile. In the living room, Shoshonah lay on the couch, sleepless and breathing, probably feeling both relief and isolation. Solitude.

Khatia dreamed that night of hurtling the couch through the picture window and into an abyss that replaced the space of the street below. Her small body was full of weightless energy, tossing the heaving object—it seemed to breathe, a beast—through the air. Blankets flew from it, floating down, billowing like woolen parachutes. Blonde hair hid within the cushions and folds, but nothing truly alive seemed to be there, not even Khatia.

The next morning, she woke before dawn. Packing her things was easy: there wasn't much. A few more books, a new sweater, actually old, from a consignment shop. A silver lighter she bought in the Brussels train station. Smoking was habitual in simply a few short days. Thank you, Juliene, she thought.

She sat in the room for a while, waiting for light to seep through the cottony dimness. If only she could reach out and break through it with her fingers. For over a year, she had held on to the safety of the past, to a person who had showed her emotions in a way Khatia did not, who did not seem to care about Khatia's strangeness.

But even this: Shoshonah *had* cared. She had cared enough to betray their pact, and then cared enough again to hide the truth from her. Being capable of controlling someone without even knowing: frightening concept. Do I really have this control? she asked herself. The power of blinded love—she did not want it. Take it back, she thought. I'm tired of sick affection.

The time had come to let go of a past that wasn't working anymore. She would always love Shoshonah, but hanging around was not the fair thing to do. Shoshonah would be all right, Khatia thought, although part of her did not believe it.

And would she be all right? Stupid, stupid: such questions were futile. She stared out the window for a while—smoke from chimneys rising, the birds quiet. A pause in the morning that smelled of jasmine and countryside rising above the stale canals, though they were in dawning of winter.

In the living room, Shoshonah slept like an angel, her breath soft and quiet. Khatia touched her face lightly for a moment. She left a note by her on the coffee table with her house keys. The door locked automatically: Shoshonah would be safe alone.

Her mother's backpack was heavy, but she heaved it on her shoulders. A smaller woman than Khatia, her mother had carried this thing through miles of trails, traversing mountains and streams.

Who was that woman? It was a question she had only recently started to face, but still, she pushed it aside. Khatia knew she should get her own backpack, one more appropriate for her size. The future lay in re–sizing.

Who is this woman? What woman?

On the train for Paris, she realized it was Christmas day.

And everyone important to her was alone or asleep.

135

PART II

Chapter One

Paris: a way station. For those who wanted, the city made a person forget to be "productive." One did not need to run around gaining accomplishments and meeting requirements. Just being in the milieu was enough, a good excuse for passing the time.

Ulrike's friends the St–Jeans were, fortunately for all, wealthy young people and had a young toddler, Anges–Mathieu, in need of an English–speaking nanny. They lived near the Javel Métro stop in the sixteenth arrondisement at Pont Mirabeau, an affluent, *chic* quarter of the city. Khatia's American accent was preferable to a British one since America was *à la mode*. Yet again, she had found employment through her voice. In exchange for taking care of their son six hours a day, Khatia got to live in a small *chambre de bonne* they owned on the top floor of their apartment building—no bathroom, although there was a toilet down the hall she shared with other *chambre de bonne* tenants, and a sink next to portable gas burners in her room—and a small spending allowance. She did not care if she were "moving down in the world," as her father would say. At this juncture, being a nanny in Paris was much more appetizing than being a paralegal in New York City.

From the tiny window of her room above the little futon, there was nothing but gray sky. If she stood on her chair and looked down, she could see the garden courtyard far below. From the St–Jeans' apartment, which ran the length of the apartment building, the Eiffel Tower came into view. On the horizon stretched endless buildings, white and pale gray, covered in soot. All built of tough, French rock. An ancient city. She could see the bridge, Pont de Grenelle, crossing the Seine where one of the miniature Statues of Liberty stood on her pedestal in the center of the river beside the bridge. She went to look at it when she first arrived in town, realizing she had never even been to the big one in New York City, seeing it only from a distance as a finger on the horizon and not much else.

Olivia Boler

The Latin Quarter. She sat in a café next to a window through which she could watch the city and its inhabitants. Bookstores, cafés, and crêperies crowded the buildings of commerce on the boulevard. Down the street, the Sorbonne, its church dome rising out from the center of the courtyard walls. After a little over a month, she knew this was her favorite part of town, the place to people–watch, fantasize that she was a young *parisienne*, receiving a socialized education with no worries other than her studies and what scarf she would wear in the morning.

Being here was too good to be true. She had always told herself, "This is what I want. To see the supposed center of art, culture, and romance in the Western World."

For most of her life, she had lived, if not contentedly, then at least un-aware that anything in her world needed fixing, until her father suddenly announced he wanted a divorce from her mother. Then her mother had died, her father stayed, and all the factors added up to a confusion she did not want to face. Shoshonah had been an oasis for a while, but there was always the underlying grief nothing could get to, not even affection. And all that was over between them anyway. When she first arrived in the city, Khatia had spent most of her free time crying for no reason, suddenly stop-ping because she had no more water in her body. Mundane acts distracted her from herself: taking Anges–Mathieu to the park, fixing his lunch in the St–Jeans' kitchen. She avoided places that would tempt her to act rashly. Bars especially. Places of darkness. At night, she stayed in her room, staring out the tiny window, reading a book, smoking cigarette after cigarette. Her family might berate her, but she ignored it. Her father had sent her two letters, asking what she thought she was doing. She replied briefly and cheer-fully, sending him picture postcards of the Arc de Triomphe. She only wrote postcards to communicate with the world outside Paris: short and sweet.

Even in the middle of winter, when the wind whips rains coats and turns umbrellas inside–out, some people can not help but be charmed by the City of Love, she thought, twisting the saucer on the table. The sky shimmered a blinding, headache–white light, the grumpy motorists honked, and Pari-sians rushed to the Métro with sour faces, hell–bent on getting back to their apartments, but for her, these urban hiccups were a panacea. Just being abreast of it all was enough. She put aside her pain for a while, letting the flow of old streets and people fill her attention.

140

Students exited their classes now, filling the sidewalks with satchels and packs full of scholarly material. Some of them came into the café, individually or in groups. All of them searching the room, looking for a seat near the heat vents. She ducked her head, blending in with the tableau of seated bodies.

An older man came in with a woman about his age. He carried an old briefcase, beat–up and oily. They found a table towards the middle of the room. Khatia watched what great care he took of the woman, taking her coat and hanging it up with his, pulling her chair out for her and tucking her in. His forehead was creased with hurriedness. He was probably a professor. The woman caught Khatia's gaze, her face relaxed. She smiled, motherly. Khatia smiled back and broke the contact as subtly as possible, taking a sip from her empty cup.

Khatia remembered her mother frowning sympathetically above her when she had to get four molars removed at age ten before she got her braces. Her face held concern and interest, but was hardly ever relaxed. Always worrying. Khatia had squeezed her mother's hand, squeezed tears out of her shut eyelids. She tried to say, "Mamma," but could not open her damaged lips; the pain would not let her.

When she was in high school, sometimes they would go to lunch, just the two of them, no Porter, no father, eating dim sum at the one "decent" Chinese restaurant in Boston. Annie Quigley tolerated the cuisine, but it was not up to the par of San Franciscan restaurants. Food: as a child, Annie ate dumplings for lunch. These were the only times they touched on her mother's childhood in San Francisco. And now, Khatia could not even recall stories of what her mother's childhood had been like. She had an impression of her mother in school, sitting at her desk in a white dress and pinafore with bobby socks and saddle shoes, hands clasped, watching the teacher with those tired, unblinking eyes. Perhaps this was the memory her mother had recalled most clearly, sharing it with her daughter. For Khatia, San Francisco was one brick school building, filled with children in saddle shoes.

She wondered if being half–Chinese had been hard for her mother. Did people call her half–breed? She was a unique looking woman, a little alien, as if she did not belong in the world beyond her home and library. Porter pursued these questions in earnest, but they weren't something Khatia had thought much about before. But identity seemed to obsess Europeans, at least, the ones she had met. America's heterogeneity fascinated them beyond politeness. All these questions people in Europe asked her—they bothered her, made her feel she was not paying attention the way she ought to be.

The vision of her child–mother disappeared immediately, as if it were only an apparition. She realized that was exactly what it was and panicked. Her mother's texture was disappearing, what little of her had been there. Think about Dad, she told herself. He's alive. He's there. If one parental unit fades, find the other.

Her father had texture, yet she did not know him, nor about him. A jock, yes. An ice–hockey player, a runner. At the time of his post–doc work, he had a shot at the Olympics as a distance runner, even had his picture taken with the team for a promotional poster before the final cuts were made. He still ran every morning before the first light of day. He spoke Spanish too, better than Russian. Once, when her mother was in the hospital but still conscious, he and Khatia had cooked dinner, Mexican. He made her speak Spanish the whole time with him, Porter slinking away from the kitchen surreptitiously. She didn't blame her younger brother. The whole time they were rolling the pin, heating the oil, and sautéing the meats, Khatia's ears were bright red, her stomach slightly clenched, blood streaming in her temples. She could not eat when the table was set. After that night, if Khatia were home, she did all the cooking and housework. That night with her father had been the changing of the guard. He mediated the switch in certain responsibilities from her mother, through himself, and down to his daughter. Willingly, obediently, she accepted, never going against his word. Once, she had tried. Once.

It was push coming to shove that made her think she could do it. What could have signaled her father to desire leaving his family? For nearly thirty years he had been married to this shy, soft–spoken woman, in their pleasant, amiable town. They had two kids, two cars, two careers, one house, one summer cottage in the White Mountains. He was a published, tenured professor of Russian Studies at a prestigious liberal arts college in the heart of the small ivy leagues. His wife, a librarian, well–read, could not be lacking as a partner in the discourse of intellectual and world affairs. The Quigleys comprised a textbook listing of the American Dream fulfilled.

Did he want a mistress? Did he want a sports car?

He needed to divorce them, he told them. He needed a change.

142

What did he want to do? the Quigleys asked. How could they help?

He did not know, nor care. Nothing. They could leave him alone, leave him in peace. Give him freedom. Yes. Give him space. He would not leave right away: during the Winter Break, when the weather was chill, and people stayed indoors, minding their own business. He would look for an apartment then, in Boston so he could be closer to the college.

So sudden, this open hostility. Numbed, the Quigley children and Quigley wife hung their heads. It was all they could do, compliant as they were by nature. Khatia left for her third year of college; Porter began his last year of high school, both of them disturbed. But no one spoke, as if ignoring the topic would make it go away. Her disappointment about not spending the year in France—she was too fond of Shoshonah, her first real friend in the world, and they both wanted to be at school for the lacrosse season(this was before they had fallen in love)—turned to relief. What if she had been an ocean away when her father broke the news?

Once at school again, taking a class in Women's Studies called the Politics of Patriarchy, her family's problems became glaringly obvious: Her father was an asshole with a mid–life crisis. How could he do this to her family?

For the first time, she was ready to confront her father. She came home that Thanksgiving and he picked her up at the bus station in Boston—

Khatia ordered another mocha, trying to put off the memory. It was not one she thought about very often. Strange, she thought, how much control I have over what I remember. Playing with Porter under the oak tree. Throwing pots in the ceramics studio. Since Shoshonah had returned from Alaska, she had not been able to control the memories as well. They came unbidden, without her selection, ones she did not even think were real, more like nightmares from childhood. "Unpleasant," as Shoshonah might say. She looked down at the new mocha in front of her. When had the waiter put it on her table? She fumbled with the handle of the cup and sipped, the liquid burning the center of her tongue. She used to dream about child–eating monsters floating outside her bedroom window.

And yet, how could she ever forget that day? It was like the day at the dentist's with her mother, clear, the pain so real she could feel it in her teeth.

Her father had picked her up at the bus station in Boston after work. She could barely be civil without immediately lighting into him, her nerves ready for combat. "Daddy, I've been thinking about it for a long time, and you can't just leave Mom. If there's one thing I've learned from my Patriarchy class, it's that Americans think they can get out of anything just by divorcing. Whatever is your problem is *your* problem, not Mom's, not Porter's, not mine. You have to deal with it yourself. If you're having some weird identity crisis, well…That's normal at your age. We did a whole unit on it when I was a freshman in my Psych class. It's sort of hard to explain but you are 'Father,'"—she made quotation marks in the air with her fingers for visual emphasis— "and you are 'Professor John Porter Quigley,' and you are a 'homeowner,' and you are a 'scholar.' You have your 'soul,' whatever that might be. I think it means whatever it is you dream at night, I mean the good dreams that you remember all the time the best. But, anyway, you are also a *husband.* Do you follow me? Daddy?"

"Yes, I follow you," he replied in his emotionless voice. She would not be fazed.

"Okay, then. Well, so you see, since you are an individual, you know you must take responsibility yourself, for whatever is upsetting you. You know you shouldn't take it out on us, right?" Strong, aggressive words: *should* and *must.* Very male.

"Khatia—"

"I mean, everything can be how it used to be. And whatever special things you want to do on your own, you can do them on your own. Everyone needs his own space."

He pulled the car into a Friendly's parking lot, parked, and turned off the ignition.

"Khatia," he said heavily. "We must talk."

She looked at him, frustrated but wary. Hadn't he been listening? No, he never did. She was surprised at herself for having spoken as much as she had.

Even though she could remember her lecture to him almost word for word, she could not remember if they had gone into the restaurant or if he had just told her in the car and let her cry into her muffler, soothing her with his grave silence. She always got it mixed up with the parking lot at the hospital. She knew she had spent a lot of time in the lot of that sterile institution, weeping silently, sobbing hysterically. Or sometimes it was humming, her mouth drawn in a clamped line to vainly hold back the re-

144

lentless sound.

He turned to her with uncontrolled weight. "Khatia, I'm not going to divorce your mother."

She released her breath. It was one of the final easy moments she would know for the next six months, and it only lasted ten seconds.

She could remember the gist of her father's words, remember the tone of his voice. Khatia, your mother is very sick. *What?* She has cancer, Khatia. *No.* Chemotherapy isn't going to help her anymore, the doctors say. There's nothing she could have done to prevent its spread, nothing we could have done. It's multiplying rapidly. That sore throat, we always thought is was a chronic cold—*No!* —The doctors have given her medicine to ease the pain. She gets good exercise, not much anymore, but she eats right. She's comfortable for the time being. She quit her job at the school. She had to give up that promotion as Chief Librarian—*No* —but she really can't work now. She needs to be home. She needs to be taken care of, Khatia. *Please god, no.* I don't want you to be emotional when you see her. You know she doesn't need any displays. *What?* She's just a little pale and weak. Thinner. She doesn't look immensely different from when we saw you in October. We knew then, but we hoped she would be better, so we didn't tell you...*Oh, Mommy.*

"Oh, Mommy!"

She didn't realize she had called out those words until her father handed her his clean handkerchief. She cried until her nose bled. She cried until she thought she would suffocate. Another father would have held his daughter, rocking her back and forth uselessly but with the best intentions. At the time, she was glad he was not one of those fathers. She didn't even have to hear it in words. Her mother was going to die. Her father had no need to divorce her now.

A *need* to leave them. Perhaps, in his strange way, her father had thought that by ripping his family apart he could bring them closer. But he was too late; Annie died, and in doing so proved that tragedy would not change them all that much.

Outside, little dogs in raincoats led their masters home, eager for a fireplace and mutton bone. She wanted to be a little dog, insensible and happy.

145

She left the money on the table, and gathered up her belongings, hurrying to the Métro stop. The wind made a person wet, more than the rain itself. Her leather jacket kept her body warm, but her exposed hands were like ice. She thought about putting her hands on one of those tiny doggies, sucking his heat away and replacing it with coldness. What she needed she could not get from a dog.

She carried her red mapbook of the city's neighborhoods. If someone asked her if she needed help finding her way she ignored him rudely. Ignore. Ignorance. She had always been good at both the state of being and the activity.

Museums were her solace. For her, they were free, and they were a heaven anyway, housing man–made art and quietude. She took the RER to the Musée d'Orsay, her favorite museum in the city.

Monsieur St–Jean owned a textile business, an ancient family business, that had served kings and noblemen since the Renaissance, probably. He was proud of his artisan, middle class roots, his nouveau–riche identity, although his family had been wealthy for centuries. Madame was half Italian. A noblewoman in Fiesole, although by marrying a commoner she had given up her noble status. Still, in summers when they went to their villa, the people bowed when she passed, calling her Countess.

All of this was exciting and exotic to Khatia, although it did not mean very much. The St–Jeans insisted she would come with them to Italy that summer, but she did not think that far ahead anymore. The only thing she was aware of was each day passing, the sun surprising her when it went down, and it was time to put Anges–Mathieu to bed.

Monsieur, because of his occupation, had a family pass to all the museums in Paris. Generously, he put Khatia's name on it, telling her to go whenever she liked. She went every weekend on her days off. She was the only one in the family who used it regularly. At dinner time, after returning, Monsieur would ask her, "Did you buy any postcards?" and she would tell him what she had bought. If she remembered, she would bring them with her and show him.

"I live vicariously through you," he told her. "Because my business and family keep me too busy to go. When Anges–Mathieu is older…" His voice would trail off, and he would look adoringly at his little boy.

Dinner was always divine. Madame actually cooked the food herself— they only had a cleaning woman come twice a week. A typical dinner: an avocado half with lemon vinaigrette in the pithole to start. A Provençal cream sauce poured over fish and green beans in a casserole with steamed rice. Baguettes to soak up the sauce. A green salad to follow with more lemon vinaigrette. Then, six kinds of cheeses to choose from with more bread. Cookies from the tin for dessert. Of course, red wine and water throughout to wash it all down. Khatia ate dinner with them every evening if they were home. If they went out, Madame left something easy to warm up on the stove for her and Anges–Mathieu. Eating out seemed something one did with another purpose than food, and she had no one to do that with, nor did she want anyone. Every now and then, walking down the sidewalks of Paris, she felt eyes pulling at her, and would look up to see a beautiful man or woman eyeing her. Was it desire or pain she exuded?

Even on her weekends off, since she was there for dinner, she would help put Anges–Mathieu to bed. She did not want to appear cold towards him. She would show them that he was more than just a job to her. She read to him, children's books in English her father had grudgingly sent upon her request. He did not seem pleased that she had moved yet again. And now she was a nanny—a *nanny?* An "au–pair," she wrote, but he would not demure. To what end could being a nanny, a house servant, a *toady*, possibly lead? he asked in his letters. What had happened to law school? She scanned the letters once with her eyes, sent him a postcard in reply.

The books had colorful pictures to keep Anges–Mathieu's interest. His big eyes stared over the coverlets. He was not, she thought, an ugly child.

His bed was a loft bed like hers, except it was a double, and eight feet off the floor while hers was only four feet high. Underneath, a wonderland of toys, games and sheeted curtains. A sultan's harem of stuffed animals. Bright halogen tracking lights on the bottom of the bed kept the secret nook warm. Sometimes, he insisted on listening to the story down there, curled up on the cushions with blankets and quilts from the hall closet. She would carry his sleeping, heavy body gingerly up the ladder, remembering times as a girl feigning sleep so her father would carry her to bed from the car after a long trip, already in pajamas, clutching her favorite blanket, her father's touch unfamiliar.

147

Olivia Boler

The Musée d'Orsay was packed for a winter day, but it was Sunday, so there was not much she could expect. It was large and airy, a converted train station with the feel of a late 1980's interior decorator of marble, steel, and acrylic. She liked it, could breathe with ease in its contained spaciousness. The sparseness reminded her of the camping trips with her family in the White Mountains—that canopy of glass and steel similar to the tree branches letting in holes of light.

She went to the section on the second floor where the pointillist paintings were housed. Seurat, Signac, Cross. Dots replacing the waves of Van Gogh. Getting as close to the paintings as the docents would allow, her eyes blurred. The dots melted into a stream of warmed honey. She could almost taste the glucose, wanted to lick the paint to be sure, although lead poisoning would likely result.

Her favorite painting was one by a little known artist, Georges Lemmen. A sunset on a coast made up of black cliffs, the sun setting on the waters, turning them marigold yellow, orange, aubergine, scarlet, cerulean—colors that opposed each other, one letting the other stand out with all the support of a worthy enemy. There were no postcards of this painting in the store; she had searched and searched. She wanted to sneak her camera in here, take a photo, but she would get kicked out into the street. It was almost worth it, to have the small painting—it was no more than a foot long—in her possession.

She felt someone staring at her, and glanced in the direction of the room's guardian, but the blue–jacketed woman was looking the other way. Next to her stood a young man, regarding her intently. She turned back to the painting, forgetting about him, her face stony the way she had learned to keep it by watching Parisian women walking quickly down the sidewalks, bitchy and with purpose.

"Pardon," he said with a terrible French accent.

She turned, showing how she hated to be interrupted by the cool look on her face.

"Dónde está la salle de bain?" Up close, the young man looked like an eager farm boy, and she assessed his pale freckles. He moves quickly, she thought. What a yokel.

"You're speaking Spanish and French, you know."

148

"Oh, grand," he said with relief. "I don't know much French, and I thought you must be Spanish, but you know English, so I'm pretty well off, right?"

He had an accent, British or something. She turned back to the Lemmen.

"Go across the hall to your right. The men's room is the second door," and she turned around, leaving him standing there to enjoy her favorite painting on his own.

Perhaps even museums were not sacred.

Ulrike had written her one letter since she had left. "Shoshonah is a good person, but God, I miss your voice! Are you sure you will not come back?"

She had written him a postcard with one line: "Come back? Please, Ulrike." Her standard answer to almost anything he said.

He had offered Shoshonah Khatia's old job after Shoshonah had called him upon finding the good–bye note, sobbing and moaning like Chewbakka, an abandoned wookie. He did not know what else to do to make her feel better. He felt duplicitous, he wrote to Khatia, as if somehow he had encouraged their break–up and Khatia's departure. So, even though Shoshonah was practically a stranger to him, he had done this kind thing. Khatia was pleased to read his words. Her crafty parts thought, Yes. Now Shoshonah will be away from Mina. But most of her did not really care.

No surprise then when she fetched the mail for the St–Jeans a few days after her excursion to the Musée d'Orsay and saw a letter from Shoshonah. Over a month. Shoshonah had waited over a month to write to her. Khatia counted the note she had written as a letter, unconscious of keeping score until she held the airmail envelope—Rules, rules, rules. She waited until after dinner to read it in the privacy of her room, almost forgetting about it as she made Nutella sandwiches for Anges–Mathieu and took him to the toy store—Almost.

Dear Khatia,

Well, you know how it is. You pick up the pen, stare at the paper, and then remember you left the light on in the other room. Once you go into

149

the other room to turn it off, you see the plants need watering. Once the plants have been watered, you realize you too are thirsty. After a good drink from the juice bottle, the taste in your mouth leaves hunger on the brain. And then you cook. And eat. Wash the dishes. Watch TV. Before you know it, it's time for bed, and the paper and pen are still on the desk, just lying there...and tomorrow is another day, Scarlett.

Don't be angry at me. Please.

I was angry at you for a long time. I think we could have done a lot more talking, and I can't believe you would do something as Hollywood as leaving me a note in the wee hours of the morning, taking all your stuff except for one lousy sock—if you want it, I'll send it, but I'm sure its partner is long gone by now, knowing you, probably a puppet for that kid you baby–sit.

I'm a head case, Khatia. I've always known that. You dealt with me well. I know it was hard to be with me sometimes, but as Marilyn Hacker once wrote, "I try to be a woman I could love." You are just as strange as I am. We're like opposite ends of the pole, crazy in different ways. The only thing that surprises me is how easily I could read you, but how you missed so much going on with me. I don't know *why* it took you so long to realize I was interested in other women.

Okay, maybe I'm still a little angry.

Another Hackerism: "Serial monogamy is a cogwheeled hurt." Let me explain.

I couldn't make the rent on my own, even though Ulrike's job pays more than my old one(I hope you don't mind that I took it, by the way. He showed me your postcard. I see you're paring down in the correspondence department). So,

150

Mina moved out of her parents' place and moved
in here—

Khatia stopped reading. These last words ran over and over, growing larger, the sloppy scrawl of Shoshonah's handwriting becoming enlarged, written as if with the side of a piece of chalk. The urge to scan the rest of the letter quickly was great, but she forced herself to read on slowly.

—It happened very fast. Really, my reasons were financial. I wanted time to recover from this, not deal with finding a smaller place and all. She's a really great person, Khatia. I mean, I still want to date other women, sort of. I didn't want to move right into another relationship. Still, here I am. Sometimes we just give into the craving without thinking of the consequences. I know. I do that a lot. Anyway, I don't want to keep any secrets from you. That's why I'm going to write what I'm going to write next. Khatia, you were always hard to talk to before your mom died. But after that, it was even harder. It's like you wanted someone to take care of you, but you didn't want it to be obvious. It made me wonder if anyone has ever taken care of you before. Talked to you like a human being. I mean your family. Every time I saw you with them, you were so different. It's like you put on different clothes and a wig, and started masquerading as this false person. But I've been wondering lately if the false person you are was the one you were with me. Confusing? Yes. True? I don't think so. I do think you should talk to your dad about your mom. About anything! Something doesn't sit right with you two. I'm not saying you should try to change him, or you for that matter. Just let him know you have a mind. A beautiful mind. He's just a man, and you shouldn't be afraid of that. I mean, I don't

151

know him at all, but, well. Anything would help.

I love you, Khatia. I will always be here to give
you unsolicited advice. Take it or leave it.

Don't get caught in the gill nets.

Love,

Shoshonah

P.S. Working with Ulrike is cool, except he's also
always asking me all these questions about life and
shit.

She put the letter in her journal, paper–clipped on the back cover. She took it out from time to time, while Anges–Mathieu played on the slide in the park, or while she watched television with the St–Jeans after dinner, just touching the envelope, remembering what was inside, remembering the person who wrote it.

Stop thinking backwards.

That weekend, the bars beckoned to her. Bars, crowded with the populous of the city, the young people listening to music, sipping drinks, talking rapidly in their language.

She chose one she had stumbled upon during her rambles around the Boulevard St. Michel in the Latin Quarter. It was near le Panthéon, a raucous, noisy bar called le Violon Dingue. The Crazy Violin. The music of the French language, the ordinary choices French people made in their words that would always render romance, even in their accustomed ears. All its drama charmed and frightened her. So much of the language, she still did not know or understand, its slang, subtleties, and innuendoes.

The international community apparently had discovered the Violon Dingue as well. The bouncer kept her waiting in line with others. A young parisienne kept turning to her, making remarks. Khatia only smiled back, fortunately understanding when the woman wanted to bum a cigarette. After a while, the woman gave up on conversation and turned back to her date who was a bore, Khatia gathered from *l'argot* she did not understand.

As she stepped inside, the words that came into her head were "European testosterone." This place was deeply heterosexual. In general, European men did not seem as hefty as their American counterparts, but they still felt their sex, the construction of their bodies and that male power which they equated.

She ordered a beer at the bar and decided to stay there. The dark, low room was packed with groups of friends, standing in small circles or against the walls. The room felt like two square rooms connected by the "hallway" of the bar itself. There was a bit of standing room across from it, and a thoroughfare for the people streaming from one room to the other. A little like Chez Manfred, except there were women *and* men here. The walls seemed to absorb the sweat and smoke that fell off bodies in profusion. In bars, the French reputation for quietness in public places dissipated. They were noisy, blustering, shouting to each other across the room. True, not all of them were French. She heard German, English, Italian—she had more of an ear for their distinctions now.

With this realization, she understood that transformation *had* taken place in her. When? Where? How? These journalist's queries flooded her mind. Europe had turned her into a more cosmopolitan person, if nothing else. It had made her aware of herself. Matter. She was made up of matter, controlled by a brain. And she mattered. She could think. She could reason on her own. A hesitant rebellion in postcards. Yes, Paris could transform, awaken, yet something did not seem completed or ready—she could not pin it down except to think that she needed more than this city could give, something beyond it. It was not a proper fit...she must continue searching.

Two men argued drunkenly next to her at the bar. Moving away from them would be best, but she was blocked in by the crowd which pushed by the narrow corridor of the bar. They both smelled heavily of cologne and b.o., the French penchant for bi–weekly bathing not just a myth, she had discovered. The St–Jeans seemed a little horrified when they realized she used their shower *every morning*. Why, the cost of shampoo alone! She could see the pores in the closer man's cheek, little cups of human oil.

Pulling out a cigarette, she fumbled for her lighter, her lazy mind listening to their conversation but not understanding.

"Attends," said the man next to her. He flipped a lighter out of his breast pocket and lit her cigarette.

"Merci," she said.

He looked her up and down, interested. "Tout va bien?" he asked.

"Oui, merci."

He frowned sharply, sensing a poser. He continued speaking in French, and she tried to keep up.

"You aren't French."

"No," she said, looking straight ahead. Except there was a mirror behind all the bottles, and she saw he stared at her in the glass. She looked down at her cigarette, letting the fire in the tip blur—

"Are you Italian?"

"No."

"Portuguese?"

"No."

"Spanish?"

"No," she sighed. Déjà vu. "American. I'm American."

A small sneer passed over his lip. "This guy and I," he jerked his head towards his friend, "were just talking about Americans. How stupidly they handle all their political affairs." He paused, as if expecting her to come at his eyeballs with her nails.

"You're probably right," she said, after a labored assembling of the sentence in her head. She wished she could just speak without translating. She wished she just knew the language—

"Ah," he said, drawing her attention back to him. The sneer again, permanent on his mouth. "So you share this basic sense of irresponsibility. Look at your nation in these last few years: race riots, the Klu Klux Klan, that famous baseball player who murdered his wife."

"Football," she said. "He played American football, not baseball."

"I don't give a fuck. All I can say is your country is screwed." He shoved his face in closer, and Khatia automatically moved the other way, into another person's shoulder. Why had she come here? The man's friend tapped him on his shoulder, speaking tentatively. He looked unconcerned, enjoy-

154

ing Khatia's discomfort, yet felt the need to pull his friend away. He probably doesn't want to get kicked out of the bar, she thought.

"And now," the man continued. His speech slurred, an alcoholic's slow motion. She wished she could not understand him. "You fucking assholes are coming here to my country, with your noisiness and sneakers and money. As if you own my country because you have no culture. Your government is turning into a police state, there's no uniformity, with your Los Angeles—"

"Really?" she interrupted, suddenly angry. She had never been to Los Angeles. She even half–believed the propaganda this man talked, had watched the ten o'clock news in the homogenous comfort of Bloomfield, quiet, old Aunt Estella nodding at the news anchors. "L.A.," her aunt would say, "should drop into the ocean any day now."

"What about," Khatia said to the man without thinking, remembering bits and pieces of words from Monsieur St–Jean's gentle dinnertime tirades after he read the newspaper. "Le Front National? What about Jean–Marie Le Pen? What about the separation of Arabs into their own little enclaves? What about—"

"Bitch! Lesbian!" the man said, his lips in her face. "You fucking cunt!"

The non–sequitur of the man's reply made sense in a way. Khatia was almost happy, her adrenaline kicking in like a death wish.

"Le FN! Le FN!" she screamed at him lustily, now on her feet, not caring there was no room, pushing into the person next to her with her imbalance.

"Los Angeles! Los Angeles!" he yelled back, spit from his words landing in her eyes and hair.

It was like opera, singing into each others' faces, screaming into the wind.

People watched them in amused and horrified fascination. They watched, this typical scuffle over politics, almost uninteresting in its commonness. They watched, as the man's clenched fist swung out, and connected with Khatia's neck, just on the bone of her jaw's hinge. She bit her tongue with the force of the blow, her cigarette flying from her fingertips. Her upper–body folded against the bar, spilling the rest of her beer.

Someone was on top of the man, hands at his throat, holding him down in the trodden, greasy sawdust. She thought it was his friend, but he was

155

standing over the heap of bodies, trying to pull the stranger off.

Before she knew what had happened, a path had been cleared, and Khatia found herself on the sidewalk, pulled and shoved, forced to leave. A common rabble–rouser. Had it been the bartender? The bouncer? Her rescuer? She stumbled against a parked car, stared about in a daze. Under the streetlight, everything seemed too bright.

"Are you all right?" someone asked.

"I'm—"

"Do you need a doctor?"

"No. I think I—"

"We can go to a doctor if you need one."

"No. I—no, I'm okay."

She did not realize she was speaking English until her companion said, "What an asshole. A woman–beater on top of it all. God!"

It was the man from the Musée d'Orsay. The one who wanted the bathroom.

She walked down the sidewalk, a little unsteady—it sloped downhill—towards the river.

"Where are you going?" he asked behind her.

"I need to move," she called back, kept walking forward, trying not to weave. Concentrating on her steps so she would not feel the pain in her jaw.

He trotted after her.

"Well, I'm not leaving you," he said.

"Okay," she said. "Chivalrous."

They walked silently. She could tell he wanted to talk, but was holding back. She cut through the small alleys of gyro stands and couscous restaurants, back onto the Boulevard St. Michel. The quay was in sight. She jogged down its steps. Found a cold, stone bench.

Lights from the ancient, gray buildings sparkled on the waters, the filthy, polluted waters of the river. What had it been like with natural, dirt banks?

Now it was all banked up by the high walls of the quay, completely a creation of man and his progress. So was the whole city. She was careful to never, ever walk on grass in any of the parks. She could find her way easily in any part of town, thanks to Hausmann's mapping of the Eighteenth Century reconstruction. A city of circles, twenty–four in all, fitting into one giant circle. Getting lost, as in Amsterdam, was virtually impossible. Just walk around and around and around like a dog chasing her tail.

He sat down next to her, about two feet away.

"Paris has always been my favorite city," she said to him. "Even though I've never been until now. When I was a kid, I'd ask my brother, 'If you could be in any country right now, what would it be?' and he'd say, 'America!' and I'd say, 'No, stupid. Another country.' And then I'd tell him, 'I like France best.'" She paused, smiling at her feet. "He would ask me why, of course. But I can't remember the answer now."

The young man did not say anything. Khatia gazed out at the river, the Cathedral of Notre Dame, that famous structure of holy worship and Quasimodo waving on the sheet of water like Poseidon's kingdom just below the surface. She knew this building by heart from all her visits there, going in to light candles for her mother and unformed prayers.

"It's probably not for my own reasons," she said after a moment. "But whatever the reason, I'm not disappointed."

He stood up, walking to the edge of the quay and peering into the waters. She took his distractedness as a sign of boredom, but decided not to let it affect her as it once might have. She was different now. Her hands shook as she lit a cigarette. Clenching it between her teeth hurt in her ears.

He stood for a while, and she sat, each looking out at the water, at the boats going by. The ferries on their night cruises. They were near one of the bridges that gave access from the Left Bank to the Right, and they could see mischief makers lurking with cartons of eggs, waiting for the open–air boats to pass underneath with their loads of tourists. A romantic couple would pass on the quay now and then, heads bent together in sweet murmurs. Or a group of rowdies in leather jackets and close, European haircuts.

Khatia felt a gap running like a thin tunnel through her body, as if one of her veins was not getting enough blood, and it was collapsing with emptiness. She sucked down the cigarette and reached for another.

157

He turned to her, looking her over.

"My name is Ian," he said.

She nodded, blowing out smoke.

"Khatia," she said.

They were quiet, looking out at the water again.

"May I ask you something, Khatia?" he said after a while.

"Go ahead."

"What were you doing in that bar all by yourself?"

She laughed. "What do you mean, all by myself?" .

"It's dangerous."

"For a woman, you mean."

"Of course," Ian said, not catching her drift. "This is the second time I've seen you, and you've been by yourself both times. I just wondered. Don't you have any friends?"

She smiled slowly.

"I'm learning to be alone," she said.

He looked slightly bewildered. "What does that mean?"

"It means what it means."

He was short, perhaps an inch or two taller than she. He had a wide face, and a dent on the bridge of his nose, between his eyes. Their color was not visible in the darkness; it seemed important that she could not see their color.

Her gaze followed the dark succession of bridges, and she imagined walking all the way back to the St–Jeans' apartment with her eyes shut, guided by the sound of the water. She let them close and the exhaustion washed over her, making her dizzy and nauseated for a moment. She swayed a little and opened her eyes.

"You know," said her new companion. "I really don't like to leave you here alone. Can't I see you home?"

She smiled up at him. "No thanks. I'm just going to sit here for a while

158

longer."

"Then, perhaps we could go somewhere? A bar or café?"

She raised her eyebrows.

"Irish," she said. "I finally figured it out. You're Irish."

"Yes," he said. "Please. I just really don't like to leave you here alone."

"Yes, I guess you do have a problem with leaving me alone," she said, blinking at him through the smoke of her cigarette. Oh, what the hell. In the Sixteenth Arrondisement, the St–Jeans slept. In Amsterdam, Shoshonah was cuddled up next to her new love. In New Hampshire, her father sat alone in his house, his wishes fulfilled. "Why don't we go get a beer?"

"Grand," he said, and offered her a hand.

Chapter Two

He is drowning in plain air.

John Porter Quigley opens his mouth, his teeth gnashing. His tongue fills his mouth, blocking the passage of oxygen to his lungs. All around his body, jagged molecules beat against objects: his bed, his nightstand, the walls, his own naked skin. It even caresses the interior of his mouth in pinpricks. The taste of it on the dried muscles inside his lips, the muscles that reach for moisture, is barely discernible, yet it is there, like a tease. He cannot remember how to take in a breath without discomfort. Like a fish on the shore of a lake, he tries relearning what to do, even though learning is hopeless. He will die if he does not get back in the water: these are the thoughts that pass through his mind in the confusion of recent waking. Waking from nightmares is like drowning in the real world.

The room is freezing; he forgot to turn up the thermostat last night before going to bed. When he sees the puffs of air coming from his nostrils and mouth like smoke, he knows that he is all right, that the dreams have not got him this time. Someday, perhaps.

The sky is pale blue outside. He does not realize until this moment that in suffocating he has sat up, but there he is, straight up in bed, on his knees, his hands on his thighs. He bends forward a little, as if that will help coax the oxygen, drive away the memory of the dream, yet his posture is a state of submission, of protection. Protecting the dream: like a parasite, it causes him to double over, to keep it in his head.

Eyes and the interior purple redness of eyelids, carbon dioxide laden blood. These images have flashed at him in the darkness of that trap. The dreams are worse now, the smells of slashed human flesh coming at him more than the images. The smell of blood, a smell like the taste of licked metal, of fork tines bitten on, the smell mixed with the sterility of rubbing alcohol and potpourri: the Lysol the cleaning woman uses in the bathrooms and kitchen to cover up, just under the surface, something unmentionable. These smells

160

intermingled cause a rising in his abdomen, both of pleasure and revulsion. He may becoming ill. Or hungry. Hungry for pungent meats—bacon, ham, anything barbecued. The meats of pigs. The meats of summer, though it's the middle of winter. Korean barbecue. His tongue pokes out of his lips a little, his eyes closed. He could barbecue; the house is far enough away from neighbors. They won't see the rising of the smoke from his grill, the smells of roasting, muscular sections charring, the carbon flaking, ingested into atmosphere and the private air of his throat and lungs. The proper Korean way: strips of meat soaked in thick, sugary sauces, red–hot spicy sauces, then placed on the coals, turned over, cooking fast. The strips are small, tenderized for thinness. Rice and chopsticks to shovel in the food, temper the spices. They eat in small bites, each one ceremonial.

The clock says 11:09. He never sleeps this late. Has risen before dawn everyday of his life since the Army. He remembers that today is the first day of his Spring vacation and the anniversary of Sung Ko's death. Last night, Dorinne took him out for drinks. Her thirty–sixth birthday. She was drunk, wanting to come back to the house with him. He said no, taking her home to her small apartment near Northeastern University. Jesus, Dorinne, he said to her. Why don't you move? Her apartment building is being renovated; young, Iranian construction workers hanging out, living in the abandoned first floor, camped out in the ghetto–like foyer of the building amidst the detritus of broken plaster and primer coats, their eyes glazing up her legs, looking for what is hidden beneath her skirts.

I *like* it here, she told him emphatically, ignoring the men, stepping over them like dirty clothes. They let me keep my dog, and the park is lovely. No hassle. I *like* it. Besides—her eyes shifted—You don't pay me enough to move somewhere more upscale.

He stayed with her, letting her cry as he entered into her alcohol–dried space, her small, drunken voice singing Happy Birthday to Me. As he left around three, she snored softly. He put aspirin and a glass of water next to the bed so she wouldn't have to stumble around in the morning.

He remembers now that he went for a run when he got home, bypassed his usual coffee, and went to his bedroom to lie down. Whistling outside: it is the wind in the bare branches of trees, the purchase of graying light.

Porter will be home next week for his Spring Break. The boy has decided to forego a trip with "the Band" to Florida and come back to the house instead. Research, he says, and says no more. Only that it is for one of his classes. John Porter Quigley is surprised at his son's quiet ebullience. A note arrived a few days before, informing the father that Porter is on academic probation. He is surprised to receive such a note, angry at the college's lack of respect for its students' privacy. Such notices used to arrive when the children were in high school, especially for the boy, and the issuance of them in college seems insulting. In any case, he says nothing to his son, except to say they will go out to dinner in town to celebrate his home—coming.

An urge overcomes him to go into his children's rooms. The maid is the only one who does anymore, and when she is in the house, he stays in his study, going for a walk when she scratches, squirrel–like, on his door. He always coughs as he passes her, his loose fist at his mouth, filling his sight; he's not even sure what color her hair is.

His knees are cramping, and he realizes he is still hunched on the bed like some penitent subject. Slowly, so they will not pop, reminding him of his age, he stretches out a leg, lowering himself to the floor. He is nude, and in the mirror, he sees his own father's body, something he has not thought about in years, if ever. His father, a man he barely remembers, a man who disappeared from his life, his life gone by an accident, a shotgun in his stomach, a slow death in the gazebo nobody witnessed.

His mother and sister. Those were his caretakers, the women. Providers, raisers. He should call them. Next time he writes to Khatia, in response to her latest post card.

Khatia. He finds his robe, walks to her bedroom door down the hall from his own. It opens silently; the maid oils the hinges at his request. Inside, it is like a storage closet, piles of books that do not fit into the bookcase, a dollhouse housing old shoes. Two boxes from Aunt Estella's place, marked BEDDING and KNICK KNACKS. He is naked, holding his robe, looking over the debris of her.

Go to her.

Porter's room is neat and cold. Both children's rooms get the southern light, the light of afternoon. Old warmth. He has the north. Annie liked this. Brightness all day.

These days, he can not get the war out of his dreams, and he can conjure up no solutions to stop them. A whiff comes back from sleep: the blood, pouring from his daughter's eyes, the slashed flesh of her upper lids. He can almost reach out and peal away the pieces, the translucent skin attached to small stiff hairs, plucked hairs. But she turns from him, mouthing words he can not understand. Closing his eyes against the image does not help. The house moans around him as the late winter wind picks up, shaking everything it meets in an uncaring embrace.

Sometimes he still hates his family. It doesn't happen very often since Annie died, but it scares him nonetheless, and he must close his eyes to himself until the fear and feelings pass, and a temporary solution is found. Part of him knows he could help his children, he is their father, but with that healing potential is also the potential to destroy.

Go to them.

He turns back to his own room and dresses.

Driving to Rhode Island takes two hours. He plays a tape, Verdi, encapsulated in his car. It was Annie's car, a present for her birthday two years before she died. A pale mint Saab. She always liked pale mint. It's in good condition, although there's a rip in the passenger seat cushion.

It's the weekend. He finds Porter's dormitory, an ugly, cinderblock building. The floors are linoleum on concrete, easy to clean. His son's room is like a kitchen.

No one answers his knocking. He decides to stroll around the campus. The students hibernate, recovering from Friday night parties and getting ready for a Saturday night. The campus grounds are deserted, a bundled up figure hurrying through the cold now and then, out one building and into another. He picks out a girl and trails her from a distance, tracking her brown, slushy footprints.

She goes into the library. It is one of the more aesthetically pleasing buildings on the campus, old brick covered in the dead vines of ivy. He enters, forgetting about the girl, the scholar in him taking it in, remembering all the time he used to spend in libraries as a graduate student. As a professor, he can afford to buy the books he needs. They are, in fact, given to him, beautiful, hardcover books, arriving at his office or house in boxes, secured in bubble wrap. Most of them are junk, poorly written with no

163

soul, and he donates them to the college or high school.

The large sitting room, with its high, cathedral ceiling, slow fans, and comfortable chairs immediately makes him sleepy. Sinking into the cushiony depths of one of the couches would be right. He remembers watching Annie do her work in the library, her body aware of his presence, her mouth set in a straight line, trying to concentrate on her work, the computer, the student, the book—whatever was before her.

Hey, someone says. The voice is from all the way across the room, small and contained, a slight echo in the expanse. John Porter Quigley turns to it, recognizing it. It is his son, sitting at one of the larger tables, papers and books spread out before him. A young woman is talking to him. She has blue hair, wears a green velvet dress and black boots, boots like the ones he wore in the Army, except these have white and pink flowers painted on them. She and Porter talk quietly, smiling, gesturing with their hands the way young people do to emphasize the importance of their words. The girl's wrist twists, her palm up then down, her fingers pointing. She bends over his papers, nodding, showing ceremonial fascination. *Interest.*

The father gets up from his chair. One of the pillars holding up the massive ceiling beckons him, and he slides behind it, watching his son with this girl, his son's hair, longer now since Christmas time, a time they spent in a restaurant in Boston, his son's hair more of a page boy, revealing its straightness. Neither of his children inherited his own waves. Porter's hair, that strange brassy color, in contrast to the girl's blue, their heads bent over his books. She runs her fingers through her own hair, touches the pages of the book, and he imagines blue fingerprints on the musty paper.

They continue to talk. Porter looks around the room, but his eyes rest nowhere in particular, going back to the girl's face. She touches his arm as John Porter leaves the building, imagining blue fingerprints on his son's white shirt sleeve.

Chapter Three

Finally: sun. It soaked into Khatia's skin as she lay in the manicured grass. Water sprayed lightly, a mist creating rainbows in the first spring–like day. The city seemed transformed, more alive. She let her eyes close half–way like a cat lying on a hot sidewalk. She could hear Anges–Mathieu's voice blending with Ian's. The boy would have a mild brogue if she did not watch their interaction. Then what would the St–Jeans say? They probably would not notice since they could not understand much English in the first place. Monsieur was proud of the fact he knew the word brownies and what they were. "Brownies for brunch!" he said one late morning as they lunched early, savoring left–over pastries from a party they had hosted the night before.

Raising her head slightly, she could see them playing on the edge of the Trocadéro fountain. Like a cannon, it shot out a fireman's hose of water every ten minutes or so, the other little off–shooting fountains rising like feelers next to it. People swam in the waters, in their clothes. Some women went topless. Khatia claimed it was too chilly when Ian joked she should do the same. They watched a man roller skate down the hillside and land in the two feet of water. Ian's mouth hung open as he looked on in amazement, his expression making Khatia laugh more than the other man's antics.

She had not laughed in a long time.

Ian was like a clown in disguise. He always wore jeans and a denim–jacket: usually a bad combination, denim on denim. When she started to pay attention, the signs of his blatant farm–boy's background revealed themselves like signs from god. There were lots of farms around her house in New Hampshire, and the teenaged sons and daughters of the farmers often dressed in crazy denim outfits on the weekends. As she passed through the downtown area of Milford on her bicycle to see Bianca or run an errand, she would see the farm couples in the diner sipping Brown Cows. Two straws in one glass. That was Ian. Two straws in one glass.

165

He was gullible like a farmboy. Everytime they went to a bar, he ordered orange juice.

"You don't drink?" she asked the first time.

"No," he shook his head and toed the sawdust like a bashful bull. "I promised my father before he died, God bless him, that I would not drink, and so I do not."

"Wow!" she said, impressed, and lit a cigarette. "But you're Irish."

"Oh, you're going to start in with the Irish cracks, are you now?" He nodded his head vigorously, but she could see he was smiling. "Go on, now. Will it be the one about the drunken Catholic? Or perhaps the leprechauns?"

"Leprechauns?" she said.

"Yes, leprechauns!"

She gave him a puzzled look. "What are you talking about?"

"You mean you don't know about leprechauns?" and he looked at her half in disbelief, half in suspicion. "Little green men! They live in the forests. Like elves or fairies."

"What?" She rested her chin in her hand and squinted at him.

"Yes! The little people. You mean you don't know? And if you catch one, he has to give you his pot of gold at the end of the rainbow." He waved his hand out the door of the bar to show her where the end of the rainbow might be found.

"Do you see these little people often?" she asked.

He stared, incredulous and lobotomized, and then he saw the look on her face. He didn't say anything, face solemn, eyes wondering.

"Okay," Khatia said. "It's your turn to tease the American now."

He smiled and raised his glass to his lips. "It's not to be tolerated."

"I don't know about you, Ian, but my nationality has never come into question so much as it has here." She blew out smoke, touching the tender spot on her jaw lightly.

"Well, I suppose that's what happens when you go abroad."

"I suppose it does."

He reminded her of some of the people she used to see at the country club swimming pool in her hometown. Her parents had joined one year when she was in junior high, forcing her and Porter to take swimming lessons. Porter loved it; he tortured the teenaged lifeguards with cannonballs, backflips, running around the pool, breaking every pool rule in existence. But she hated swimming, although she went to the lessons and performed obediently. She watched the other people, those in her lesson group and the adults around them. Some people would stride right up to the pool as if they were on a Sunday walk through the park. They would not even stop striding when they reached the edge, but kept on going as if the concrete deck were still there, and they would plunge off into the chlorinated waters, sinking down, the water engulfing their heads. They would pop up immediately, and go striding off again, this time using their hands to propel them forward. That was Ian, plunging into anything with all the trust in the world, always going forward, plowing through.

Then there were people like her. Those who strode up to the edge with the purposefulness of a provoked buffalo, looking very much as if they were plungers too. But Khatia would always pull up short, lace her fingers together on her chest, gaze down tentatively into the waters of the pool looking for sharks, wondering what degree of heart attack the icy drink would produce. She would walk back and forth along the edge, perhaps dip in a toe, and then ease in, slowly, painfully, never believing she would enjoy the plunge.

Let's jump.

Khatia sat up to make sure Ian and Anges–Mathieu had not drowned. She blinked as her sunglasses slipped off her nose for a moment, and the sun's reflection on the water blinded her. Once, when they had only been in Amsterdam for a few days, Shoshonah had urged Khatia to jump off one of the bridges into the canal waters with her, holding hands. Sewage, Khatia thought. Insanity, she thought. Absolutely not.

She wondered what would have happened if they had.

"Khatia! Look at this!" Ian called.

She stood up, stretching her muscles. Her legs were hairy and pale, exposed by the short skirt she had pulled out of the bottom of her back pack.

167

She would get those freckles like Porter if she were not careful. Khatia tanned deeply in the summers spent hiking and laying out by the lake at her family's cabin using a select mixture of cocoa oil and sunblock lotion. Madame had given her sunscreen that morning to protect young Anges–Mathieu, and Khatia had smeared a little on her own limbs.

On the water floated a small paper boat. Ian looked at it and back at her.

"Look what we made," he said to her. Anges–Mathieu cooed like a turtledove.

"Boat," Ian said to him. "How do you say it in French, Khatia?"

"Bateau," she said. "But we want him to learn English, remember?" "Right. But I need to learn more French."

Ian was an electrician working for an Irish construction company, and was now doing work on a new shopping complex in La Défense, the business district on the edge of Paris. The company would be there for a few months, so their boss had encouraged his men to learn French, although all Ian knew was slang and cuss words from the bars he and his friends went to. He insisted Khatia and he speak French together so he could practice.

"I like speaking it with you," he told her very brokenly, with lots of incorrect verb tense, "because you talk slowly, and I can understand you."

"Gee," she said. "Thanks."

Such compliments did not go over well, and they soon returned to English–only conversations. Still, she had to admire his tenacity.

They had been spending free time together for almost a month now, and he was always a gentleman. Even the St–Jeans had met him. After bearing their teasing for a few nights— "Ah! Finally, the romance of Paris has hit our young American guest. She never eats dinner at home anymore, always out with her suitor."—she invited him over for a weekend lunch. The St–Jeans liked him, proclaiming him a handsome young man, and very subdued for an Irishman, although he did smile quite a bit. Khatia knew he was only subdued because he did not speak their language. If he could, he would have talked a blue streak. But they especially approved of the way he coddled Anges–Mathieu, playing with their son in the harem of animals while the others watched TV.

"I come from a family of ten children," he explained.

168

She was not attracted to him. She let him know her politely, with the barest of details. Letting him know all about her life, her family, Shoshonah, her strange thoughts, would not be fair. He knew she had come to Europe with a friend, but that they had a falling out and gone their separate ways. She filled in the time they spent together with a lot of conversation fillers, things she had learned to say, like what it was like to see a French supermarket's salad bar and compare it with an American one. He seemed to like hearing about her daily life.

"My brothers tell me about all the fantastic things they can buy in supermarkets over in New York City, but I never really believed them. They keep gigantic supermarkets open twenty–four hours a day, don't they?"

"Actually, they just keep one aisle open after midnight."

"Really?" His eyes grew big.

He did not threaten her with his masculinity, although she saw that kind of interest in his eyes, knew that it was important. Could see it now as he looked up at her from the little boat for approval. She ignored it, aware only fleetingly that the way he felt about her was probably the way she had felt about Ulrike: an infatuation with newness, with the unexplored. Fleeting. But Ian would push it soon.

He was courteous. A gentleman, always walking on the outside of the sidewalk. She found the dent in his nose, received from an accident playing hurley ball as a teenager, comforting. Yet, she could not take the plunge.

He had lost his father, she, her mother. He seized this connection, and she let him.

Tea time. Ian observed it strictly, albeit in McDonald's. It was like eating in a strip–mall on an interstate in New Jersey, yet they were in Paris, France. McDonald's: the ubiquitous comfort food of her nation. They sat in the fast food restaurant, she with a vanilla milkshake and fries, he with Chicken McNuggets, a Big Mac, fries, Coke, and apple pie. Always the same order for him. Anges–Mathieu squealed in toddler–delight at his Happy Meal prize, making a little raccoon–driven car fly.

Khatia pushed the flesh on her arm, seeing the white impression of her thumb in the pink skin. She would be sore in a few hours, the burn easing into her pigment. The glare at Trocadéro had got her. It would melt into her skin in a few days, turning a warm golden–yellow cast.

"I have to go home next week, to see my mother," Ian was saying. "I'd love it if you would come with me. I've told her and my little sisters all about you, you know."

"What are their names again?" she asked quickly, trying to hide the fact his words had caused her to choke on a fry.

"Alice, Barbara, and Siobhan."

"Right." She sucked at the straw, swallowing the thick, goopy substance. They seemed fresher, Parisian McDonald's milkshakes, as if the cow and vanilla beans were out back by the dumpsters.

"Well, what do you think?"

She swiped at Anges–Mathieu's mouth with a napkin.

"Hold still! About what?"

"Going home with me?"

She frowned at Anges–Mathieu's messy face, aware of Ian out of the corner of her vision.

"It sounds fun, but I can't really leave Matt and the St–Jeans. Can I? Huh, Matthew? You'd hate for me to leave." She dipped her napkin in a cup of ice water and went after him again. This time he held still, enjoying the cool, paper cloth on his face, moving around so she could get behind his ears.

"Nonsense!" he said. "Of course you can. You can leave whenever you want. And it would be a good vacation. Besides, don't you need to get your passport stamped?"

That was true. She did need to do that. Nearly three months had passed since she came to France, and she needed to leave the country and re–enter in order to avoid immigration.

She looked towards the main doors. A woman came in with her little Yorkshire terrier and put him on a table, telling him to stay while she ordered her food.

"Would you look at that," Khatia said. "I mean, people have to *eat* off that table." She shook her head. "Paris."

"It'll be an adventure. You'll love Ireland. County Clare. My county. It's the most picturesque place on Earth, I swear to you—"

"On your father's grave?"

She immediately regretted her words. He looked at her in bewilderment. She opened her mouth, wanting to apologize. Instead, she glared at him as if to say, "How dare you be offended."

They stared at each other for a few moments like rude strangers.

"Are you a singer, Khatia?" Ian asked after a while. The question surprised her.

"Do you mean, do I like to sing?"

"Yes. Because I love to sing. When I was growing up, I was in the choir. Now I hardly ever enter a church. I know it disappoints Mum. She doesn't ask me if I'm going or not while I'm here."

"Lord knows, there's plenty of churches to choose from in this town," she said, sighing a little. "It's okay, Ian. It's your choice after all."

"But if my father had asked, I would be going everyday. He wasn't as serious about it as Mum." He scooped up the apple turnover and bit off half of it.

She smiled. "You're a very honorable person, Ian."

He looked up. "Are you, Khatia?"

Again, he startled her. "I think so."

"Did your mother make you promise her anything before she died?"

"No. She was in a coma."

Ian looked a little ashamed at her flat words. She was not hungry anymore, and she had been very, very hungry.

"But did she make you promise her anything in life? Before she entered the coma?"

"I don't know what you mean. Talking about dead people is bad luck." Her mother had said that to her once. Also to never wear a green hat.

171

Khatia had wanted her mother to wear one on St. Patrick's Day once. "That's not my holiday," her mother had muttered, pulling it off the moment Porter put it on her head. "It means you're a fool and a cuckold to wear green." Ireland is green, Khatia thought, looking at Ian.

"How did your parents meet?" he asked.

She tried to remember. "Graduate school, I think. I mean, my mom was in graduate school, my dad was an assistant professor. Different departments though. How about yours?"

"High school sweethearts. And they were third cousins twice removed."

"Not surprising on such a wee island as Ireland is."

He narrowed his eyes slightly. She was having problems playing the nice–nice game at the moment and wanted a cigarette very badly. Because of the boy, she would have to wait. Her fingers drummed the tabletop. She reached for Anges–Mathieu's paper cup so the sound would stop.

"Here you go, Matt." Khatia handed him his soda and picked up her milkshake, her lips fumbling for the straw.

"Let's try this again, shall we?" Ian said. "I've never met a person like you, do you know what I mean?"

"Well," she said. "That's neutral."

He shook his head. "You say the strangest things."

"Someone has to," she said, more relaxed.

"I think I could marry you, Khatia." His face was humorless.

"What?"

The Yorkshire terrier woman returned with her tray of food, and Khatia glared at it as she set it down next to her beribboned pet, his tail wagging. His tiny white teeth snatched a French fry.

"You're the best girl I ever met."

"Woman. And no I'm not," she said without thinking. Denying goodness was so automatic. "Besides, don't you have to be in love before you get married?"

"Then I love you."

172

She looked at the crumbs on the table, her eyes roaming all around except on him. Anges–Mathieu was getting restless, twisting in his chair, wanting to pet the terrier.

"You can't possibly."

"I do."

"Then why are you bugging me?" she snapped, the vehemence in her voice like a tonic. "I just don't want people to bug me. Can you understand that?" She slammed down the paper cup of her milkshake with an inverted thud. "Why are you doing this? God*damn* it!"

"What?" he asked.

"This weird thing you're doing! Asking me all these uncomfortable questions, then saying these things. We've barely spent any time together at all. Do you always do this to women? Half the stuff I've done...You just don't know, okay?"

"I want to. And I don't mean to make you uncomfortable. Darling—"

Darling? That word. She hated that word. It was a Mina word. But Mina did not even matter anymore—just the word, the word and everything a word connoted—a weapon to make her wince—words for arguing, for finding truth, for asking her father"Why?," and her mother "Who?," and a divine power "How come?"—

"Let's go to London and get married."

"What? Is that like Las Vegas or something?" She wanted to shock him with irreverence.

Outside, a passing car's chrome bumper sent a slip of glistening light over Ian's face, accentuating the dip in his nose and the part underneath his eyes.

Khatia looked closely at those eyes. They were gray. And seemed kind. She had not registered that fact very seriously before. She knew she could hurt him.

This power added to the pressure on her chest.

"Ian, do you mind if we go now?"

"Khatia, I—"

173

"Let me think about all this for a while. Okay?"

"Of course," he seemed relieved. Perhaps this was more than he had hoped for, and she sensed his confidence as he reached over for her hand, holding it, patting it. Hers was slimy in his dry palm, and she wanted to wipe it on her skirt. She removed her hand from his grasp, patting his in return before she drew it under the table, squeezing her paper napkin into a gummy ball.

Disappearing into his work, Ian gave her time to decide whether she wanted to go visit his home. He promised not to call her, and if anything, he was a man of his word.

As spring caressed Parisians out of their apartments and onto the sidewalks, the American tourists descended like the circus come to town in their brilliantly colored nylon sweat suits and athletic shoes. Khatia cringed, seeing with French eyes.

"Oh *honey!*" their battle cry seemed to be as they peered at paintings in the Musée d'Orsay. "Look at that Monet! The waterlilies at *Giverny!* Gawd, aren't they *gor*geous? We hafta go see 'em owselves." They pronounce Giverny with a hard g, loud and honking. Their theme music was "Yankee Doodle Dandy." She had never noticed just how honking Americans were. Or maybe she had. Maybe that's why she had left them.

"They can't help themselves," she said to Anges–Mathieu as they sat on the bus to Giverny. As soon as she said it, she looked down at her lap. Here I am, she thought, Trying to be a person, a nationality, that I am not. She felt that emptiness in her belly, a hunger for something she could not name.

"It's my birthday today," she whispered to Anges–Mathieu.

Today, she turned twenty–four, and no one around her knew it except for him.

The bus arrived at Claude Monet's home–turned–tourist attraction, the site of his famous garden and waterlily paintings. The flowers were in full blossom, welcoming April, and for the moment, Khatia forgot her troubles in the sleepy warmth of the spring outdoors. Anges–Mathieu would sometimes grab onto her skirts and point at things, sounding out the first letter of their names: "Ba," for bee, "fa" for flower, "wa" for water.

174

They walked through the garden: row upon row of flowers. Paths ran next to the flowers, trellised every so often. The flowers were color–coordinated into a subdued orchestration. Purples, cerulean blue, pinks, oranges, mauves, lavenders, ivories, marigolds. This was better than sitting in a room of paintings. Miles and miles, it seemed, of non–stop shapes and hues. Hues. Khatia licked her tongue over the word. This was almost more than she could stand. She thanked the powers that be that she was not blind, and wished everyone in the world could witness such beauty.

They ambled down the rows of flowers, cups of color nestled in greenery and feathery grasses. Some flowers pushed forward on trestles. She took pictures of Anges–Mathieu in front of them framed in the downy beds, counseling him not to touch the silky blossoms and warning him about the bees.

"If you pull a flower, they'll getcha! They're guarding against naughty little boys who want to break the rules."

He seemed to believe her, keeping his poky fingers flat by his sides, and she wondered how much longer this obedience would last in his life. Taking words at face value. When would he begin to doubt the sagacity and motives of those around him?

They walked over the little green bridge that Claude Monet had so lovingly painted in a blur of green and lavender, his sight failing him. Still, he had known what was in front of him and what was simultaneously in the back of his mind. His paintings were renderings of fond day–dreams.

Khatia closed her eyes, trying to paint her own pictures. She let the colors slide over her burning, dry eyeballs until they formed into images: Mother at the library, stamping overdue notices. The Quigley house. Amsterdam at sunset. Shoshonah in bed, stroking her hair. Anges–Mathieu saying words in English. Ulrike in his suit in Brussels. Ian on the quay of the Seine. Her father, running. What did she really know about these people, and what did they think of her? Perhaps if she knew that, she could know in what way to see herself. Monet's blurs, Van Gogh's waves: she touched the material of her skirt, rubbing it as if to convince herself of its existence.

She ignored Anges–Mathieu's babbling voice for a moment longer. Just a little bit of stolen time. Images swam together slowly, slowly, and she could feel the watercolor wash over, conjoining them. They became fluid, one running into the other. A giant pooling, liquefying inside of her. She could feel the moisture in her eyes.

175

She did care about Ian. He found her exotic. Didn't exotic imply out of place? They could go to Ireland together. Perhaps that was the place for her. Perhaps if she found her place there, she could *stop* as the old man in Amsterdam had promised. Find my place, she thought. *Then* I can stay still.

She looked at herself in the green–brown waters of the pond, shocked out of the wash of colors. The light refracting on the surface, like cracks in a ceiling.

"Why does he want me? What can I give him?" she asked her sage companion. Had her mother asked these questions when her father proposed?

"Bah!" Anges–Mathieu answered.

"Exactly!" she laughed. Exactly. That was it. Bah. The French equivalent of "Uhhhh…" The American equivalent of "Whatever."

"Happy Birthday to Me," she smiled at Anges–Mathieu, picking him up and spinning him around so he laughed until he was almost scared but not sure why.

Chapter Four

Two nights later, Ian took her out to dinner. They dressed up. Khatia did not have a fancy coat, only her leather jacket. It was like her purse and utility belt all in one containing proof that she existed: wallet, identification, wads of tissue, pen, paper, Altoids, sunglasses, old receipts, cigarettes, lighter, back–up matches.

As they were leaving the restaurant, Ian put something in one of the pockets as he helped her with her jacket.

"What is that?"

"A present."

She took it out once they were outside and stood on Pont Neuf. A small jewelry box.

Lighting a cigarette, she looked at it.

"What's this?" she said, her fingers trembling.

"Open it," he said, hopping back and forth from one foot to the other as if he had to pee.

She cracked the box slowly. Inside was a Claddagh ring: two hands holding a heart with a crown. It was silver with a small green stone in the middle of the heart.

"I asked my mum to send it," he said. "It's very Irish."

"People wear them in the U.S. too," she said.

They looked at the ring in its box.

"Ian," she said. "I need to tell you something."

"What?" he asked, smiling.

"It's about a relationship I've had…Someone I loved," she held onto the

177

box.

"No, Khatia. You don't have to tell me anything until you're ready."

"I'm ready now. And you should hear it. There is so much we don't know about each other—"

"I have no problem with your smoking!" he said. Chuckle, chuckle. Make it harder, Ian, she thought.

"That's not what I'm talking about," she said, throwing her hands back. "I'm not referring to *bad habits.* I'm talking about life. Style. Lifestyle. Whatever." Bah.

He swallowed, waiting.

"My friend, whom I came to Europe with—"

"Sharon? Was that her name?"

Khatia paused. "Shoshonah."

"Shoshonah. Hebrew or something."

"Yeah. Well. Anyway. Shoshonah and I have known each other a very long time. For almost five years now. I love her very much."

"Sounds like a wonderful person. How come she didn't come to Paris with you?"

She shook her head. Taking the plunge, taking the plunge.

Let's jump.

"Because we broke up."

Ian stared at her for a moment, and there was nothing behind his eyes. Then, Khatia learned that understanding is a process that can be witnessed. Slowly, the fire spread, and a blue flame lit up his gray eyes. Everything became engulfed in knowledge.

Her hands were shaky, and without thinking, Khatia slipped the ring out of its little cushion, and began to slide it onto her left ring finger, waiting for his words.

"Wait."

Ian was breathing more heavily as if he had just run a long way. She even

178

thought, as they stood in the cool night air, she saw some sweat on his brow.

"You're telling me that you've coupled with a woman?"

Laughter almost squirted out of her tense lips, but she answered in a solemn voice: "Yes."

He did not say anything.

"We were friends before we started going out."

"For how long?"

"How long did we go out, or how long have we been friends?"

"Going out."

"Almost three years."

He coughed, and put his hands on his hips like a schoolmarm. "That's a long time, Khatia."

"Yes."

"You must have been pretty serious. You two. You two girls."

"Women," she said, automatic and dull. "Serious and demented."

"What?"

"Nothing," she said, and realized she was trying to ignore the forceful panic in Ian's voice.

"Look," she said. "I don't know if you've met very many…bisexual people before, but giving you a sociology lesson is not my job. There's nothing that's different than a heterosexual relationship, I don't think," Her voice rose. "*Jesus*, Ian! It's over with her now. It probably should have been over a long time ago. I felt like I was breaking some rules or something."

"So, you know it's not right, do you?" His hands were still on his hips.

"What?" she said, shocked and uncomfortable. "No, not at all! I love Shoshonah. Of course I know there are no rules. That's a bad way of putting it." She could not ignore it any longer. "Ian, what is going on?"

He looked away from her, not answering right away.

179

"Khatia, it's wrong."

"Excuse me? I couldn't hear you, I have some earwax in my ear. It sounded as if you said something profoundly idiotic, but I know that *can't* be possible."

He let out a huffing breath and looked out at the dark horizon. They were near the Seine. Always the Seine—the breast, the life–giver. She followed his gaze, seeking answers in the river the way she had the time they met, but she could see nothing of what had been there that night. The rainbows of her previous, brief happiness were an oil slick on the waters. She could find no solace now. She had heard about this kind of thing happening, had tried very hard to avoid it. Maybe there *were* rules. The waves on the river lapped gently against the banks, and she thought again of Van Gogh, his waves, his rules: non–rules. Her cigarette had gone out a long time ago.

"In the eyes of God," Ian murmured, and she glared at him. "It's wrong." How could he be saying these things? With a straight face? "It's not natural."

"Not drinking because your father asked you not to and then keeled over is not natural. Pretending you are smarter, stronger and better than I am because you have an impediment swinging between your legs is not natural. Believing in only half the stuff God tells you to do and not the other half is not natural." She stopped herself, realizing she did not know how to argue. It was a learned art, something she had never needed before. "I had doubts about telling you, Ian. But I did not think this would be such a traumatic thing to learn about me: that I loved someone?"

"I don't know how I feel about—homosexuality." He said the word in a clipped, proper voice, as if were he to say it casually, it might bite him on the ass. "I'm sorry, Khatia. It doesn't feel right to me." He sounded almost ready to cry.

The river flowed, and Ian searched its waters too. Khatia could see the wetness on his eyes, like marbles submerged in baby oil.

"If it had been a man…Three years with a man," he said. "It would be different."

Khatia dropped her head, feeling the weight and tension in her back, the muscles in her neck bunching into little bouquets.

Somehow, they had hurt each other. A new friend. A lost friend. Her list of lost friends grew as the list of current ones shrank.

The ring was still in her palm, like a sweaty penny, metallic and stained. She looked at it for a while, thinking of what she had just lost, how she had not been sure if she had wanted it. What did she feel? Relief? Grief? She wiped the ring off on her cotton blouse and put it back in its case, closing it with a snap.

Love: he had given it readily, and then aborted it, snatched it back in a bloody, flushed out clot.

She placed the box in his hand, and all her bravery crumbled as his fingers closed over it.

"Your sisters will be disappointed," she said, knowing she was about to cry. She was so sick of crying. "Not to meet your American friend."

A final shock: Ian's mouth dropping open in a mixture of revulsion and relief.

Let's jump.

She could not bear it. The river flowed, and Khatia put her hands on the wide stone railing of the bridge. Not so far below. She pushed herself up on her hands, and remembered playing on bars as a little girl, the muscles in her abdomen strong enough to heave the weight of her legs. She leaned forward, plunging, falling towards the water, towards the Seine. It was freezing, inundating, covering her head for a few moments. *Take me away from here. I don't belong here either.* She swam, listless under the water, pretending she heard Ian calling after her, although she knew it was not true. Her mother used to tell her a bedtime story about the black pearl that was really an egg, and when it cracked, a water–dragon was born. Khatia slithered. The water cushioned her body. She floated, unnoticed and dark in the waters until she saw some stairs. A few long strokes of her arms brought her to the walls and she arose, soaked in the river's waters. Washed.

181

Chapter Five

Airports housed the coming–together ceremonials of peoples all over the world. Employees had to be versed in more than one language. Families greeted each other and departed, both tears of joy and sadness falling from their eyes. The sameness of most airports comforted the traveler; they were like Catholic churches in their uniform nature. One knew, more or less, what to expect.

Khatia felt the same way about sunsets. She had watched the one yesterday, showing it to Anges–Mathieu on the balcony of his parents' apartment. Changing colors: the drip of the sun into the tops of buildings on the horizon fascinated the little boy, and she did not need the pieces of bribery candy to keep him sitting still. The sunset did it all, as she had hoped, the cooked–yolk orb holding the boy's attention; she had to warn him, through his child's awe, not to stare into it too long.

"Look away for a little, then look again," she whispered to him.

There was an omnipotence to sunsets, and they were her church, she realized that evening. She had watched sunsets with Shoshonah, had watched them on a hillock with her brother, had watched them in Amsterdam and Paris. And she passed the tradition on to Anges–Mathieu. Perhaps he snuggled close to her legs, reached absently for her hand, because he knew it was their last night together.

Hesitating in line with her heavy backpack, Khatia scanned the people around her. The de Gaulle airport was like a ride at Disneyworld: tubes transported passengers to their destinations, up, down, around corners. People could watch their loved ones being escalated away through a glass dome.

The ticket–buying line was getting shorter.

She had given the St–Jeans two weeks notice. That had seemed the right thing to do, although they insisted she leave more immediately, if it were

182

convenient for her.

Air France had lovely international service, and a smoking section. They, like most airlines with transatlantic crossings, served free alcoholic beverages during the fligh,—but their champagne was in more abundance than their competitors, Monsieur had joked. Khatia stayed in their line, wondering if she would be able to get a flight out that day. The traveling season was in full effect, even to the United States.

She knew, at least, she wanted to go *there*. But this was not running away.

The meals on Air France were supposed to be exquisite as well. Madame and Monsieur raved about the duck they had feasted on the last time they went to Italy. Even on such a short flight—*Quel service!* Definitely. Air France. And flying coach class was not so bad. So they heard, *quand même*.

And, she could smoke, they told her, sniffing a little.

Yes, she knew all that.

No one mentioned Ian. In the St–Jeans' eyes, he had offered their employee a potential romantic interlude. Something quaint and refreshing. A distraction from her little duties to their son.

They were just trying to be cheerful. Her news was bad, and they had to help keep her spirits up. How they hated losing her! Such a wonderful American girl, the best thing to happen for their son besides having them as his parents. *Zut!*

Only two more people in front of her, then she would be facing the counterperson. Khatia wanted a cigarette very badly.

To have her deepest, unlabeled fears made flesh. To have a passing insecurity solidified by another's belief. A wounding blow, and she had been wrong in thinking she could take it, could take anything after all she had already been through. Theory was theory and reality was pain. That was the scandal which mortified her to her heart's end. Khatia had never loved Ian. She had liked him tremendously, had thought they could be friends. But he had shamed her out of herself, confirming what she had often suspected: she was an aberration, a perversion. Being gay or not had very little to do with the more abstracted idea that she had it all wrong, that she was wandering through her life making mistakes, false choices, enemies. Inside her head, these fears were mere fancies, dust motes of her paranoid conscience. But to think of oneself as a monster and to have one called such by an outside source—Khatia found that "truth" existed, became real, when voiced by another, confirmed by someone other than herself.

Home seemed the only place to go, the only place available to her. Wounds must be licked. After almost nine months, the gestation period for a human foetus, she would go back, back to the looks of quiet disapproval, the curious glances from Bianca, the concern from Meredith. Porter, with his increasing neurosis. Well, she would like to see him, at least. He might be her only friend left in the world. Maybe Shoshonah, although it was too soon. Ulrike might be a possibility, but then she definitely would have to see Shoshonah. *Too* soon. No one from New York or college could help her.

She dug around in her pockets, searching for her pack of cigarettes, readying herself for a designated airport smoking area. They were not in her pockets. She put down her back pack, looking in the smaller outer compartments, places for water bottles, first aid kits, maps. She found a wad of papers and letters, neatly rubberbanded, and could feel the cigarettes beneath them. Madame had helped her pack, and must have tried her best to hide them. A French family who did not smoke. Odd. They did drink wine. Gallons of red wine.

The person in front of her moved forward to an open space at the counter, placing his luggage on the scale.

At that moment, the rubberband around her letters chose to burst. It was dried up, a dead earthworm betrayed by the sun's rays. The papers spilled onto the floor. Khatia put her cigarettes in her jacket pocket, cursing softly as she scooped everything up. The woman behind her watched, offering no assistance. Khatia tried to arrange the letters into a workable stack, straightening them clumsily on the surface of her backpack. A yellow slip caught her eye, and she pulled it out of the chaotic pile. Ulrike's slanted handwriting, more precise than usual: Cree Brown.

"Madame?"

Khatia looked up. The man behind the counter beckoned to her efficiently with a flick of his wrist: Hurry up and get over here. She stood up from her crouch, shoving the rest of the papers back in the zippered compartment, holding the yellow slip in her hand.

"Bonjour," the man said. "Destination?"

Her voice cracked a little, but she did not hesitate. "San Francisco, s'il vous plait."

Telling a lie had not been hard. She was getting very good at lying. The truth was what gave her trouble, perhaps because she was hardly ever sure of it.

"Quelque chose à boire?" the flight attendant asked.

"Champagne, s'il vous plait." Champagne with the duck à l'orange.

She sat in back with the other smokers, most of them businessmen.

Omissions: she had been omitting details for a long time now, perhaps all her life, but they were different than out–right lies. Words spoken were taken as truth, so trustingly: she had believed this; that she could be wrong, even about this, was not hard for her to accept.

The flight attendant brought the champagne, a small bottle, and handed Khatia a plastic flute. She uncorked it and poured, letting the fizz die down, then pouring more. Taking a piece of duck with the crispy skin into her mouth and then a swallow of the bubbling wine, she held them there, the pieces of meat with the liquid; they sizzled on her tongue and on the walls of her inner cheeks. Delicious. Decadent. This was, after all, almost the last of her savings. What would her father say to that, if he knew?

"My brother is very ill," Khatia had told the St–Jeans. "He has some problems. They aren't sure. Maybe hepatitis or mononucleosis. Perhaps Crohn's Disease." She savored the lie, almost believed it. It thrilled her more than simply omitting.

"Oh, you must go home, *immédiatement*! Your family needs you. Your father must be beside himself with worry." Madame and Monsieur understood. They had a child too, after all. If Anges–Mathieu had a sibling, which could be within the year, of course they would want the family together in times of need.

She gave them her home address but neglected the phone number in case they called. Letters were okay. Her father would respect her privacy, but he did speak French, and she did not want to be caught in a lie; she could think of nothing less mortifying or dishonorable.

Monsieur gave her some bonus money and drove her to the airport, gallantly carrying her bulging backpack to the curb. Guilt and money seemed to go hand–in–hand, especially when someone left the premises. They kissed on the cheeks four times: one two one two. A sign of closeness.

It wasn't really a lie, in a way. Porter wrote in his last letter that he had started seeing a psychologist because of his "distractibility." It was affecting his school work, and he was on academic probation. Only half a lie rested on her shoulders.

Dipping her fork in the small strawberry pastry, Khatia noticed her hand trembling. San Francisco. The impulsiveness of her decision hit her, and she had to put the fork down, call the flight attendant for another bottle, light a cigarette—the man next to her offered her one. Insane people did this. Crazy, lunatic. She had never been to a therapist, priest, or self–help book after her mother's death. Nothing. Maybe Porter had the right idea. She should be going to a counselor, not to yet another city. Strange cities had not worked for her so far.

But San Francisco didn't "count," not really. In a way, she knew it better than Milford, for it was the one place her undeveloped imagination conjured up: her mother's childhood home, a city where being half–Chinese was not seen as so exotic by the populace.

Perhaps she and the place would fit. Not to be an anomaly—it was too much to hope.

Darkness surrounded the airplane; they were above the clouds, in the stars. She did not have a window seat, but the view outside was black anyway. She picked up the pastry, and placed the whole thing on her tongue, swallowing, chewing only a little.

No. Seeing someone, "seeking help" was not for her. *This* had been her direction all along.

Chapter Six

On the small beach, Dorinne tans her gradually sagging skin. John Porter watches her with little interest. Every thirty minutes she turns from her stomach to her back or her back to her stomach.

The old summer cabin seems smaller with only the two of them. Strange: one would think it would feel more empty.

John Porter observes a moment of silence as the sun sets into the lake, a lake so wide he can not discern its other shore. This habit of silence is ancient, and he can't remember when it originated. Probably from his mother and sister. When he was thirteen, and his father had shot himself in the gazebo, the women in his family had turned away from their Episcopal roots to the Quaker Church. Her mother had her husband buried with all his guns so that he could take his act of violence with him and leave them in peace. She watched her son carefully, the new man of the family, watched him for signs of fury from that day forward.

In a way, the same thing has happened to Khatia: she has been left in a family of men, the only woman. And what signs must he seek from her?

Old Man Sun dips into the water and disappears. Dorinne continues her ludicrous sacrifice to a god that now ignores her for sleep.

His daughter is in trouble. He shifts his feet, thinking about answers to questions she has not even begun to ask. Porter has, but the boy does not worry him as much, although he is unsteady. It's Khatia's tenacity that makes her vulnerable.

They will get hurt some more. There is nothing he can do about it. Having created the hurt with their mother, and then tucking it away, John Porter senses that a time is coming when they will know everything about him, about themselves. Whether they decide to love him or hate

187

him afterwards, he cannot control. Perhaps aging has made him this way. But he knows this is no excuse: truth revealing itself is inevitable.

He welcomes it.

Chapter Seven

A commuter bus took her from the airport into the city. She tried to watch for it from the tinted window, the way she had watched the Eiffel Tower on the horizon, but all she could do was sit in a daze; no one knew where she was. The sky was white, as if the blue of the sky had become ill. Into the whiteness rose smallish skyscrapers, the famous Transamerica pyramid building. A silver bridge took cars off to the East, but she did not see the Golden Gate.

She got off at a youth hostel. A busy boulevard next to a fenced in lawn, stretching out towards white buildings and beyond to the bay. Walking towards the buildings, she could see their understated ornateness, stucco columns rising on a portico with plain horizontal lines as its only carving. Militant. Non–Parisian.

This was the scariest thing she had ever done. To prevent hyperventilation, she lit a cigarette and sucked on it, long, slow inhales.

She was fortunate to get the last bunk of the Fort Mason Youth Hostel.

"You don't want to go to the other hostel," the attendant told her, shaking his dreadlocks emphatically. "It's in the Tenderloin. Addicts and prostitutes. They just had a murder there last night."

"In the Tenderloin?" she asked.

"In the hostel there." He shook his head again, the hair flying away from his head like ruggy snakes. "Bad mojo. It's much better here."

She was in America. Again. Three thousand miles across land, her father and brother walked the same soil as she. What was the difference between here and there and the there of Europe?

The hostel only allowed smoking outside by the kitchen's side door. They provided pamphlets next to the ashtrays from the American Lung Association. "Take one," read the container.

189

Olivia Boler

America.

After a shower, she fell into the bed and a deep, fourteen hour sleep.

Strange the way the ringing of a phone, listened to from a pay phone, sounded so hollow. The phone rang and rang, a small whine of technology in her ear. No one answered, no machine picked up. After twenty rings, Khatia put the receiver back on its hook and asked the youth hostel attendant where she could buy some food. He pointed her in the direction of a supermarket, just a couple of blocks away. She went there, buying an orange and poppyseed muffin. They tasted wonderful, and she tried to eat slowly; the last thing she had had was a croissant with lots of butter and jam and café au lait on the airplane.

The day was bright, but not sunny. Wind blew, and she could see sailboats taking advantage of it, heading out of the marina into the bay. Windsurfers skipped mellow waves, their neon–bright sails like dyed birds' feathers on the slate waters. From the supermarket, one could see the Golden Gate Bridge reaching across the bay into hills, green hills against white sky. Beyond them were others, densely packed with houses. Khatia could not blame people for wanting to crowd the hillsides: they must have a beautiful view of the city's landscape which changed as she trained her eyes around: skyscrapers to low brick buildings to trees. And beyond, the hills with its own congestion of buildings, some elaborate, others more humble. Looking back towards Marin County, she wondered how the hills could support all those houses on sticks, at least from a distance they seemed to be on sticks. This was earthquake country, after all. What if they tumbled down on each other?

The bridge itself was an orange red, not gold at all, and she couldn't help allowing a little disappointment. After all, the Emerald City was emerald; the Golden Gate Bridge should be gold.

At a corner drugstore she bought postcards, stamps and other supplies. One of the skyline for her father. A cable car—she hadn't even seen one yet—for Meredith and Bianca. The Bridge for Porter. She scrawled on each one "Surprise! Will write more soon, Khatia" and popped them into a mailbox before she could change her mind.

Then, armed with a bus map, a tourist book, and her journal, she went in search of Ulrike's friend. Maybe he just did not want to pick up his phone. The map was easy to follow, and she figured two buses would get her to his home. She walked up to a wide, highly trafficked boulevard, Van Ness, and soon caught a bus heading south. She stared out at all the people getting on and off, walking down the sidewalks, doing whatever it was they did. Industrious homeless people stood on concrete islands between moving traffic, holding cardboard signs: OUT OF WORK. PLEASE HELP. WILL WORK FOR FOOD. MUST FEED ME AND MY DOG. HAVE TWO KIDS. SPARE CHANGE PLEASE. This boulevard used to house large mansions, the homes of San Francisco's elite. Now they were apartments and stores. The types of buildings changed as the bus traveled down the street, from restaurants, car dealerships, to the city hall, opera hall, and then to Market Street, another large boulevard leading to more commerce. It was like a scaled down version of Paris, she thought. Except there weren't just Europeans here. There were Asians, Hispanics, African Americans.

Her mother had not mentioned the people. She had never mentioned their beauty. Fat, thin, baggy clothes, chic Chanel, brown, blond, kinky Afros, smelly, made–up, doused, athletic, elegant, crazy, rich, poor—Everyone.

On Market, she descended stairs to the Metro, the underground train. After a while, it went above ground, and soon she got off in a little neighborhood with cafés, bookstores, grocers—it felt a little like Greenwich Village without all the brownstones. The book called it Cole Valley. The buildings here that housed shops on the sidewalks were mostly stucco or wood, painted in a variety of colors, from pastels to earthtones. She supposed those were Victorians: Painted Ladies, her book called them.

She walked up a hill, away from Cole Street where she had got off, admiring the trees along the sidewalks and the shrubberies in front of the houses and apartment buildings. The neighborhood was peaceful. In the distance, she heard the rattle of a bus and the shouts of children from a nearby schoolyard.

Cree's apartment address was two blocks up–hill. Khatia's lungs wheezed, and she stubbed out her cigarette into the sidewalk. Perhaps she should lay off them for a while, although she had only been smoking regularly for a few months. Could her alveoli deteriorate that quickly?

Finally, his building. The steps led up to four separate doors, all in a row and all with their own apartment number. She inhaled deeply, patting her hair, wishing she had thought to put on clean jeans before leaving the hostel—the French influence of owning few clothes, laundering occasionally. Her watch informed her that getting here had taken nearly an hour. An hour! How far away was the youth hostel? How big could this city be? Dinky compared to Paris. She twisted her neck from side to side, the vertebrae cracking, and knocked on his door. After a brief moment, she rang the bell too.

"Coming!" she heard someone yell. Impatient. The sound of feet tramping down stairs. Maybe this was a bad idea.

A man opened the door. He was tall, perhaps a head taller than she, but it seemed he could stand eye to eye with anyone. He had dark, brown skin, and black hair kind of grown out of a hair cut; it was in his eyes, which were a strange color: pale topaz rimmed in black. There was no other way to describe them because that's exactly what they were. His nose was large and slightly rounded at the end as if the gods had decided not to follow the standard rules of beauty. His mouth smiled when he saw her.

"Yes?" he asked. He seemed to be expecting her.

She stuttered. "I'm sorry to bug you. Are you Cree Brown?"

"Yeah," he said, and she recognized his voice, immediately at ease.

"I'm Khatia," she said quickly. "Ulrike's friend? We talked on the phone once a few months ago? Just for a little bit."

"Of course," he said. "Come on in." She followed him up the stairs which led directly into his apartment. "I just got home from work. I was going to make some tea. Would you like some? Or is coffee more your thing?"

"Tea," she said. "Tea would be wonderful."

Chapter Eight

I just got a tattoo on my ankle. It hurts like a motherfucker, and I bled slowly the whole time. Drip, drip, drip. I still have a gauze bandage on it, and when I pull it away, my skin is all purple and bruised, like I just shot up down there or something. Ankles are supposed to be tough, I thought. Plenty of skin, layers of fat, all that. Muscle. But bone. The body's armor, yadda yadda yadda. Anyway, it's a Chinese character. *Yü–eh*: the moon. I love the moon, and I love the character, the way it looks like a Chinese lantern, or the Moon Lady's window. She looks down on us, makes sure we have light in the night. All she wants in return is some lucky money and a few oranges. It also looks like a rabbit. A rabbit is supposed to live in the moon too. My Chinese teacher gave us some lucky rabbit candy. It tasted like sweet condensed milk solidified, and as it melted in my mouth, all I could think was, Lactose breaking down into simple sugars. Glucose. Glucose. Fatty acid.

I know for *sure* now that I'm in the wrong major. Being a doctor is my dad's idea, and it sounded good at first because everyone else in my family is humanities driven, especially with languages. My sister with her Art History and French and Spanish, my father with his Russian and liberal arts pedantics, my mother...I don't really know if she spoke another language besides the standard college French and Latin. But she was half Chinese. Sometimes she sang lullabies to me in what I've always thought of as my baby language. I didn't listen too closely, but it was probably Chinese. Cantonese, Mandarin, Shanghai, I don't know. It makes me ashamed. And the sciences are getting to me. I'm just not...*good* at them. I try really hard. Really. But honestly? I could care less. All that math. I dropped Calculus II and Introduction to Physics. My dad will be disappointed in a livid sort of way. I can handle the blood and guts. I can handle all that. Like, I can handle the bruise on my ankle. The tattoo is on the inside, near the bone and the tender spot that curves back, where they got Achilles. It doesn't reach that far of course—I'd probably be a gimp if it did—but I can imagine it reaching back inside of me, the ink seeping through my skin and down, out the other side eventually, a sort of mirror image.

My sister is in San Francisco now. That makes her fourth city in a little under a year. I got this cryptic postcard from her. So did the old man. He nearly flipped his lid, in his own controlled sort of way. Called me up and said, "What is your sister doing? Has she finally gone out of her mind?"

Strange that she should go there now, because I've been thinking of heading that way this summer to find my mother's parents. Dad would *not* like it. For some reason, he doesn't like California, particularly San Francisco, and it's weird because that's where his wife grew up. I've been wondering more and more: what is he avoiding?

Good for her, I say. Good for Khatia. She's going through one of those mid–life crisis things early. That happens to the truly repressed. I know this from my American sociology class. And that's why I want to go to San Francisco.

Don't get me wrong. I'm repressed too. It's just that, I'm sick. I have a legitimate excuse. The therapist hasn't pinned down a name for it yet, at least, not one he's telling me, except to call it a "bi–polar disorder." He might put me on medication. Great. I would love that. Maybe then I'll stop being such an asshole. I mean, I've always been a little loopy, a bit of a goof. But just this year, I can't seem to control it any longer. I get so distracted. I'll sit at my desk and start to work on a paper or a lab report, and then I'll hear a bird chirp out my window, so I go outside to find it. When I do, I start to follow it. Sometimes I have to leave in the middle of a class because I'll start wise–cracking, giving the TA or even my professors lip. I got kicked out of my physics lecture last week, which I took as a sign that I was not meant to be there. Period. I just kept cracking jokes with the people around me, making them laugh outloud. The prof finally caught me and gave me the boot. Good for him, I say. Serves me right.

If I were ten years younger they'd probably call it Attention Deficit Disorder and put me on Ritalin. I think they still could, even though I'm nineteen. A legal adult. Maybe that's what the doctor is going to prescribe for me, but he's too embarrassed. It's a kid's problem, and he doesn't want to diagnose me the wrong way. Well, I have to see the psychiatrist before that anyway, just to be sure.

The only thing holding my concentration these days is this genealogy project I'm working on for my Asian American History class. Not too many Asians out here in Rhode Island, and I'm only a quarter. One of the guys down the hall saw my books and said, "Why you taking that chink class?" A real class act, that one. God! I wanted to kick his ass. I said, "Because I *am* a chink, you Nazi bastard." Always play the Nazi card. It shakes people up to be called a Nazi. Except the Skins. They think it's a compliment, sick bastards.

People always think I'm Slavic, or some Vietnam Love Child because I'm such a freak with my slanted eyes and Anglo nose. And this crazy red hair I got from my dad. Who knows, maybe I am a Love Child. The way my parents showed affection, I'm surprised they have any kids at all. Anyway, they do, me and my sister, so I therefore have ancestors I want to look up.

When the old man said, "And why San Francisco of all places," I nearly expected him to add, "She knows I forbid that place. Above all others, I forbid that one region." We've never been there. We've never seen her parents either. I'm not even sure she had siblings. It's just not something we ever talked about, and she and my dad always looked irritated if we kids tried to ask questions. No one asks questions in our house. No one talks really. We've been well-trained: silence is golden. I'm starting to talk to Khatia more, at least, I talk through the letters I send. I think she wants to talk back, except she's stuck in this holding pattern with this abbreviated form of communication. Postcards, man. She and her best friend got in a fight, and Khatia just ditched her. In the middle of Europe. My sister. She continues to surprise me. The woman has got some *cajones*, as my bandmate Jorges says. He's taking Chinese too, and he plays drums. He's all into the Buddhist stuff, keeps writing music about "zenning out."

My dad would flip if he knew I'm taking Chinese. But the class Beginning Chinese is only offered every other year, and next year a famous scholar is going to be a visiting professor on our campus. He's from China, and you need to know some basics to even be considered for his class. Translations of erotic monk poetry.

He's never said it in so many words, but I don't think my dad thinks Oriental culture is of any scholarly value. I tried to ask him some questions when we went to dinner the other night. For Easter, as if we celebrate. I asked him questions about my project without letting him know what it was. He wouldn't understand why I'm taking a class in Asian History. He got all tense. Well, more tense than usual. Maybe because he fought in

195

Korea. No one really had a choice though. The draft was in effect. We don't talk about it at all, of course. I'm not sure what we talk about when we're together. It must be something because the time does pass by, and I don't think it's all in silence.

I poked around the house while I was there for Spring Break. Found some old letters, but I haven't had a chance to look them through. Writing this genealogy is going to be a bitch. That's for damn sure. No cooperation anywhere, and no one to ask. But I'll figure something out. I'll figure something out all right.

Chapter Nine

He invited her to stay. The apartment was one of four in the building, each door leading to the top or bottom of the back or front. Cree's windows looked out over a backyard that had the feel of a wild yet controlled English garden. Someone loved roses, jasmine, and baby's tears. An old sycamore tree grew up, reaching the narrow laundry porch off the kitchen. Khatia stood on the porch to smoke while Cree prepared tea each evening. One could look into the neighbors' backyards for what seemed like blocks, their apartments and houses slanting to catch the hillsides cemented in with streets and sidewalks.

Everything in the residential parts of the city seemed bright and colorful, like a bouquet of wildflowers assembled by someone on the side of a road. It had to be colorful, for the sun coming out was an occasional phenomena. Sometimes it would peek out from behind a cloud for about five minutes in the middle of an afternoon and not again for the rest of the day, and other times the sky was mostly blue. One could never predict. She learned to layer her clothes, shedding them like a madrone sheds its bark.

Madrones were her favorite trees. Cree took her across the Golden Gate Bridge to Bolinas Ridge, the highway twisting its way towards nestled hill towns and beach villages. Before watching the sunset above Muir Beach(he agreed that sunsets were his universal place of worship as well, but the sunsets he saw above Muir Beach were his home place), they hiked in the hills. Cree spotted trailheads on the sides of roads, pulling his old Volvo onto the shoulder, taking her up into the trees or down to a creek no one else seemed to know about except for those who had forged the trails. That could have been deer and cougars for all she knew. Wild boar. He showed her the trees and grasses, pointing out the eucalyptus, which were non–natives, brought over from Australia for lumber and wind breaks, but spreading like a plague, choking out the natural timbers of cotton wood and willow.

The bark of a madrone was like clay smoothed over: life imitating art.

"Feel the water inside," Cree told her. "They're called refrigerator trees because they're cooler on the inside. You can almost squeeze the moisture flowing up into the leaves." Her fingers pressed into the bark, its coolness shooting up through her skin into her bones.

They drove down the coast, south, back through the city, and he showed her the redwood forests, the valleys of giant conifers. They lay on their backs in the middle of "fairy circles," a ring of trees climbing up into the sky, the ground beneath them a soft red cushioning of needles and duff. Cree taught her how to guess the ages of various trees.

"That one," he said, pointing. "Is about two thousand years old. Probably older."

She watched the tree. It was enormous. The top wasn't even visible from the ground, swaying somewhere up above all the others, as tall as a small skyscraper. They would need about fifteen people, arms stretched and hands held, to hug that tree.

"Is that how you know? Because it's so wide and tall?"

"Yeah, but look at the scorched places on the bark. This tree has been through I don't know how many forest fires. It's moist inside though. It keeps itself alive partly through hydration. Can you imagine, Khatia? This tree was around during the time of *Christ.*"

She looked at it again. Something alive. It breathed the ground, she thought, and had no reaction to them.

Being with Cree was like having a family. He was lovely like Shoshonah without her fawning. But then again, Khatia admitted to herself that she had probably encouraged Shoshonah that way, their insecurities, when stirred together, did more harm than good. Cree was not like that at all. She had never before met a person so at ease with himself who was not an asshole.

He insisted she stay with him, especially since she was so poor. The couch in the living room was comfortable, and she got used to the smell of dog that permeated it, forgetting about it after a while. His dog's name was Artichoke, a medium sized mutt, a scaled down version of an Australian sheepdog with labrador and beagle thrown in. He was a Frisbee dog. An independent film–maker had even paid Cree to put Artichoke in a scene of one of his movies. Two hundred dollars. Not bad for doing what he did nearly everyday: going to a park, chasing the soft, nylon disc, jumping up, and catching it between his gleaming white teeth. Artichoke mostly ignored her, unless she had food in her hands. He followed Cree with devoted dog–eyes wherever the man went.

Cree was a nurse. He worked at the University of California Medical Center rotating from pediatrics to urgent care to admitted patients. When she met him for the first time, he had just come home from a graveyard shift, still in his teal blue scrubbies. On his off–time and weekends, he played the guitar with his friends at coffeehouses and tutored middle school children in the Mission District, a predominantly Mexican American part of town.

"What do you help them with?"

"Math, spelling, self–esteem. You name it, I do it." He grinned. He grinned often. "I'm a jack of all trades."

She knew she could fall in love with him. Attention mixed with fond attraction. The formula was right.

One hundred dollars in cash. That's all she had left, and one un–maxed credit card. Khatia needed a job and soon. Cree asked around the hospital, but nothing was available. She considered law offices but with a shudder. Nothing so oppressive and cog–like.

"I don't want to be a lackey again. I want to do something different. I'd rather help people the way you do."

"Oh, how sweet."

"Shut up!"

He laughed, throwing his head back, mouth wide. She wished she could laugh that way.

"My profession was an accident, really," he said. "I was going to be a childcare teacher. I worked for the YMCA, grew up going to camp in the Santa Cruz Mountains. I didn't want to go to college, and my parents didn't push it. We were fairly poor, and they thought I should be making money. Not that child care is money–making, god knows! But I thought I could work my way up to some sort of administrative position. It beat shoplifting, and that's what most of my high school friends were up to, if not worse shit. Anyway, I had to take some classes at City College to get my early childhood education units. I took child psychology and it was really fascinating, learning theories about why we are way we are, because of genetics or abuse and also because of the way our inherited personalities react to whatever environment we're born into. I'm lucky I have such a calm mother because I'm a real hot–head. If she had been a hot–head too, I'd probably be a career criminal or something."

"I doubt that," Khatia said, sipping her tea. They were in Cree's kitchen, and he was baking chocolate chip cookies wearing an apron with the phrase: Besa la concinera. "I'm a more likely candidate than you."

"Well, we won't know, will we? Unless we just go nuts someday." He paused while he beat the eggs with his electric mixer and then poured them into the flour and sugar. "Anyway, I found my career because of what I felt were my *social* obligations. Most of the women in my class—I think there were only three guys out of twenty or so people—were going to become nurses. They became my friends, and I was afraid that after the class was over I'd never see them again. So for fun, I kept signing up for the same classes they were taking. Could you hand me the chocolate chips? Thanks. Pretty soon, I had more classes towards the basic degree requirements than I did for my own major! Do you like nuts? Me neither. Anyway, I transferred to San Francisco State, got my degree in biology, and went on to nursing school." He began dropping spoon–sized clumps of dough on the cookie sheet. "Pretty funny, huh?"

"You are not so selfless after all."

"I'm not Fred Nightingale, it's true. But I like kids well enough. That's why I go back to my old neighborhood. I mean, my parents didn't care if I got a higher education. Well, that's not true. They *cared*, but they were realistic. Anyway, if your parents don't push you, who will? The teachers? They know what the parents think, and they're underpaid and have these rowdy kids in the first place. I don't know." He shrugged and slid the cookie sheet into the oven. "So, I push myself. It's all I can do."

"I do that too, I guess," she said. "Except I get rigid. I make up rules for myself. That's a reason I like smoking, I guess. It's bad for me. So say the doctors and society. Of course, society says women going out with women and men going out with men is wrong too…"

"Who is this guy, Society?" Cree asked. "I've never met him."

She smiled at him and shook her head. He flicked flour at her nose.

"So." she hopped up on the counter, forgetting her parents had trained her it was vulgar. Cree hopped up too. "You're Mexican then? How did you get the name Brown?"

He held up his hand and began ticking off: "Mexican and Hupa Indian on my mom's side. African and Chinese on my dad's. Some Viking, I'm sure, on both sides." He grinned pointing to his topaz eyes. "Can't really escape it. How about you?"

The question did not seem out of place or odd anymore because of her experiences in Europe. Besides, she had brought it up.

"White. Whatever, you know. And a quarter Chinese on my mom's side."

"No," he said, and she began to prepare for the usual fight: you're Italian! Spanish! Portuguese! "You've got more than a quarter."

"What?" she said, surprised. He wasn't kidding.

"I can tell. Believe me, when you live in this town and you're a mutt yourself, you can spot them a mile away."

"Well then, too bad you couldn't meet my mother because she was half Chinese. I wonder if you could spot *her.*"

"Do you have a picture?"

"Yeah. In my wallet." She went to the living room for it and came back. It was a black and white picture someone on the school newspaper had taken while doing a feature on the librarians there. Her mother sat at a desk, smiling up at the camera shyly, a pencil in her hand poised over her desk—blotter as if she were simulating work for the pose.

Cree studied the picture for a while. Khatia waited, looking at it over his shoulder, not noticing that she leaned on him. His arm was comfortable. She could feel the muscle under his cotton shirt, warm, the bone beneath it. He smelled like the soap and shampoo in his bathroom, and a little salty, the natural fragrance that would always be a part of him, no matter what.

The timer chimed. It was time to take the cookies out. Cree moved, and only then did Khatia realize how close she was to him. She stepped away, getting a glass from the cupboard and filling it with water from the tap.

201

"What was your mom's maiden name?" he asked, taking a spatula out of the drawer.

"Chew. C–H–E–W, I think."

"Hm. There must be thousands of Chews in the city alone, nevermind the Bay Area. Her father was the Chinese one? Or was she adopted?"

"God, I don't think so," Khatia said. "Why would you say that?"

He shrugged, handing the picture back to her, but pausing before releasing it into her fingers. "No reason, really. It's just unusual for the man to be the minority in mixed marriages, especially with Asians. Ahh..." he said, making a sound reminiscent of Ulrike. "I won't give you a lecture right now."

"Once, I rented an American movie to watch with Angel–Matthew," she said. "It was about three young brothers who happen to be a quarter Japanese, but they were probably just white actors, and their Japanese *grandfather* is teaching them how to be ninjas."

"I think I've seen that one in the peed ward," Cree said.

"Of course, the character I related to the most was their mother—I *guess* she was supposed to look half–Japanese—but all I could think about was the way she was stuck in the tract home in suburbia making sack lunches for her sons and husband."

Cree did not answer right away.

"You don't want to have kids and be trapped in suburbia?" he said, and she felt relief that his humor still existed, that the conversation was not a tense and heavy as she thought it was becoming.

"I want to have kids. Someday. I guess. Procreation is not my all–consuming obsession."

"What is?"

Khatia drew into herself for the answer with a sigh. But inside, all she could picture was a river and the outline of a pearled sea dragon just below.

She pointed to the cookies and waggled her eyebrows.

"Yummm..."

The spell—or trap—broke.

Cree shook his head with a grin and handed her one.

"So," she leaned her arms on the counter. "What do you think? Can you spot her?"

He laughed a little as he scooped the cookies onto a dish. "She's an unusual looking woman," he said quietly. "Hey, get the milk out. We'll need it for dunking while they're still warm."

After she was sure enough time had elapsed for her father to receive his post card, she called him to let him know she was okay.

"I'm staying with a friend of my old boss from Amsterdam," she told him.

"Another Dutch?" he asked. "Can you trust her?"

"No, he's not Dutch, he's American. And yes, I can trust him. He's a wonderful person."

"You're staying with a—" her father stopped himself.

"I'm going to look for work around here. Something temporary. But I really like it here, Dad. I wish I had come sooner." She waited in anticipation and fear; would he suck in his breath and yell at her for coming to this place that seemed to repel him?

Her father did not answer. In the silence, she thought of asking him about what Cree had said. Her mother's photograph: he had acted oddly, she thought. But this was her father, and without even realizing it, she dropped herself into her daughter–role—no laughter, no questions. Habit was so comfortable like a worn, familiar piece of clothing, weakened in spots to fit one's curves.

"Well, I hope you find something decent around there," her father finally said. So much unsaid under his words.

"I'm sure I will. Tell Porter I'll talk to him soon, the next time you call him, okay Dad?"

She realized she had not heard her father's voice, nor her brother's, in a very long time.

Even though she had no experience, she found a waitressing job with relative ease. A nice little bistro in Cree's neighborhood, one of hundreds in the city, that served seafood, salad, and pastas. They showed her how to fold linen napkins into little angels, set the tables just right, carry four plates on her arm. How not to burn herself. She would go into work early and earn extra money by prepping the food for the chef. His name was Giovanni, and he was also the owner, but the restaurant was named after his long dead mother, Simonetta. Giovanni and she would take smoke breaks together in the little courtyard off the kitchen, and he would give her advice about which baseball teams to bet on, assuming she was interested. Khatia did not mind.

Neither she nor Cree talked about finding her another place to live. She continued on the couch, slowly saving money. Tips: wads of cash. When she opened a bank account, she gave Cree's address as hers.

They called Ulrike.

"Guess who's here?" Cree asked him, looking at her and wriggling a little as he waited for Ulrike's impatient, transatlantic answer. He winked at her, his partner in conspiracy. "No," he said, a laugh about to burst out of his throat. "Guess again. Nope. No. Okay, okay, okay." He passed her the phone.

"My name is Khatia, and I like tennis, sewing, and chess," she said in her language tape voice. "What is your name?"

"Khatia!" he cried. "So. There you are. The St–Jeans told me you left. Shoshonah and I were going to call your family tomorrow if we did not hear from you."

"I'm glad you didn't. How are you? How are Sofie and Frithe?"

"Fine, fine. Everyone is fine. We miss you very much, my girl."

She missed them too. She missed him and loved him, but she did not want him.

Her next question, bold: "And Shoshonah? How is she?"

"Fine. Still living with that Mina woman, though they both see other people."

"Really?" Khatia thought about it. Maybe Shoshonah was not a serial monogamist after all.

"She will be sad you did not call us at work."

"Tell her," Khatia said, not knowing what exactly to say. "Tell her I think about her. Tell her I hope she's doing well. And we'll talk soon."

"Shoshonah," Cree said after she hung up the phone. "She's your lover, right?"

"Ex," Khatia said. "Ex–lover. Ex–girlfriend actually. We never really called each other *lovers*. Bleck. It's so cheesecake." A formality, a sexualizing she could not relate to.

He nodded. They sat on the floor. Cree leaned against the couch where she slept, and Khatia was next to the telephone, near the window. She looked out of it at the morning sky. It would stay blue today. Cree had come home from another graveyard shift, waking her up with the idea of calling Amsterdam.

"Can I ask you a personal question?" he said.

"Of course."

"Do you only like women?"

"Do you?" she said.

He considered her question. "Well, I've only been with women. Although, when I was a little kid, I pinched my friend Rico's pee–pee and he touched mine. We were bathtime buddies."

She laughed. "Good to hear you like experimentation," she said.

"You haven't answered my question," he said.

She nodded. "I like men too." She spoke without thinking. "I like kind people. Beautiful people. People who can find something in me to like."

"Ah," he said. He crossed his arms.

"One more question," he said after a moment. She looked out the window, her back slightly tense.

"Go ahead," she said.

"May I kiss you?"

205

She looked away from the window. His arms, shyly crossed over his chest, his legs stretched out before him, also crossed, in hiking boots. A little mud caked on the bottoms. Ian had never even asked her for a kiss. He had asked for her soul in exchange for a ring. He had wanted to join in a mysterious union of the spirit without a sampling of the flesh. And Shoshonah? Shoshonah had assumed her rights, correctly yes, but still, she had been cocky. So sure she had done the right thing in bringing them together. She had taken without the asking, Khatia it realized now, so that Khatia had never had the opportunity to make an answer.

Much like her life.

Khatia waited until Cree looked up, and she could see his eyes, topaz rimmed in black.

"Go ahead," she said again.

And he did.

Chapter Ten

He listens to the boy while watching his own hands; one holds a knife, sawing into the animal flesh, seared by the grill, and the other steadies his fork, piercing the meat, keeping it in place.

The voice of his son is only half audible in his ears. Soft music, a Tchaikovsky piano concerto, pours from another part of the restaurant. When the children were very young, he took the family to a production of *the Nutcracker*. It was after Christmas Day, perhaps even after New Year's Day, for he remembers the tickets were discounted. The children were small, sitting neatly in their seats wearing the new camel hair coats he bought them for Christmas. Their manners filled him with pride that day—it was the matinee showing—not wanting to take off their coats, their love for the gifts he bestowed upon them.

Now he knows it was only fear that made them keep the coats on. He realizes this because his son is skirting around whatever is really on his mind. The word "genealogy" has come up, and "research." And one of those etymological inventions of identity politics: "Asian–ness." A frown must be clouding his face because Porter's voice becomes more and more soft, his body sinking further into the wooden chair, spine curving.

John Porter looks down at his hands again, concentrating on the sawing motion. They are old hands, the veins bulging through his softened skin, blue edged in brown. His son's hands are the hands of a man now, hands he used to engulf in his own while crossing a busy street. I am an old man, he thinks. Soon, I'll be trembling.

Porter is trying to ask to go through Annie's old things, and really, there aren't any more reasons to say no. Not that John Porter Quigley has ever had to say no to his children. They usually know when to stop a line of inquiry simply by his look, by what he casts at them: parental rule. The unspoken knowing, the understood authority. They've been well–trained.

207

Olivia Boler

But now his daughter is in San Francisco. Of course he could not keep her from that place forever. It's inevitable. She is so much like her mother when Annie was that age. Pity she did not live to see it. Alone. Becoming old. He is becoming old and alone. Alone, facing his own sicknesses.

Go to her.

He catches the word "roots" coming from his son. His roots. Even though he is only a quarter Chinese, he wants to know his roots, he says. Choosing to know is his right. Perhaps his sister is not interested—he hedges here—but he is. Maybe the knowledge will not change the course his life will take, but at least he will have it.

Nodding, he listens to his son, putting an aromatic piece of meat in his mouth and chewing. It is animal flesh and stinks only of animal. John Porter is sure if he lets his son do this, the nightmares of bloody, burned faces will end. And then, he will sit back and wait to see what the children will say. This is something he has been dreading his whole life it seems, although he only acknowledges this to himself now, in this restaurant. And he is so calm. Never again, he told himself years ago, as Annie, blinded by her own blood, cried in pain, shock, betrayal—*You were supposed to take care of me forever*—never again would he lose control. Never again would his demons and misconceived hate—he had been so naïve and young and stupid, but never again—bring him or those he loved to their knees, their knees caked is Asian mud and blood—

His son has fallen silent, poking a spoon into the Yorkshire pudding, nibbling at a sliced morsel.

What miracles his children are, John Porter thinks. He has to quiet his fears and love them. Whatever happens, he will have to let them know that he cares.

Of course, he tells his son. Look through her things. You don't have to ask me. She was your mother.

Porter stops eating for a moment, his fork held between his fingers as if he has forgotten something. As if he wishes it were a pair of chopsticks.

I know, he says after a moment. I just wanted to make sure you knew what I was doing.

John Porter signals to the waitress and orders coffee. He crosses his legs

208

and adjusts the linen napkin over his knee.

"I always know what you're doing," he says.

Chapter Eleven

Giovanni showed her how to make meringue kisses. Khatia perched on a barstool holding the pastry bag against her arm, slowly squeezing out rosettes onto a piece of parchment paper. Cooking and its tools were beginning to appeal to her under her employer's guidance. The kitchen had never been a turf she explored in much detail until her mother died, and she had to do the cooking for the men during school vacations. In junior high, she suffered a period of frantic "baking from scratch," although she did not remember the taste of her creations. She would bake half a dozen cakes, freezing the layers, bringing them out to thaw for special occasions such as Porter's birthday or the Fourth of July town picnic and parade. Once she surprised Meredith and Bianca on their birthday—they had the same birthday—with a lopsided carrotcake rendition of the water–tower next to their house. What would it be like, spending your birthday in a hospital, your orifice opening up to accommodate something the size and roundness of a honey dew? What would it be like on any day? She shivered a little, touching her flat tummy. Now that she was sleeping with Cree, she had to think of these things.

"You got a handle on that?" Giovanni stood in the open doorway to the courtyard, teeth biting on a cigar.

"Yeah, I got it," she said without looking up from her work.

Parchment paper. She loved the way those words sounded together. Giovanni cooked almost all his seafood specials baked in parchment. Khatia's mother used to use wax paper to wrap their lunches: chicken salad sandwiches drenched in mayonnaise dressing, nestled in wax bags to prevent leaking.

"You gotta get it right, you know. That wedding's coming up sooner than you think."

"I know," she said, bending in closer to the industrial–sized baking sheet.

Simonetta's often catered special occasions, serving up whole dinners of

210

the parchment wrapped seafood, salads, breads and desserts; or, they only needed to make hors d'oeuvres such as canapés, stuffed mushrooms, polenta triangles, and other kinds of small but delicious foods. This couple wanted meringue, had explained to Giovanni and Khatia that it was the first food they ate together, feeding it to each other while consuming a bottle of champagne on one of the ferries that cruised the San Francisco Bay. An inside joke. Romantic endeavors, Khatia thought, seemed to succeed with the body's basic necessity for nourishment. A found passion for cooking and her growing relationship with Cree: could the two events be mere coincidence?

"Cream a'carrot soup, beef stroganoff for the meat eaters, flounder turbans, antipasto..." Giovanni muttered the menu to himself. She wondered what he dreamed about as she placed macadamia nuts in the center of each meringue. He was probably a sleep–talker, rambling off menu lists: *garlic potage, trout almondine, tiramisú...*

The only wedding she had attended was a long time ago. She was ten years old, and the groom was one of her father's colleagues. It was held in the campus chapel, a plain, Protestant type building with one, huge rose window glowing an earthy orange. After, they went to the reception, she could not recall where. Her parents had danced cheek to cheek to the slow band music. Khatia looked away from them in embarrassment, as she looked away from the image now, setting down the pastry bag and rolling her stiffened shoulder until it cracked. Still, she had somehow known to enjoy the moment of her parents' closeness, because of its rarity. Briefly, they had really been one unit, connected by her father's hands on her mother's back, the fronts of their bodies touching and their feet shuffling.

Khatia slid off her stool. The cookie sheet filled, it was time to put it in one of the ovens. She carried the heavy pan carefully to the other side of the kitchen. One had to be patient with pretty food.

That same year of the wedding, her mother had driven the children to school one day, although they usually took the bus that picked them up at the corner of their gate. But that day, Khatia was providing cupcakes for a classroom party. What was it? Halloween? Valentine's Day? The weather was chilly. The cupcakes were from the local bakery, fancy rainbow jimmies and homemade butterscotch frosting. Her mother drove them so the cupcakes would not get crushed on the school bus.

"Khatia," she said. Her daughter always sat in the front seat, Porter in

211

back. The privileges of age. "I'm thinking about going away for a little while."

Even then, Khatia knew so much more lay beneath her mother's words than the words themselves, like volcanic streams under the earth, waiting for a shrug to push them upwards. Perhaps her mother would have gone on to explain. Perhaps she herself would have continued, putting Khatia's fears into the strong stone of words, letting them become reality, making them more than their potential. After all, her mother could mean she was going on a trip to see friends, or a librarians' conference. That would not be so strange; she had done it before. But Khatia knew, at the age of ten, an age adults often take for granted, especially with shy, quiet children, what her mother wanted to say was more than that. It was the introduction to permanence. It was the proposition of a life–changing move.

"No, Mommy," Khatia said softly, from instinct. A child's instinct— Don't let her go. Make yourself small and vulnerable. You are her young who needs her care and provision. You will suffer, maybe die, without her. She looked at her mother's profile as she drove and could not look back, keeping her eyes on the road. Her nose was small, and her mouth was small too, with an unusually full bottom lip and almost no upper one. Her hair was shiny black, coarse. And those dark brown eyes, with strange lines in the folds, lines as smooth and fine as thread, lines make–up seemed to emphasize, not hide, although her mother continued to apply it each morning. Seeing her mother without it was a shock that occurred only when they happened to bump in their hallway late at night, each on some nocturnal errand. The woman might not hug her the way she had seen Meredith hugging Bianca, but she was her mother.

When traffic slowed down, her mother looked over and down at her daughter, the little girl with long, soft braids, a crooked part from the haste of the morning, and the same dark eyes as her mother's, slightly more slanting, open and cat–like. Khatia saw her mother swallow, and look back out the window. The appeal to mother–instinct at work.

"Okay, Khatia," she said.

Jesus, she thought. The oven door slammed shut with a bang, making Khatia jump. She leaned against its warmth. She hadn't realized how cold her hands had become, and stuffed them in her hip pockets so they could absorb the heat of the ovens and not get burned. It wasn't her father who had wanted to leave the family first. It was her mother.

Hours passed, and she was waitressing in a daze, still shocked by the surfacing of memory.

"You okay, Khatia?"

The big concerned face of Giovanni hovered bodiless through the small order–window. A film of sweat seemed to cover him from his forehead down to his neck. It could also be the steam from all the simmering food, or a combination. The chef's perspiration mingled with the food she served to the patrons. It actually seemed right, a bit of the cook in the cooking.

"I'm fine. I'm sorry."

"You've been distracted all evening," he poked the dishes he had placed through the order window. "Table four."

The plates were hot on her arm, even through the material of her white, button–down shirt. She was used to this now. Her skin was toughening.

"Could we get some water when you get a chance?" asked the man at the table.

"Certainly," she said.

She went to the back of the restaurant to refill the water jug. It was a beautiful example of Majolica pottery painted with whirls and fruits, but a bitch to carry when full. Her wrists were getting stronger too, not bending as much at a painful, straining angle.

"Here you go." she poured the water into the couple's goblets with a steady hand. The man's eyes followed her movements. Simonetta's was an elegant restaurant. Small, intimate, with not a lot of room. Giovanni, while training her, had told her to respect the patrons privacy. Never make direct eye contact. Smile demurely. No big laughing or dramatic behavior: he did well in hiring her, reserved as she was by nature, except she did not feel equipped to *serve* people. She did not know how to smile, nevermind demurely. She had been in many restaurants, of course, as a customer, but even in that capacity she was inadequate; the relationship between server and served continued to baffle her. Gratitude often overwhelmed her when in a restaurant or store, even though she knew the person was just helping her to make a living. The false security of a friend made through the exchange of money. It puzzled her.

And when a customer broke the boundaries. Took some human interest in her. What to do then? Khatia continued to avoid the man's gaze, and was just about to turn away.

"Miss?" said the man.

"Yes?" she turned back, let her eyes flick over his face and then rest on a clear spot of the white table cloth.

"I'd like to ask you something rather odd. Do you mind?"

She shook her head. Probably drunk. Eccentric. Or both. She would extract herself with grace—

"Okay," he said, rubbing his hands together. "Would you say, 'KDDG, dig it' for me please."

Khatia laughed a little, glancing in the direction of his companion, allowing herself to get the impression of a tanned woman with long blond hair.

"Sure," she said. "KDDG, dig it."

The man looked at the woman. Khatia could tell they were smiling at each other.

"Wow," he said. "Tell me, what's your name?"

"Khatia."

"Khatia. Super. Khatia, I'm George Almeida, executive producer at KDDG." He held out his hand. She had to set the water jug on the table to take it.

"Do you listen to our station?"

"Um," Khatia glanced over her shoulder towards the other tables. Some of the customers were listening with interest, for the man had a loud voice. "I don't listen to the radio very much—"

"So, I take it you haven't worked in radio."

She laughed again, picking up the jug and walking away. "That's one thing I haven't done," she said over her shoulder.

After serving other tables, she went into the kitchen to wipe her hands.

"Eh, Khatia," Giovanni said. She looked up from her towel. "What did Georgie Almeida want?"

"Oh," she shrugged. "Just wondering if I've been in radio."

"Yeah," Giovanni said. "You got a pretty voice. Shouldn't smoke so much though."

"You should talk."

"Now, now." Giovanni scooped some soup into two small tureens. "He's a nice guy. Regular. Having him on your side would be a good thing." His voiced lowered. "He's connected."

"Capice."

"Hey, I didn't say capice."

"You might as well have."

Khatia ignored Giovanni's glare and merrily dolloped sour cream and a sprig of parsley on each soup while the theme music from *The Godfather* swelled up in her imagination.

"Okay, he's connected. I'll remember that."

As "Georgie" Almeida paid his check, he placed one of his business cards in her hand.

"Come by the office some time next week. Let's talk over options." "Options?" Khatia said. "I'm sorry. I guess I'm unfamiliar with radio talk."

"Maybe we can set up a test. See how you sound on the air." He stood up and helped the tan woman with her coat.

"Sure," Khatia said, reminded of Judy Garland in *The Easter Parade*. Except she did not rip the man's card in two before putting it in her pocket. Food, romance, and potential jobs all seemed to go together; after all, Ulrike had found her and her voice in a public house, ordering beer.

215

Chapter Twelve

Cree poured the soup Khatia had brought home into a pan to warm. After work, they met at a café near the hospital, and he introduced her to his friends and co-workers, mostly women who looked her up and down subtly, taking in the woman who had made their Cree smile so much lately. They stayed for a while, Khatia answering their questions, remembering to ask some, and gulping her tea with impatience, wanting to be alone with him now, no matter how nice his friends may be. They could get to know each other and exchange Cree–stories later.

"Which radio station?" he said now, after she had told him about the Georgie Encounter.

"KDDG."

"Hey!" he said. "Dig it! That's a great station. They play 'classic rock.' You know, the Rolling Stones, Eric Clapton."

Khatia nodded. "I don't really pay much attention to music. My brother's the one who's in a band. They should talk to him."

Cree stirred the soup slowly.

"Mmmm...Lobster bisque. I'm starved." He looked over at her leaning against the counter. "Remember what you told Shoshonah once?"

"No. What?"

"That time she asked you what you really want, and you said people's respect. Even of people you don't know?"

"Yeah?" Khatia opened the door to the back porch and stepped outside, lighting a cigarette.

"Well, maybe this is the answer."

"What do you mean?"

"Maybe," he said, pouring the steaming liquid into a big bowl. "Maybe you were actually talking about fame."

"Fame?" she repeated.

"Yeah. I mean, don't famous people get the respect of strangers?"

She shrugged. "Maybe. I never thought about it that way." She tried to picture herself famous; what did that mean? Standing around signing autographs in a crowd? Staving off hoards of admirers in the grocery store?

She smiled. It could be fun.

Cree sipped his soup, and she looked at him with mock–guilt in her eyes.

"You must think I'm selfish. Especially since you're Fred Nightingale."

He shook his head, taking her seriously. "Remember that the point of the question was supposed to be a selfish desire? We all have them, Khatia. I think everyone would like a little glamour. It's just a sign you want to be treated well. Being a nurse can be really crappy. Sometimes I want to throttle the patients. Most of the time in fact. Liking my job is just a side–effect for surviving everyday. There are no martyrs in this apartment."

"Yeah. Just people who have *torrid* love affairs."

He tossed a dish towel at her. She habitually teased him about Ulrike's description of the woman in Brussels.

"I was very naive, and she stripped me of my innocence," he would always say, and said so now.

The phone rang and Khatia went into the living room to get it. It was Porter. This was her first telephone call from her brother, although she had been in San Francisco for about a month now. After their shy greetings, smothering their joy in actually speaking to each other, he dropped some news on her that made her say:

"You got a what?"

"A tattoo. You've heard of them, haven't you?"

"Yes, I've heard of them. Smartass." She paused, looking at Cree. "Well, what does it look like?"

"The Chinese character for the moon."

217

"The moon. Interesting choice. You'll have to send me a picture. Why did you pick that?"

"I wrote to you I'm taking Mandarin, right?"

"Yeah."

"Well, it's my favorite character so far. I want to watch it get blue as I age."

"Neat," she said.

"You should get one too."

"Me?" she laughed. "Whatever for?"

"It would be like a pact. Between us. A brother–sister thing."

She didn't answer. She could feel a stirring in her throat. What had taken them so long?

"A sibling pact?" she said. "That's a good idea. I'll think about it. Where is yours?"

"In Rhode Island."

"You're such a toe booger. On your *body*."

"On my ankle. Hey, Khatia, listen."

She sat next to Cree on the couch as he read a book, slurping his soup out of the bowl with no spoon, dipping a chunk of sour dough bread into it every now and then.

"Go ahead," she said.

"I told you about the genealogy I'm working on, right? Well, I found some old letters when I was home over Spring break. Check this out, Khatia: they're from Dad to Mom."

"No kidding?" Why did she feeling like changing the subject? She didn't want to think about her parents's courtship, a time when they were young, perhaps spirited, perhaps different people then the ones she knew, perhaps people she could befriend.

"Yeah. And they're dated from the early fifties, when Dad was serving in Korea."

"Is that possible?" she asked. "I don't think they met until the sixties."

"That's what I thought too. But they're from him to her, and they're sent from Korea through the USO. And I also found a letter written in Chinese. It doesn't have an envelope, but it was in with the other letters."

"Can you read it?"

"Not yet. I was going to take it to my teacher, but what if it's private? I want to try translating it myself first."

"Porter, you've only taken a semester of Chinese. Aren't there like a zillion different symbols?"

He didn't answer.

"Okay. Have you asked Dad about the letters?"

"No. I didn't start looking at them until yesterday. You know what else? I think the address on them is the address of our grandparents."

"You mean Mom's parents?"

"Right. She was only a girl when Korea was going on. Khatia, the address is in San Francisco."

She paused. "So? That is not a revelation. She grew up here."

His end was quiet, and what he wanted began to dawn on her.

"Khatia—"

"No way, Porter."

"Come on! It would mean a lot to me."

"Then *you* do it!"

"Khatia—"

"They didn't even come to her funeral, or send flowers or a card or anything!"

Cree looked at Khatia, and she glanced back at him, her breathing a little off.

"Well, wouldn't you like to know why?"

"For all we know, they're dead."

219

"For all we know," Porter repeated. "We won't know unless you look."

"If you care so damn much, you go look." She almost hung up the phone, but reached for her cigarettes instead. She could not name why this was making her so angry.

Porter did not say anything for a while. Cree had set his book aside and was looking at her with concern. She closed her eyes.

"Okay, Porter. This call must be costing you a set of guitar strings, at least. Why don't you give me the address."

"I'll do better than that. I'll send you the letters. And...thanks."

She shrugged, as if he could see her. "What are sisters for?"

They were both finding out.

The letters arrived three days later in a packet, and Cree was at work, so she had the time and luxury of looking them over alone. Porter sent a brief note in his hasty scribble asking for them back as soon as possible. The one written in Chinese was on top. It was written in bright ink that resembled tomato juice or blood. Porter said Chinese words were called characters. They were symbolic drawings of their meanings, hieroglyphic in a way, metaphoric in combination.

"Whites are called ghosts by some Chinese," he wrote. "And African Americans are black ghosts."

Khatia stared at the letter for a while, trying to feel what it meant to her. It was written on rice paper, a thick, cottony paper. She could not understand the language. Was language heritage? No emotions overwhelmed her; the sense of "yes, this writing is a part of me, new, but a part of me" did not present itself. She was still a young woman with an unhealthy addiction, falling in love with a man for the first time in a place she loved for the first time. Yes, she felt an affinity for this place—so close to hills and trees of water, full of people both angry and beautiful—perhaps a person could *just know*.

The choice was to learn about her heritage, she supposed; she could have done in college what Porter was now doing, taking classes, learning the history of a quarter of his being. A quarter. She traced her finger across her stomach and then from the top of her head to her pelvic bone. Dividing herself: what could make a person whole, the sharded pieces coming together seamlessly? Finding out her mother's story, events she did not really know about, was that really what she needed? Would knowing about Chinese people enable her to write to Shoshonah, "I forgive you, I'm in love now, and I know who I am"? What choice? She closed her eyes and saw herself on Bolinas Ridge watching the sun go down in a bowl of fog, the dry grass scratching at her ankles, the squared peninsula of San Francisco beyond the hills, concrete building containing breathing humanity, jutting toward the sky, anchored to land. All of them, herself, hills, buildings—anchored.

She held the paper against her chest for a moment and then put it down on the bed, the bed she shared with Cree. So far, Porter had translated the date, although it was in the lunar calendar, but he wrote the letter had been sent around the time their parents got married. The other letters were in their envelopes, each addressed to an Anna Chew, her mother's maiden name. Porter had put them in chronological order.

Dear Anna,

It was very nice to get your letter in the mailbag. You are right. We do not get too much entertainment out here in the field, so it's always refreshing to get letters. That is a mighty fine program your school is doing, having you write letters to the GI's. I'm pretty sure I remember you from your classmates. Pigtails, right? That was a good day. I'm glad you enjoyed it. I don't blame Billy for wanting to join up as soon as he is old enough. The army holds a great opportunity for many young men. I plan to go to college after I come home and to study medicine. So, I am sure we will meet again someday.

Yes, my mother writes to me almost everyday. She and my sister live in New Jersey. That's pretty far from San Francisco! Have you ever been to the East Coast? It's beautiful. Not the same as your town, but seasonal. There are real winters there with snow and the works. They have snow

right now! Hard for me to believe in this heat.
But I'm sure your people are used to that. It rains
nearly every other day. A strange combination
with the heat. I think about those few days in
San Francisco with fondness. I can't wait to get
back to the fog!

Well, Anna, I look forward to your next letter.
Don't worry about the mail delays. I'll know it's
coming.

Best regards,

Private Quigley

Khatia's mouth dropped open on a slow hinge as she read the letter, her
brow furrowing. Her father had met her mother when they were practically children! She flipped through the stack of envelopes, checking the
postmark dates. They had corresponded for almost a whole year before he
was sent back to the States after getting wounded. She did not know much
about the wound, except that he had a scar across his chest, the skin slightly
mottled and red. Napalm: she had once overheard him talking to someone
on the phone about it, probably his internist. He had a purple heart and
other decorations for bravery beyond the call of duty.

"Combat," he said to her once when she was writing a term paper on
Eisenhower for her American History class in high school, "is not something you should worry about. Stick with domestic politics."

A whole new history evolved in pieces before her.

She skimmed through the other letters. Chatty: not a word she would
usually use to describe her father, nor his letters, but these were. Flirtatious,
even. The letters of a nineteen year old boy, the same age as Porter, writing,
unknowingly, to his future wife, a twelve year old girl in the States. They
were pleasant letters, describing the cities and scenery of Korea. He could
have been on vacation instead of in the middle of a police action. He did not
refer to her "people" again. Perhaps being on foreign soil made him aware
of how American a half–Asian girl could be, probably an avant–garde concept in the White America of the 1950s.

222

One was written in someone else's hand—writing. A long time had passed between letters, perhaps a couple of months. Her father had been wounded and was in the hospital. A nurse wrote the letter because he had lost a lot of blood and was too weak to hold a pencil. One of his companions had stepped on a land–mind, and Quigley caught shrapnel in his chest and legs(What about the companion? Khatia wondered). But Annie, as he had taken to addressing her, should not be frightened. He was going to be fine. Sent home early. They were even going to give him a medal: the coveted Purple Heart.

And yet, that did not happen exactly as Khatia had always vaguely understood, not really ever asking for clarification; some things she just seemed to believe, and could not recall how she had learned to believe in them. Her father got his medal, but he did not come home right away as she had always thought. He continued to write to Annie for another two months, working as a translator in Seoul. He knew some Russian, and could thus play a vital part in interrogations.

One letter, the second to the last, caught Khatia's eye. She read it twice. Apparently, her mother was having "boy trouble."

My dearest Annie,

Thanks for the sweet, funny letter. Your use of the word "obfuscate" was quite accurate, as far as I can remember. It's been a while since I've been able to get a hold of any good books around this joint. I think I've read the latest Agatha Christie six times over now! But I guess your mother doesn't let you read that sort of thing. I hope you get a break from studying occasionally. It's great your folks finally got the radio fixed. I don't know where my mother would be without hers. And television! Don't get me started on that crazy thing. My mother finally got one. I can't imagine it in our house. We only listen to Beethoven and opera, usually. And I have to comb my hair with Vitalis every night for supper. Out here I have permanent Vitalis it seems, only getting a

shower ever week and a half or so, even in town.
Well, the interrogations keep me busy...But this
is a hateful place, what they make me do is hateful, but I go along with it. I'm weak that way,
Annie. I take orders as every good soldier should.
They've given me something to hate, but I don't
know if it's myself or these people, the enemy. It
has to be one or the other...But we're all starting
to look the same. We're all the same.

Khatia stopped for a moment. "It has to be one or the other." How very
like her father she was, dividing up the world into order, black and white.
Poor man. Didn't he realize, as she did, that the world was chaos, especially
the world of war, and he would not create order in it? She continued reading.

So, has that boy Stanley still been bothering you?
You would think telling him that you aren't allowed to date until you go to college would have
given him the hint, but some boys are real block-
heads. I should know, I used to be one! Maybe
the best thing to do would be to tell him that you
already have a steady. Tell him that the guy is
overseas, fighting for democracy in Korea. That'll
impress him. Who knows, Annie? Maybe when
we meet again, and the world is a different
place...Anyway. You keep up that studying, and
I'll be hearing from you soon.

Yours,

John

The last letter was brief, informing Annie that he was finally going home,
and he gave her his address in New Jersey.

Her parents had lied. Or, at least, had not told everything. A whole
romance existed between them. Before, their first encounter seemed silly
and dull, with a touch of "their eyes met across the crowded room, and from
then on, it was pure magic": meeting at a graduate student tea at Simmons

College where Annie was getting her Master's Degree in Library Science and John Porter was a lecturer. That dull image fit with what she could see of her parents's marriage. Nothing heightened like a nineteen year old soldier exchanging letters with a twelve year old girl in pigtails.

If only she had her mother's letters! What had her father done with them? Part of her was glad she did not have them; already, she felt like an invader of their intimacy. Respect privacy, they had taught her. And she did. But—

Here, in these moldy pages, was the tenderness Khatia had hardly ever seen between any of her family members. Here was the kindness, the humor, the companiate warmth. It was not the soundless drinking of coffee, side by side, ruffling through the newspapers. It was not brown loafers and beige L. L. Beane skirts and blazers. It was a breath of the living.

What had taken over that voice of the father she knew? Why didn't he show his family this side of himself?

Omissions are not accidents.

The phone rang. It took a moment for the noise to register, drawing her slowly out of herself and into the living room. She had been sitting in the bedroom for almost three hours, and the stiffness in her back made her groan. It was Giovanni.

"Khatia. I got a message for you."

"For me?"

"Yeah. Georgie Almeida. He was serious the other night. He really wants to talk to you. Left his home number and everything. Why don't you give him a call?"

"Are you trying to get me a new job or something, Giovanni? Is this your subtle way of telling me I'm an awful waitress and prep assistant? I'd rather you be straightforward." She stretched her legs out in front of her carefully, rustling the letters spread everywhere, wincing in stiff–muscled agony.

"Kid, I wouldn't blow sunshine up your ass; you're the best. But I know I can't give you health and dental. Maybe Georgie can. Anyway, here's his number."

225

The radio station was South of Market Street in a neighborhood going from the slightly seedy to the yuppified gentry of live–work studioes, galleries, and restaurants. It came alive after the moon rose with nightclubs and bars.

Perhaps if she had not had these letters in her possession, in her head, she would have ignored the persistence of George Almeida, but she needed distraction. Leave it behind for a little while.

"Hey, that was Carole King with 'It's Too Late,' and you're listening to KDDG, dig it, the Bay Area's best in classic rock. This is Khatia Quigley, and in the next hour you can give me a call at 478–KDDG for the all request Dead Lunch Hour. Which doesn't leave many choices since it's only the Grateful Dead you can request—"

"Khatia!"

An instant buzzing occurred over the speakers, in her earphones, and in the sound booth, as if an angry tsetse fly had found its way into the wires.

"Sorry! I'm sorry. I guess that counts as opinion?" Khatia squinched her face into that of a rabid fruit bat, looking out of the glass over all the dials, sound needles, and monitors to Grant, one of the producers who was "testing" her and also teaching her about the equipment. They were also teaching her about curbing sarcasm and watching out for those times when she may want to say something that would make the station look foolish.

The equipment was pretty easy to understand, and after observing the DJ who was on the air and then going into a smaller booth to try it out herself, she found she could probably do this. Push buttons, slide controls, speak with her lips brushing the microphone's foam head. The constant changing of the carts—cartridges that looked sort of like eight–track tapes and contained one song or commercial—kept her moving; it was a lot like waitressing, constantly being aware. She would have to write to Ulrike; he would find the image of her in yet another sound booth amusing and just.

Her voice had found her a place to be for the third time, and, perhaps, the best place: She did not have to speak as if she had acute angina. She did not have to talk baby talk. With the headphones on, her voice sounded bottomless.

226

"Khatia, Khatia," Almeida stood up from his desk and opened his arms as if she were the prodigal daughter dragging her battered self into his golden palace. He was one of those ex–hippies turned executive. His peppered, receding hairline was left to do its own thing, and he wore a big turquoise ring on the ring finger of his right hand. It matched his deep green shirt impeccably. He sighed a lot and called his assistant, "babe." All his employees probably said, "dig" even the young ones.

"Are you tired? Of course you are. It's been a rather busy day, hasn't it? Did you enjoy the booth? Good, good. Grant tells me you sound like an angel on the mic. An angel. No, he really said that. And I trust that man. He's like a brother to me, and he's not one to bullshit. So, what do you think?"

Her eyes were dry and sticky. She watched Almeida in a sleepy haze.

"It could be fun," she said. "A lot of fun. But…Why me?"

He leaned forward. Slick, she thought. He's a schmoozer all right.

"One, I think you have the potential to become a very good disc jockey. You have a wonderful quality to your voice. It's very warm and throaty, yet smooth. Very feminine. You smoke, don't you?"

"A little."

"That's where the throatiness comes from. You shouldn't smoke more than a pack a day, otherwise you'll probably lose it. Get grainy." Grainy, like her mom's voice before she died. Khatia pushed the thought away, laughing out loud like an autistic savant on a Ferris wheel reeling backwards.

"Do you always pull people from off the streets just because they smoke?"

"Only if they have a great voice and they're pretty."

"Pretty?"

"This brings me to number two. We like to have," Almeida paused. "How can I put this delicately? Well, I can't. We like to have DJ's that not only sound good, but look good. May I say, you are an attractive young woman?"

She blushed, looking behind his head out the window. Schmoozer, she thought.

"Khatia," he said again. He seemed to enjoy saying her name. "We often

227

do promotional events for the station. We are the classic rock station of this city, and we often host concerts, fairs, festivals, premiere movies, walkathons, things like that. Our DJ's are local celebrities, so naturally, they participate in promoting these events, either by introducing acts or doing a remote with the fans in public like at bars or shopping malls."

"Bars or shopping malls," Khatia mumbled to herself. "Lovely."

"Hey, that's the crème de la crème! Wait 'til you promo a tire shop! Ho ho! It can be a lot of fun, making a little money, meeting new people, becoming a local celebrity yourself. But the first thing I want to tell you is, don't quit your day job."

"What?"

He laughed.

"What I mean is, I want to offer you a start. A beginning. And I think very rapidly, you'll move forward. You see, I don't really have any positions open up yet, and besides, you're green. You still have to take a written and practical test to get your license with the FCC—don't worry. It's cake— and there's a lot of hours you need to get in practice. That's cool. What I'm thinking of is starting you as a roving correspondent. Send you out looking for cars with our bumper stickers on them or people wearing our baseball caps and t–shirts. You know, be the prize patrol. Give 'em CD's and trips to Maui, stuff like that. Then, because this is a promotion that the listeners know about, I'll have you on a remote or a phone, talking to the DJ's in the booth. You'll do a conversational, tell 'em what you see, where you are, trade some wit, yadda yadda yadda, and then hand out some more prizes, be cool, put on a good face for the station, more conversation, about every half hour. Y'see, we're really targeting people your age, eighteen to thirty–four, and they need to see that we are still hip and vital, dig? We *know* we got the thirty–fives to sixty, but it's a matter of keeping the music alive, because it deserves it, y'know? I mean really, man, this is the music that brought the conservatives to their knees, their fucking *knees*, and it's not over yet, baby. I don't think so, no way. It's all there, in Dylan, in Hendrix, in Joplin, in the Stones. Good people, good music, good messages. So, after a while, and I know this is going to happen for you, Khatia, we'll switch you to the weekend. Saturday shift from two A.M. to seven. Ouch, you say! But hey, if I moved you right in, the bosses would have my nuts for hors–d'oeuvres. That'll be in about eight, nine months, I don't think it'll take longer than that. After that, you'll probably go to weekday graveyard, then, who knows? The morning show banter? Anything's possible when you're young. What do you think?"

Her mouth was open and dry. Khatia looked down at her lap checking for lost drool. What did she think? This was a brave, new world. She pictured the postcards she would write to everyone when she got back to the apartment.

Chapter Thirteen

The bright lights of the twenty–four hour copier center lent a sense of sterile, white happiness. Khatia wondered if people who used these places or worked there were afraid to leave, to go back into the simultaneous color and bleakness of the world outside the glass doors. Copier machines chugged away, providing white noise and soothing one's mind from completing a thought.

"This is really exciting. We should go find them. Definitely." Cree nodded enthusiastically, reminding her of the cheerleaders in high school who loved everyone—popular or nerdy—during the rallies and games.

Khatia put the letter in red ink on the glass plate of the copy machine, holding it like the powdery wings of a butterfly she did not want to destroy.

"Man, Khatia. All this stuff is happening to you. What do you *think* of it all? You never say."

She looked up at his topaz eyes. She still could not get over his beauty, the mahogany of his skin, making her feel pale and washed out, especially under the lights. Candles. She still preferred candles to soften her body, give it the illusion of weight.

"I don't know," she said. "You ask me that, and I try to come up with a word, but all I feel is blank. And then I feel bad, like I should be giving it more thought."

"Dig it," he said, tickling her sides. Cajoling. Always cajoling. He picked up one of the envelopes, looking at her mother's childhood address.

"Let's go there," he said. "Right now, after you finish this up. Or, we'll take the red letter to Mindy." Mindy was a friend of his who spoke and read Chinese. "She can translate it, and then we can go find them. Maybe take them out for pizza. C'mon c'mon c'mon. What do you say?"

"I have to think about it—" She shrugged him away. Sometimes his exuberance tired her. Yet, she was jealous of his constant smile, needed to see it.

"No!" He stopped her from pulling away. "Don't think. Act!"

"Stop speaking in exclamation points."

"Make another copy of that letter and we'll give it to my friend. Come on. I have the car anyway, so you have to do what I say and go where I go."

"I have a Fast Pass; I am as mobile as the next Muni bus."

He bit her earlobe, and her shoulders went up, pinching him away from her.

"Hm," he said, seeming to calm down. "You didn't squeal."

"I'm not a squealer."

"Yes. You'd make a very good spy. Even under torture no one could get any vital information out of you."

Something he said made her wince, and she did not want to think about the reason why. Her eyes moved to the pile of letters on top of the copier. Like an escapement in a clock, a piece clicked into place: her young soldier–father conducting interrogations in Korea, her mother resting her eyes each day, Khatia ignoring what was in front of her, closing her own eyes to knowledge.

She shrugged. "It's my upbringing."

"Let's go find your grandparents. I have a lot of questions anyway. I mean, I don't know many interracial couples their age. I'd like to hear their stories."

She finished the last copy and looked up into his face again.

"This stuff really interests you, huh?"

He nodded. "It's history. My history. Yours too."

She shook her head, making another copy of the Chinese letter in red ink.

"Not really," she said, pulling out the access card to the machine. "I can't force myself to care about this. I can't make it a part of me." Liar, she thought. Try harder.

He waited for her to continue.

"I mean, getting a job with this radio station, being here—with, with you—means more to me than all this. I'm curious, yes. But I have this feeling..."

Her voice trailed away, and she shrugged.

"What?" he said.

She looked around her. People were making copies, using the computers. What were the secrets they kept? Her brain felt like vapor. All this stuff was happening to her, and she did not know what to say. Act, he had said. Don't think. *Find out what you feel. Move.* She had tried moving with Shoshonah all the way across an ocean, but discovered that a different kind of movement was what she needed.

"Fine. We'll go. Before I lose my nerve, we'll go."

Cree kissed her on the cheek. "Life's little adventures. You can't avoid them."

His friend was not home, so they left a copy of the letter with an explanatory note under her apartment door. Khatia was glad Cree drove; she probably would have turned the car around by now. This was so impulsive; she thought she would have more time to prepare. I'm doing this because Porter asked me to, she told herself. Then why did she have an exhausting urge to cry? If she let her throat swell and ears ache, she would cry. These people: why didn't they want to know their grandchildren? Why didn't they ever call their daughter when she was alive? She took a deep breath, facing questions she had never allowed to take shape before; they made her angry beyond comprehension.

The house was grayish blue in the weak afternoon sunlight. It was one of many houses that looked exactly the same, marching up and down the sloping streets of the mostly residential district. They were stucco and small, with the garage on the ground floor next to the front gate, and the window of the living room above the garage. Some had slight variations: a cornice here, a tiled roof there. Some people chose to cement or tanbark the small front yards while others cultivated small gardens. All the houses were squished together, with barely enough room to fit a dime between their outer walls.

Rose bushes grew supported by lattices affixed to the walls of the Chews' house. In front, there were small patches of dry grass.

They spent some time sitting across the street in Cree's car, looking at the house in silence. Khatia was surprised to feel so calm. She lit a cigarette. No matter what Almeida said it did for her voice, she thought she should quit soon. The dangerous image that had so attracted her months before was losing its importance to her.

"It's called a bungalow," Cree said after a while.

"What?"

"That kind of house."

"Hm," Khatia said.

They fell silent.

He spoke again. "I always think of bungalows as being made out of grass or something. Like a hut, you know?"

"Yeah, I guess," Khatia said.

"Shall we do this?"

Getting across the street was easy enough. It was even easy to ring the bell next to the metal gate. The next few seconds were hard to endure, stretching out like hours, like time spent in hospital waiting rooms. They huddled by the gate as if to take shelter from the blinding grayness of the sky. She looked around inside the ornamental iron bars at the swept Spanish stairs rising in a curve to a place she could not see. There was a door just inside the gate to the left leading into the garage. Khatia tried picturing her mother as a young girl. She could imagine the young Annie walking down the stairs with a packet full of letters from a GI overseas, and they were to be transported across the country to her new home and life as keepsakes, and then stored for a daughter and son.

After what seemed like an eternity, they heard a door open from above.

"Yes?" said a voice. Man or woman, it was hard to tell from the pitch and echo.

They had not anticipated such a barrier, a voice without a body. Khatia looked at Cree, and he shrugged.

233

"Is this the Chew residence?" Khatia called after clearing her throat. She tossed her cigarette butt into the rose bushes, running her tongue against the roof of her mouth to scrape the taste away.

"Yes?" the voice said again.

"May I talk to you for a moment?" She hesitated. "I have a message from New Hampshire."

Nothing. Khatia could feel a pulse in her temple.

They heard the door close and a shuffling of steps. They seemed slow and careful, as if the person wore slippers with no traction. A great sigh emanating from above. The young interlopers heard a soft, mumbling echo, and they could see the shadow on the wall of a person coming down, and then a second shadow.

Out of the darkness, two small figures emerged, one thin, the other round in a skirt or dress. For now, they could only see the silhouettes, but Khatia began to pick out the woman who wore a skirt. The man seemed bent over, his back in a slight hump like an old cartoon vulture. The woman hung back by the stairs, shrouded by the dark. The man came forward, and they saw that he was an ordinary old man, wearing a wool vest over his blue button–down shirt, and brown carpet slippers from Chinatown. His gray hair was thin on top, and his eyes were a little watery, big and questioning like a cautious bird. He had age spots on his forehead and around his ears. Khatia tried not to stare at the spots, but they were fascinating, a map of his thoughts.

He peered at them through the gate.

"Yes? Well? Who has the message?"

Khatia looked at Cree who gazed at the man, a smile in his eyes. Breath held.

"I do," she said. "I—I think you're my grandfather. Was your daughter Anna Chew?"

He frowned at her, looking her up and down.

"I don't know you," he said.

"I'm Khatia," she said. "I'm Annie's daughter."

234

The old man's head jerked back, as if he had been struck in the eyes by sand. A sound like that from a conch shell came out of his mouth. He looked her up and down again.

"Are you her father?" Khatia asked.

"My daughter is dead. She died thirty years ago."

"No," Khatia said. "She only died four years ago. My father, John Quigley, he must have sent you a letter. Or called at least."

The woman called something in Chinese, and the man replied. They had been speaking softly at the gate, and the woman could probably not hear them. She can speak Chinese, Khatia thought, knowing that there was significance to this, but not making the connection.

The old man replied to the woman, this time sharply, but the woman mumbled something back, sounding perturbed. They argued for a moment, and then she walked to them out of the darkness.

Her hair was short, obviously died a blue–black, and her skin was a pale color, as if powdered with ivory sugar. She had brown eyes, and a pug nose very much like her daughter's. Khatia stared. Not only were her eyes dark brown, the lids lacked a fold, smooth straight across, slightly bulging forward in the sockets.

She was Chinese.

It was Khatia's turn to step back, as if struck. She gasped a little, feeling like a swimmer emerging from a long dive. No one spoke as they took each other in.

"Khatia," said the grandmother after a moment. "I am happy to meet you. Yes, Annie was our daughter. I can see her in you. You have her mouth."

"You have her eyes," Khatia whispered. Or, the woman had Annie's eyes if they had had a fold in the lid. Something was wrong; she frowned at the woman: her hair, nose, the shape of her face. She was a sculpture, a mold, poured bronze into a cast. The old man looked at one then the other, and Khatia suddenly remembered her mother's way of slowly blinking, swinging her head from one object to the next, taking it all in. Memories of her mother's nuances rushed at her: the way she held chopsticks, her soft soprano, the difficult smile on her lips which turned down in natural lines like

235

a puppet's mouth. This woman—this grandmother?—her voice was very much like Annie Quigley's: it could sing songs in Chinese about silkworms falling in love.

"You're supposed to be white," Khatia whispered. "You *can't* be my mother's mother."

The woman's face dropped, contained by a tightness Khatia could not explain. They looked at each other, an expanse of years and recognition in one moment; they understood the answer to something that had not even been asked.

"John never told you," the woman said.

"No," Khatia said, breaking their eye–contact, looking at the ground. "I have a brother too."

"We know," the woman nodded, her voice was soft, as if she were practicing lines from a script. "We've seen you before. Annie used to send us letters, pictures of you. And now you tell us she is dead." She put her hand on her husband's arm. "She is finally at peace. *Wu Shan* tells us she is at peace."

"What did you say?" Khatia asked. But she knew: it was her name— Misty Hills. What her mother had given to her, naming her first born after the place she loved.

Khatia turned, pushing an object out of her way—it was Cree— and ran down the street , down the cement hill of the sidewalk. *She is at peace, she is at peace, she is at peace.*

236

Chapter Fourteen

The sky opened up, pouring rain all over the city, drenching it in a way that was not cleansing, but merely soggy. The noise, like pellets on the roof, penetrated her dreams, and her first thought was, I am glad to be in this place rather than anywhere else. Upon fully waking, Khatia looked through the blue–black darkness, illuminated only by streetlights, out her window and at the old oak tree in the neighbor's yard, its leaves wet. Staid tree.

A few months ago, she had been in another dark room, the bedroom she had shared with Shoshonah in Amsterdam. Had only eight or nine months passed since she left Aunt Estella and her steady joe–job in New York? It seemed like a lifetime. For a moment, she missed the old, bored feeling of rootlessness; it wasn't necessarily gone, but replaced, in a perverse way. She was happy here with Cree. A year ago, she would have fallen apart to find out that—

It was too hard to think about concretely. She buried her face in her hands, feeling the despair, the need to find a comfortable lie. She realized she was still in her jeans, the hard parts of the canvas–like material leaving marks in her skin. Stretching her legs out, she lay back down in the bed, still keeping her hands on her face. Why did she need to know all this? All her life, her parents had set up rules for the raising of their children, rules that Khatia obeyed, added to, and now she longed for that blanket of ignorance and omission, because all along, her parents had been breaking some other kind of rules, ones she could not yet comprehend.

She had never wanted to know this much.

"I am bigger than my problems," she said into her hands. A quote from a poster she had seen while wandering downtown after fleeing the Chews', looking for a gesture: she smoked three packs of cigarettes, more than she had ever smoked at one time before. Her throat was numb; she actually could not feel it. Perhaps she was not so much bigger. In fact, she propagated the problems.

237

"You are," said a voice. It was Cree. She removed her hands, sliding them down her face, smearing her fingers into the skin of her cheeks, and sat up again to look at him. He sat in a corner of the room, a beautiful young man, his arm resting on one knee. She could feel the filter of his eyes. If he could see her, she must be there. "You *are* bigger than your problems."

She broke their gaze and looked out the window again. Wind and rain pounded the tree. Again, she was reminded of another time: Paris, sitting in a café, remembering her mother's death, remembering her father holding her, about to speak, to let all the stones and marbles of his emotions spill and pelt her. Yes: that would have been the right time. But how would she have taken it?

"I'm the kind of person who likes to read instruction booklets. You know, the ones that come with new stereos or furniture kits? They tell me what to do, what to expect from myself. And I like tags that come on products and suggest how to use them. Like that silk eye pillow you gave me last week: it says on the tag to use it for five to fifteen minutes on my *eyes.* I would never think of putting it in my sock drawer to make my socks smell better like you did. I use it on my eyes for five to fifteen minutes. No more, no less. And that's all. I need that—so that—"

"So that no one can accuse you of being wrong."

"So that no one can accuse me of making a conscious mistake. Of doing wrong. Of being a bad person. Immoral. Unethical. Evil. Depraved."

He smiled down at the floor, and she sighed, shaking her head.

She understood about secrets. She even believed in them, buried her own inside so that she could not recognize them herself. But there was no way everything hid well. Someone would dig. Porter had started to dig. She wondered what he was feeling, and how she could be the one to shatter the fun and adventure of his genealogy study.

"I remember when my mother died, and Bianca's mom gave a eulogy." Khatia continued to stare out the window. "She said that the clock marches on, and our pains and joys just become part of some giant tapestry that could care less about what makes it up, that doesn't give a shit about our pains and joys, even though we hand them over as threading material like gifts or sacrifices. We make up the tapestry, and so we should know not to make a big deal about our lives or our pain because we're just specks compared to the Appalachians, and the oceans, and the ozone, and the Milky Way."

"Maybe," Cree said. "But without us, the tapestry wouldn't exist. It comes from our own making, you know? Pain and joy gives it textures. Beauty, well, it couldn't exist without ugliness. And you know what? There's even beauty in ugliness." He paused. "It took me a long time to accept ugliness as well as beauty. That's why I love this city. I can see both the good and bad in it. There's paradox in the tapestry too, like a secret."

"You know, I'd like to believe that sort of thing. I mean, I really would. But when I feel pain or joy, especially pain though, I feel as if my body and mind are a small universe, and that suffering is taking up every quadrant. I can't escape that landscape, even though I'm good at ignoring it after a while. I can make myself believe that everything is all right. Maybe its denial." She turned around on their bed and faced him. "Is that a rationalization for selfishness?"

"It sounds like survival. You worry too much," he said, "about being selfish."

"I worry too much," she said. "Period."

She lay down, reconfiguring her lineage. She and her brother were *half–*Chinese. Their mother had been all Chinese, although she had not *looked* Chinese. She had always looked like herself: unlabeled and strange. Khatia was half. She looked at her arm, tried to imagine her face in the mirror. Her bronzy tone, pale compared to Cree's brownness, yet glowing and deep, suggesting a resistance to sun, a Mediterranean warmth: *Are you Italian, Portuguese, Mexican, Jewish, Native American?* An Asian warmth?

"It's just skin," she said.

"You're right."

"I'm still Khatia Quigley."

"Right."

"And eyes."

He did not answer.

"What happened back there?" she asked.

239

"I had tea with them."

She sat up again.

"You had tea with them?"

"Yeah."

"With the people who abandoned my mother?"

"Your grandmother asked me inside. I only stayed for about twenty minutes. I wanted to see where you went; I was worried."

She shrugged. "I went up to Turtle Hill and watched the sun go down. Then I went to Haight Street and almost got a tattoo declaring myself a half Chinese woman so people will stop asking. You know, I do have a nice little sibling pact with my brother to honor eventually."

"Did you?"

"No. What did they say?"

"They were nice. Your grandfather seemed a little pissed off. He didn't talk much. Your grandmother talked about your mother. They hadn't seen her since she told them she was marrying your father. There's more to it, but I don't know. They say they told her they didn't approve of him. In fact, I think they hate him. I guess your mom insisted that he was a decent person. She defied them."

Khatia looked down at her hands. "He interrogated prisoners in Korea. My father did."

"Oh, yeah?"

"Yeah. I know that from the letters," She hesitated. Asking probing questions did not come easily to her. "Did they say anything about the way she looked?"

"No. I tried to bring it up, but they refused to talk about it. They said they shouldn't be talking about her as much as they were because, in their eyes, she was dead long ago. A ghost–child who hadn't really been born. But I got the feeling there was more to the disowning then they let on. I mean, back in the sixties, many people inter–married, especially on the coasts because that's where the most diverse populations are. Look at me; I'm living proof of that. So are you. Your grandparents must have seen it all around them. They couldn't be that irrational." He paused. "People deal with their pain in all kinds of ways. We can't pretend to judge or understand them."

"It doesn't mean they thought interracial marriages were okay. But...her face," Khatia stopped. She didn't want to cry. Her mouth moved over unspoken words.

She looked at him, sitting in the corner, this man she had not known for very long, yet trusted. Things could change just like that.

"Come here," she said holding out her hand.

He crawled the few feet to the bed and climbed in, wrapping his arms around her shoulders, breathing into the skin of her forehead until they both fell asleep, dealing with their pain.

Chapter Fifteen

In impatience, Porter gave up on the struggle to translate the letter himself, and asked his professor to do it. Within a day, Porter and Khatia received the translations of the letter written in red ink and sent copies to each other, the envelopes passing each other in postal bags across the country.

> Mei Ching,
>
> You have made your decision, one which will dishonor the family for as long as the name of Chew continues to exist. It died with your brother in China, so your dishonor is doubled. You are dead to us now as well, child, unless you change your ideas of marrying this white devil. He fits his race well, especially after what he has done to you and to the family.

("Here," Porter's professor noted, "the script changes. Someone else is writing now, but with the same ink, and probably the same pen.")

> Daughter, you must reconsider. I know in writing this letter, I am making you dead to me, but I must let you know that this marriage will destroy you. Losing my son to the pestilence was painful enough. It almost ended our lives. But we still had you, our daughter and our hope. How can you live when you are creating a lie of yourself? I do not need to write to you in order to kill you—you do it with your own actions. He will never let you have children. You know that, don't you? He will find a way to keep you unhappy, rob you of prosperity, longevity, and health. Your father has never once in the time I have known him, touched me or his children in anger. You will

242

not tell me the details, yet you should, daughter, you should. I am your mother, and when I tell you to talk to me, it is your duty to answer. You have not earned the rights of silence; you are not made of mountain rock. Your father is a stern man, but not a violent one, and I had always hoped you would find a man like him. This man fills you with lies: he promises he will not touch you again, that what he did to you he did *for* you. His words are devil smoke, drugging you into belief. Can you not see that? What he did to you, to your beautiful face, to your body...And then, filling your head with ghost whispers, telling you that you would heal, be more beautiful than you were. More beautiful, he said. You say you believe him. You say you have never loved anyone this way. But daughter, do you not see the beauty you had? Does it take such a letter as this one to make you aware of it? Do not be foolish. The damage is done. Perhaps we could forgive your marriage to an American, but we cannot forgive your betrayal of us, of your culture, of who you are. You say he is full of love, that his battles in Korea made him do what he did, but I cannot believe that. He will always walk with death and pain in his heart, even if he does keep his promise to you. Is a childhood delusion worth this, daughter? It is this place, this America. We should not have come here. We should not have come.

The letter ended there, unsigned. Porter, on his professor's note, wrote that in the Chinese culture, writing a letter to a person in red ink meant the writer never wanted to see the receiver again, that he might as well be dead.

"That's why they said she was dead thirty years ago," Khatia said to Cree after he read the translation. "They had already killed her."

He shook his head. "I think they rationalized. To them, she killed herself by marrying your father."

"But it's not so simple," she said. "Something happened to my mother, something they blame my dad for. I mean, they call him a destroyer. They call him evil. Evil! They say he did something—something *violent* to her. I don't know what, but something...perverted."

Cree looked as if he wanted to speak, but held back.

"What?" she said.

"Well, it seems pretty perverted to have cosmetic surgery and then lie to everyone new you meet, telling them you're something you're not."

Khatia's eyes widened. She stared at the wall, wondering how her hand would feel if she slammed the knuckles of her fist into it. Would the bones splinter? Would the pain cancel out the reeling in her head? A brain can vomit, she thought. It can explode and still exist in agony afterwards.

"My father's not a violent man," she said. "And *I'm* not a violent person. But I feel like being one now." She put the letter down on the kitchen counter. "Maybe it's latent. Genetics."

She sighed, closing her eyes so she would not see the wall.

"I must have been dropped on my head as a baby because right now I fully believe that I am mentally disturbed."

He brushed back her hair, soft as a butterfly.

"Oh, Khatia," he said. "We all do."

Ulrike had once said she looked out of windows a lot. She opened her eyes again and did this. Yes. No answers, but respite from searching. "I'm not what I thought I was. Do you know how that feels? To suddenly know something like that?"

She felt Cree's arms come around her shoulders and pull her against his chest. He held her tightly, but with enough room to move around. "What would be different? If you had known all your life your mother was a full–blooded Chinese woman? Wouldn't she still act the same way? Wouldn't she raise you and Porter in the same way?"

Khatia shrugged out of his embrace. "I'll never know."

"Right. You'll never know."

They waited quietly, listening to the outside noises of slow, electric buses hissing down the hill, children's rising voices, birds chirping, a neighbor's stereo mumbling talk–radio. Khatia picked up a bottle, half full of olive oil. She pictured her mother's face, the smooth skin, her small nose and strange lips. That glow, slightly golden, not ruddy like other people. Like white people. And her eyes. Those eyes with the fine web of creases in the folds of her lids. Scars, and the lids pulled back artificially to form folds, drying out the membranes, forcing her into darkened rooms.

"I need to, Cree," she said. "I need to know."

"I love you, Khatia."

She looked up from the bottle, and they held each other's gaze for a moment. The sunlight shifted over their faces as it began its orange descent. He loved her: he was happy with who she was, this troubled young woman, who could not stay still. She understood now: to keep moving did not necessarily connote the physical. She could stay here, inside herself, embittered and immobile. Or she could go on. She could find out.

"I'm not so angry about losing twenty–four years of who I thought I was," she said. "I don't feel all that different. Despite it all, I feel quiet." She shook her head. "It's the lies. The omissions. If anything, it's the lies."

Cree kissed her palm and held it against his cheek, closing his eyes.

"Is identity in race? Or is it in geography?" she asked. She put her lips against his with a quick, darting movement. "You don't have to answer." She spoke against his mouth. "I love you too. I mean that. I think I mean that forever."

Cigarettes: smoking gave her a sense of comfort, and she ignored George Almeida's advice, smoking at least two and a half packs per day. It was punishment, but she had to go on.

The radio internship, as Almeida called it, would start soon, and she needed to be ready. Get a scooter license so she could ride the company scooter around the city looking for cars with KDDG bumper stickers and for people with their t–shirts. She had to study the manual and guidelines, learn the ways of the studio, prepare for the FCC written exam and studio practical to get her disc jockey license.

And work continued at the restaurant; she had to earn money. Cree was not to give her any charity she decided. She had gotten through death and break–ups. She would get through this. What was this new thing—this crisis— but a fragmentation of who and what she was, things she did not even really know in the first place? *Yeah, right.*

"Yeah, right," said her brother.

Porter was livid when she called him to tell him about the Chews. He cursed, questioned, whispered filthy epithets about their father. Khatia did not try to stop him. You are so young, my brother, she thought. She wished she knew how to hold him, even with her voice over the telephone. Shoshonah and Cree were the only people with whom she could initiate the hug. She had not learned how to do that, how to be affectionate, with the members of her family or other friends like Bianca and Meredith.

She did not call her father, but she did make a phone call to a different number in Milford.

"Khatia Quigley? Is that you? Good heavens, when are you finally coming home little Miss Globe–trotter?"

Khatia let Meredith go on for a while, asking politely about Bianca, telling her briefly about San Francisco. Then she asked her.

"Meredith, what do you know about my mother's parents?"

There was a pause on the other end.

"Not much, dear. I know they did not get along with your mother, nor approve of your father, which is odd since he's from one of the best families in New Jersey."

"I met them, Meredith."

No answer.

"Meredith. Tell me what you know. Please."

Khatia watched the second hand on her watch sweep a full minute and twelve seconds. Finally, she said, "Everything is unraveling, and I really need some answers."

Khatia wished she could see Meredith. What could her expression be, three thousand miles away, breath held? She started slowly.

"I know that, for what it's worth, your parents were in love. When your

246

father wanted to leave, right before Annie fell ill, he still loved her. He didn't want to leave because he had a mid–life crisis as everybody said. It was for her. Everything he ever did during their marriage was for her."

"But why? Why leave? What could that do?"

She heard Meredith sniff. She was crying. Khatia had been waiting for her to start crying. "Well, to make up."

"Make up for what? Talking her into changing her face and denying part of her heritage?"

"Khatia," Meredith said, her voice tender and patient. A mother's patience, Khatia thought. *I want a mother again.* She tugged at her hair so that the pain would take over the tightness in her chest. "You don't know everything," Meredith continued. "*I* don't know everything. I didn't know your mother before. She did it because she loved him. Those two would do anything for each other, for you kids. Don't judge them until you know."

"I don't know if I want to know, Meredith."

"I can understand that, kiddo. But if you're asking questions, you must want to. I'm not the person to ask. Talk to your father."

Khatia remained silent.

"Anything I tell you is just second hand. She only told me about the surgery because I guessed. You know how nosy I am. I don't think anything but death could keep those two apart. It might not have been a regular relationship, but it was genuine. How many people can say they have that? When you get to know a person a little better, you meet their dark side. You also find more of their deeper light."

"That's my problem, Meredith," Khatia said. "They never let me know them."

247

Chapter Sixteen

I am so fucking angry.

Well.

Doesn't it all make sense?

I can make it all fit in nice and neat. Little compartments for each insanity: why I am on medication, why my parents were both so fucking tweaked, why we never met our grandparents, why the rainforests are disappearing, why ethnic cleansing goes on in the world.

My own small theories are on the verge of exploding in my head. My father and mother did their own experiments with ethnic cleansing, didn't they? It was probably all him; he cowed that woman. She was weak all her life. I don't know how she lasted as long as she did. I really don't.

Khatia called just now. She tells me she met the grandparents Chew. Lovely. They're just as cowardly as their daughter. I don't believe in all this disowning bullshit. Maybe that's the "American" or "white devil" in me, tainting their pure, unpolluted Chinese blood. Maybe I've been corrupted by Manifest Destiny, Imperialism, Separatism, the Protestant Work Ethic. Dementia.

Oh god, here I go.

I refuse to talk to Dad. He's called here, but I don't answer the phone anymore. My roommates don't appreciate it. I left a message with Dorinne, my would–be step–monster, at his office. Told her to tell him to stay the fuck out of my life and I wish he were dead, I wish he had received a *posthumous* purple fucking heart in Korea. Those exact words. Maybe *I* should write a red ink letter. Sure, I wouldn't exist if that happened, but, yippee–fucking–skippee, I wouldn't *exist* if that happened. I wonder if I was meant to exist. I mean, I wonder if they wanted me and my sister in the first place or if we were just big uh–oh's.

248

Why did they do it? The letter implies he coerced her into plastic surgery. Did she fight him? I can't see her fighting him. She was always subdued. Both of them were. I'm angry at her too. And maybe he was angry at her for the way she looked.

But, was it everything? I mean, in her face. What did he touch? What repulsed him? Was it just the eyelids? The cheek bones too? Nose? Mouth? Hair? Skin?

My mother.

This elaborate, stupid scheming. He didn't change her language though. She *did* know Chinese, even had a Chinese name.

It's not fair. I could have known Chinese the way I know English, without even thinking, like a part of me, like breathing.

I think I know what happened. He freaked out during the war—wars fuck people up, as we've seen from Vietnam, Bosnia, Israel—and couldn't handle her face, but for some fucked up reason, he wanted to marry her.

Maybe that's what love is, and that person we find is someone we paradoxically love and hate simultaneously. They are a mirror of what we love and hate in ourselves. Marriage: we're all looking for the perfect mate. Well, I'm not, but some people are. I think Shoshonah was my sister's lover. She doesn't talk about it, but silence can't hide everything. Now she's with a man, this Cree guy. I wonder if he'll be good to her. You can never know what will set people off.

People don't do what my mother did. Do they? Maybe they think about it. I know I used to wish I were black. When I was a little kind taking swim lessons, I'd watch Kenny Burkman get out of the pool, the way the water would roll off of his hair like a duck—I was so jealous. But I know it couldn't ever be. Ever.

To actually do it. To find a person malleable enough to say, "Yes."

Is that a sign of love? Despair?

I'd kill Dad if I saw him right now.

My mother. She must have hated herself so much. People who scar themselves: plastic surgery is just expensive scarification.

Not that I regret the tattoo. I'm happy now, more than ever, that I got it.

249

It's all I have, really. I don't have the language. Yet. I don't have the culture, history, stories. Traditions. Neuroses. Only what they gave me. Children don't have the power to make those choices. If I could only start over...I should have gotten the tattoo a long time ago.

I want to leave here, Rhode Island, but Khatia says stick it out. I only have to take my finals. I won't do well, but I'll take them anyway. Then I am out of here. I can't be tied to that man anymore. He makes me want to cut pieces of my flesh off, starting with my chest.

Chapter Seventeen

The young man, the friend, directs him back down the street to the neighborhood shopping district. That's where she works, he says, in a restaurant called Simonetta's. No one is eating there now, but the chef has her in training. She's a wonderful cook, the man adds. John Porter Quigley looks him over, this Cree Brown, an odd looking man. Exotic one might call him, an African–Tahitian mixture, like an undone cocktail. He smiles knowingly. John Porter resents his sympathy.

Finding the restaurant is not difficult, and he stands outside of it for a while, across the street. On one side of the restaurant is a bookstore. On the other is a green grocer, the display of summer fruits and vegetables adding color and life—green peppers, red tomatoes, bananas, mangoes, strawberries.

Perhaps she will be a restaurateur; she could do worse.

He crosses the street and knocks on the wooden part of the door, peering through the glass at the tiny room. She is the one to come out from the back in response. She pauses as their eyes meet, wiping her hands on a towel attached to the belt of her apron.

How like her mother she is: the look of surprise, of dread and relief, maybe even delight, crossing over her face, a face that refuses crumbling. Stoic: like her mother, her people. He might as well think these things now, released from confines that have become a part of him for the last twenty–five years.

His daughter calls something back towards the kitchen. She approaches the door and unlocks it, opening it, not looking at his eyes until the wood and glass no longer separates them. Then she does look at him, all over him, as if he were a statue in a museum she needs to memorize.

She puts her arms around his torso, and he is startled by the motion. The feel of her small body against his own, even through the raincoat he wears.

251

Her smell is in his nostrils for a moment: shampoo, cigarettes, dog, and something else familiar. It's a smell like Annie, bittersweet like her milk. She nursed the children for a month before going back to work. Khatia and Porter will always have that smell of their mother; it's in their blood, passed from nipple to gumming mouth, into them, protecting them. At the time, watching them drink from her, he was jealous and thankful.

He cannot remember his daughter in a familiar way. She has not initiated contact with him since she was a little girl, asking to sit in his lap while he read her a story. She pulls away, does not look up into his face as a lover might after such an embrace, after almost a year apart from one another.

She removes her apron, gets her coat, that ragamuffin leather thing she insisted on buying in a New York thrift shop. The first time he saw it, he winced at how right it looked on her. They go to another place, a café down the block. He orders coffee drinks for them. She says she needs one. The two first fingers of her right hand are slightly browned, and her gums seem a little gray around the creamy enamel of her teeth. She has taken up smoking he sees, something he had feared would happen in Europe. Such temptation is great over there. He smoked when he was young, of course. Everybody did.

Why are you here? she asks after a moment.

It is not a hurtful question, although some parents might take it that way. She is only scared and curious.

Are you dying or something? Is this some last ditch effort to make some connection?

She does not usually talk to him this way. Perhaps the year abroad has given her some fire. But he sees right away it is just smoke: she turns pale, regretful.

Actually, he says, and he can not help but be satisfied with unnerving her a little, I found out I won the directorship for the college's program abroad to St. Petersburg next term. True, I have a distaste for loose ends. I simply came because...you've found out.

Porter told you. I know. You should be visiting him. Why come all this way to see me? I'm not the one exhuming skeletons.

John Porter sips his coffee. You prefer to leave them in their graves?

252

She shrugs and nods and the same time.

He did not tell me, exactly, that you two had found out, but he left a scathing message at work and will not return my phone calls.

He's upset, of course. Shit, Dad. We trusted you.

Her arms are crossed over her chest. She hugs herself, holding herself in. She seems thinner than he remembered, the delicate bird–like sliding of her collarbone in relief.

You've lied to us, Dad, all our lives and about so many things. Why did you do that? I think I can live with what you were covering up. It's the covering up I'm not sure about.

He does not answer, frowning into his cup. She leans forward.

Are you ashamed of Mom? Were you ashamed to marry a woman who wasn't white? Is that why you made her into a, a postiche?

She continues to hug herself. Leaning forward, her breasts push together slightly, and he can see the cleavage in her loose blouse.

You want to know the truth, he says. But it's not all that strange. You see, we tried to be normal and unobtrusive. That's all we wanted. Things happen, though. Things one cannot control. We did not lie to you directly. Encouraging what your childish minds made up wasn't difficult. We would have simply not told, except that you decided for yourselves what the story was. You asked and answered. Both of you, inquisitive children. And there were practical matters: you would need to know things like your mother's maiden name. We couldn't hide everything from you completely, even though we had forgotten for so long...You weren't born until we had been married for almost eight years. Children. So unpredictable. Even though we tried to drill into you the importance of privacy...Well, one cannot stop natural traits.

She is looking at him, his mouth in motion.

You tried though, she says. You and mom—

I know, he says, putting up a staying hand. I know. I will tell you the facts, Khatia. That's all I can do. You know as much as I do because I allowed it.

She turns her head, mutters to herself—*Bullshit*.

253

Olivia Boler

Do you think Porter would have found my letters if I had not let him?

She looks contrite under a strong visage, and John Porter feels a swell of power in his ego he must quickly subdue.

He sips his coffee and begins.

I was drafted into the army to go to Korea. It was my own fault. I should have gone straight to college as my mother and sister encouraged. They wanted me there. Needed a man close by. My father had killed himself five years before. Accident or suicide, I don't know. But I was just a boy, and I had all kinds of romantic notions. I told them I wanted to take a year to do a little traveling. What I really wanted, although I never admitted this to them, was to be drafted into the army. My mother and sister had converted to the Quaker Church after father's death. They were peaceful women, against the war and violence.

I told them I had deferred from Princeton for a year, but when the draft letter came, they knew I had not even applied. They wept when I got on a train for boot camp in South Carolina. I pretended to weep with them. I was really crying for joy, I think. I was eighteen, ready for adventures.

Boot camp was everything I dreamed it would be: a homosocial environment, much like your college experience Khatia, but mine was complete with grueling drills, indigestible food, and no women anywhere. I thrived in the pranks the other boys pulled, in the "bitching out" the sergeants gave us. It was everything that small kernel of rebelliousness in me had longed for, that which my sister said I had inherited from our father.

The soldiers were put in special units. I had requested a medical assignment. My mother had aspirations that I would follow in my father's footsteps and reopen the doors of his office someday. But somehow I put it off and got assigned to cryptology and languages. Mostly languages. I already knew French and Spanish, and a bit of Russian, so the commanders figured I was good at languages, and I was. They taught me rudimentary Chinese and Korean.

After three months, my troop had orders to go overseas. But first, we had some lag time in San Francisco.

The American people, on the surface, were so sure their boys should be going into battle. After all, we had defeated the Germans and Japanese, we could do it again with a Red–Yellow Menace. There was a lot of animosity from ignorant and paranoid people at the time towards Asians. They were sometimes vocal as well, always reminding us that Asians couldn't be trusted, that they were unknowable. I didn't pay too much attention. I just wanted to live a moment of the picture shows. John Wayne and Gary Cooper were my boyhood heroes.

Strange that red and yellow make orange. I find it a comforting color. It's the sun at daybreak.

It's the sunset too, Khatia says.

Yes.

They watch each other for a moment. Her father orders more coffee and some biscotti. She nibbles at it.

In any case, he continues. It came to my commander's attention that there was a particular junior high school in San Francisco with many Chinese children, and *they* had been suggesting that perhaps it was not right to go to battle in Korea, or at least, to uphold slogans about the Red–Yellow Menace and slant–eyes and coolies. These children protested by writing. On Veteran's Day, their teacher asked them to make signs for the soldiers, and most of them read: "We are Americans too. Please do not forget that."

Now, it just so happened that I was a darling of my platoon because I was a star in track and field. My commander, drunk one night at some party, bragged about me to the coach of the Stanford team. They made a bet: me against his best man. For that reason, I was allowed to stay behind my platoon. Imagine something so completely frivolous; I'm about to go overseas into combat, and I'm getting recruited for a meet that shouldn't be happening in the first place. My commander justified this show of favoritism by telling the others that I was to go to this school where the "incident" with the children's signs had happened, and talk to them, show them that the U. S. Army and America were on their side. I remember my commander said, "Even if they are slopeheads." He had served for a while in Shanghai in his youth, and seemed to think he knew the ways of their race.

The students were in a history and geography class. I remember knocking on the door and going in, and the first thing I saw was a classroom full of black hair and brown eyes. I admit, it did make me pause. There was one white child. It turned out he had speech problems. The teacher was also white, a woman.

255

I talked to the students, answering any questions they had, although it seemed obvious to me they only asked questions because their teacher had coerced them before I arrived. And if they did have questions of their own, they were not asking. It was an uncomfortable half hour. But one student approach me after the bell rang.

She came up to me after class, just looking at me in my uniform. I said hello, and she said, "Do you really want to kill people?"

I didn't know what to say, so I told her, "I want to help my country."

She just stared at me for a while, and then she said, "Our country doesn't need any help in Korea."

I was just a soldier, a boy. She was twelve. Her speech did not seem to need any help. She spoke as clearly as any American. I sensed she knew more about the issue than I did. I guess she just left me standing there, going on her way to her next class.

I spent the day at the school, visiting other classes. The school had whites, Asians, and a few blacks, but somehow, the administrators had managed to segregate the classes, owing all to the "speech problems" the Asian students had. They moved in a pack from classroom to classroom, taciturn yet attentive, doing their school work, answering questions when called upon, hanging about together in the schoolyard, as children are wont to do.

I spent three days there, visiting the school. On my last day, two days before I was due to ship out and join my troop, the class gave me a gift. It was a scarf, and they had put their money together to buy it. They also gave me a list of their names and addresses in case I wanted to write to them, which I did not, and I gave them the address of the Army mailbag.

I didn't go into battle right away. I spent some time in Tokyo, then in Seoul working in offices there. I suppose I was lucky.

And I began to receive letters from Anna Chew. She asked in her first letter if I remembered her. How could I forget that accusing look? She wrote that she was the one who had talked to me that day, and that she had long, braided hair.

I did not answer right away. I even forgot about it. Honestly, it was sheer boredom that made me write. Finally, I was seeing some "action," but that only meant we had been sent in to guard an old convent with a good view on a hill. We couldn't even hear any shelling. I had the nightwatch, and after I got off duty, I couldn't sleep. So I wrote. I wrote to your mother.

John Porter takes a parcel out of his coat pocket. It's a bundle wrapped in a chamois cloth.

Her letters, he says. Khatia looks at the bundle and nods.

You're in control, Dad, she says, and he deflates. What a man you are.

She makes a noise and shakes her head. Go on, Dad.

He takes a deep breath. John Porter was wrong about his daughter's strength earlier. It has been slumbering but now wakes.

She wrote back almost immediately. I began looking forward to her letters more than my own family's. She asked hard questions, told me about her days. There was something alive in her letters that made me happy, like a good novel can make you happy, or a sunny day. A visceral reaction, I know. I even memorized some of them, and when we marched from one place to another, I whispered them to myself while watching my friends get blown up. Watching my own life spared time and again by chance.

But one night, I was unlucky, and I was not only wounded—he touches his chest— but captured. He pauses in the telling. It was a horrible, cruel experience.

What happened? she asks.

He stops short of answering. This answer he could give her. The terribleness of it cancels out any desires for lording over his children, over anything. Everything is meaningless to him with his atrocious acts.

I don't want to discuss it.

She withdraws inside herself, looking at the worn table top.

I don't mean to sanitize war for you, Khatia.

She shrugs, still looking at the table top. He sees that she expected more from him.

He sighs. He will have to give her more where he can.

Man has not lost his love of torture, he says, but she still stares at the table top. I was given no medical treatment, no food or water. The kindest thing they did to me was to pour vinegar on my wounds like some kind of Communist retribution towards the white man's Christ. Basically, I was their plaything. They were trying out brainwashing techniques on me. Seeing if they could bring me to their side, just to amuse themselves. Then, they might kill me. They were angry and disorganized, resentful of everything about their situation, and not well–regulated. Either were the Americans for that matter.

He watches her face, but it does not change.

I grew to hate them. I would think of your mother, and I would hate her. She was not Korean, but she was Oriental, and it was enough. He pauses, seething with the vividness of memories, the colors and smells, the hissing voices assailing him. He swallows. *Control. Control.*

In a way, he continues, the brainwashing worked. I understood our society's ignorance and paranoia. I believed in it too. It did not matter to me if Americans did these same things to their POW's, I just knew what I had to endure. My captivity probably only lasted three or four days, but that was all it took to kill something inside of me. The romance of war was a myth, and I had found out the hard way.

Khatia is shaking. He almost puts out his hand, but he realizes she is just jiggling her foot under the table, keeping time to some internal rhythm. Pulling back is easy for him. They are moving away from each other as he has feared. But he must keep talking.

The Koreans traded me and some others for their own prisoners. Perhaps the Red Koreans chose me because I could communicate with them a little, and in the end, instead of killing me, they felt some brotherly sympathy. I don't know. I didn't see it that way then. Life was something I deserved, not something I needed to earn. But a soldier can't think that way.

I was sent to the American hospital in Seoul where a telegram from my family was waiting, wanting to know if I was all right. There was also a letter from Annie.

I answered it, although I did not want to. I hated her. Yet, I desired her. I had fallen in love, you see, and I resented it. It got in the way of my new hate.

Khatia shifts uncomfortably in her chair. Perhaps she has to go to the restroom, he thinks, but ignores this, caught up in the drug of remembering. He has not talked about this to anyone, and the process, one he anticipated would be so simple—he's only talking after all—exhausts him into nervous wakefulness.

Before I was sent home, I was asked to do a favor by the colonel for whom I had clerked in Seoul. An interrogation. I watched my own fellow soldiers hook a prisoner up to a jeep battery. As I asked him questions in Korean, Chinese, and Russian, every language I knew, another soldier would flip a switch—

I don't want to hear this, Dad.

He stops speaking, but he is caught up in the memory, one that has never really been buried in his subconscience, but is always there, manifesting in his dreams, finding new players in the forms of his family, influencing his demeanor—reserved—his actions, particularly on one night almost thirty years ago towards his young wife. John Porter Quigley remembers how—

they watched with detached interest, the man writhing in agony, the smell of cooked meat licking at their nostrils. His name was Sung Ko. The man would not answer the questions in any language, and seemed to make up his own tongue, hissing to himself, cursing their lives with his tears. When blood dripped out of his ears, they stopped and put him back in his cell. One of the other soldiers suggested cutting his eyelids, giving them the fold they needed to make him "human." I'm sick of these fucking slant-eyed, buck-toothed gooks. His companion laughed. Make Quigley do it. They tried to hand him a razor. It flashed at him, drawing him in as he remembered the POW camp, the napalm seething on his chest, no aid—He backed away—

I know, he says. I know. I'm sorry.

He squeezes his eyes shut. *Finish this.*

I returned to the States. After the summer, I went to school. My sister had married, and she and her new husband moved into the house and were taking care of Mother. I went to Princeton, but I hardly ever went home. Annie continued to write to me, but I did not answer. After a while, she gave up.

I was doing post–doctoral work at Simmons College when we met again. I was waiting for my dissertation to be published and a university position. Simmons was good school, not a prestigious school, but the money was fair.

Olivia Boler

We met at a faculty–graduate student tea. It had been at least eleven years, and Annie was now a young woman. She approached me, the way she had years before. The braid was gone, but her hair was still long. Much like yours, Khatia.

"It's because of your letters that I came to the East Coast for graduate school," she told me. "The way you wrote about the autumn leaves." Always so bold. She had received a scholarship, and she was one of the first Asians to be accepted to their excellent Library Sciences school.

Bold? Khatia says. Do you mean for an Oriental?

He goes on, ignoring her brief reactionary zeal.

We met for coffee. I was only being polite. But we began to date after a while.

He pauses in the telling. *Annie.* Her energy back then, that which could drain him of all protest, still surprises him. She was not what he thought she would be as a woman. Actually, he had never indulged in thinking of her beyond pubescence; she was exquisite.

But still, he loathed her in a way. He looked at her face. He saw those eyes, and he recalled his tormentors. He hated them. He saw her eyes and remembered. He hated himself. He hated the prisoner he had helped to interrogate. He hated the soldiers who had handed him the razor, big kids torturing a human grasshopper, pulling off its legs, watching it gimp around. He wished he had taken the razor then. And used it on whom? When to take it? When would it have made a difference?

She often spent the night at his apartment, and sometimes he would have dreams about her as they lay side by side or entwined. In his dreams, she was the tormentor, keeping him sick and in pain, laughing at his tears as he shit his pants. He would wake up with a start, look at her sleeping form, and he would have to curl his hands underneath his body to keep them from going to her fragile throat. She did not know what he had suffered in that other place. All she knew was that she had loved him all these years, and somehow they were together again.

When he got the offer of a permanent position, she suggested marriage; her parents would not approve, but they would not protest either. He stared at her, thinking to himself, he must leave her now before they were both ruined. But he ignored himself, lost in the realness of their happiness.

And one day, coming home from a lecture, he ran into a man on the street. One of the interrogators. The man said he was a bartender now. John Porter tried to circle away from him on the sidewalk, but his former colleague wanted to talk, to unburden himself.

Remember that guy we lit? Well, Franklin finally poured kerosene on him and gave him a cigarette. Man, it was beautiful. Fucking poetry.

John Porter laughed and the bartender joined in. Creature from the Black Lagoon. They went to the bar where the ex–soldier worked and shared drinks for hours.

That night, carving a roast she had cooked for him—Chinese foods she knew how to prepare best upset his stomach—he looked down on her, sitting at the kitchen table, slicing lettuce or something for the salad. The tops of her eyelids that did not *fold* the way eyelids were meant to fold, as Franklin had said. He could help her. He loved her; it was his responsibility. He stopped carving, one hand starting in a caress, encircling her neck—his arm a flesh necklace—the other holding the carving knife—

He looks at his daughter. She has the eyes of her mother, the old eyes, only with the fold in her lids. They are shiny now, from exertion, from listening to him, from understanding the changing waves on his face.

There was an accident, he whispers.

What? Khatia asks.

She had to have reconstructive surgery—on her, on her face.

Khatia's fingers are blue. Bad circulation, he thinks. Smokers have bad circulation.

She looked—different. Afterwards. After the surgery. We decided to hold off on children for a while until we could figure out how to explain— She said she didn't want any. That was fine with me. I wasn't sure how they would look, you see, or how to explain your mother's—

He breaks off again, looking up at his daughter.

You didn't want us? she says. Were we *accidents* too?

We started a new life, he continues. In New Hampshire. We built the house together, far away from town. She found a job at the school. We were together. Her family abandoned her when we went to her home to

261

meet each other. They despised me. And they despised her. For the accident. But that's what it was. Khatia, it was only an accident.

He is shaking.

Do you ever have nightmares? he asks. Ones that seem to take over everything, and that vanquish reality?

What was the accident, Dad? What did you do to her?

My dreams come true. I can make them come true. I am the creator and I carry them out. But Annie forgave me, Khatia. We helped one another when no one else would. Yes, you were an accident, but we were relieved, in a way. When you were born, we worried that you would not understand. Except, you didn't look Asian. You looked white, mostly. Unbelievable. Like a Latin–European. And it didn't matter, as long as you didn't ask. And you didn't. You learned the smokescreen. You were so beautiful. You and your brother. You are beautiful children.

He is crying now, and he can see his tears disturb her. He wipes his face with a napkin, and they are gone.

Do you understand the need to recreate?

She shakes her head. He senses the fury in her. She resists his words.

Why keep secrets? Khatia asks. Why not just tell us about the accident?

He sighs. Too horrible. Too horrible. *I swear a change.* The violence left him that night.

He takes a sip of coffee.

How is Shoshonah doing? Have you heard from her lately?

She looks down at her lap, her face a combination of ash and crimson. Last I heard she was fine.

He can see the impulse in her face to tell him what he already knows about her, what she knows now that he knows. But it is just an impulse, and she is stubborn.

If your grandparents weren't going to accept you, why bother teaching you about a culture that would not forgive? Why make you believe yourself inferior?

Dismiss a culture because of two people? Your family *is* your culture and your culture is who you are. Don't you know that? Have you learned nothing?

She pauses, and he can see the frustration on her face.

You're confusing me, she says. *You* were the one who wouldn't forgive. And what was there to forgive? Ghost crimes. War crimes an innocent, American, civilian girl had nothing to do with.

Her hands are between her knees and she is rocking back and forth in her chair. He knows that look. She wants a cigarette. He almost tells her to go out and smoke one, but old habits are hard to break; they can not help but respect what is unacknowledged, pretend it is not reality.

It was better for us, he says, nodding his head as if convinced. They didn't want her anymore, and I did. I took care of her.

Then why did you almost leave us?

He starts, claws his hand in his hair, squeezing it down to the roots. Khatia watches people outside. They wait for each other.

It is the hole in his carefully constructed life.

You know what? Forget it. His daughter can not wait. I have to go back to work, she says and stands up, putting on her jacket. Please don't try to see me again. I can't talk to you for a while.

But Khatia—

No, Dad. She stops him. I'll—I'll let you know when I'm ready.

He does not watch her leave, instead, plays with the twine on the bundle of old letters. He remembers the day Annie died in the hospital. She slipped away quietly, her eyes closed in her sunken face as if she were only asleep, and he could put his arms around her and feel the warmth emanate from her body.

Chapter Eighteen

Khatia understood the variances of perception. What was an accident to one person was sabotage to another. *Put yourself in his shoes.* For most of her life, she chose to blind herself to emotions. Her father chose to blind himself to facts. In the end, there was only one person left to ask, and that person had died years ago, as foretold in a red ink letter.

The excuse of going back to work was a lie. Khatia had asked Giovanni for the rest of the day off. She asked Cree to borrow his car. He did not press her to explain.

Sitting on the edge of the lookout point over Muir Beach, Khatia thought of flying off the cliff, smashing onto the rocks, or perhaps to the tiny beach hundreds of feet below to her right, directly onto the nudists. Her vision was as keen as a bird, and she breathed deeply the smells of wind–toughened beach grass, tangy air, and cold mist. In the next life, let me have feathers and wings. The city lights twinkled and sparkled out beyond the natural landscape of water and earth: her home.

She saved the cigarette butts, making a small hill of them to throw into a garbage can after the sun had given her its show.

Yes, they had loved each other, her parents. But four years ago, her father realized how their love, as they chose to name it, was killing them. Their ruse, they thought, was forever, but they had refused to deny one aspect of humans: they change. Desires, sentiments, beliefs—Perhaps he was not violent anymore, but his past had reached forward as a past *must* do, its traces touching his children despite his cautions. He had tried to leave, too late, tried to tell them, but couldn't.

"It's not too late for us," Khatia said to herself. She lit a new cigarette as the sun dripped into the ocean. The cigarette burned, the smoke rising off the tip. She imagined breathing in the smoke, the path it would travel through her esophagus, down into the cushiony sponginess of her lungs, the alveoli, seeping into her blood stream with a sucking sound audible only on the inside of her body. Lowering it into the sand and grass, she ground it out and placed it on top of the pile of butts.

Epilogue

Hands pushed and reached out to her. Fingers clutched, wanting a prize: compact discs, t–shirts, coupons for sodas and French fries at fast food restaurants. She had become used to this push of humanity on her, its ever–present nearness. It wasn't an easy thing, being surrounded by so many people, people who wanted to be close to her. For so long, she had been one or two, but hardly ever more than two. Family had once been four, but four separated into their compartments, their invisible walls.

"Khatia! I love you!"

"Give me one of those t–shirts. Hey, did you see my bumper sticker?"

"Dig it, Khatia! *Dig it!*"

"What did I win, Scooter Chick? Look, I got the list: Top One Hundred of this year. C'mon, what did I win?"

She looked out at the crowd. Seven months ago, it had been the prizes they wanted, the free stuff. Anything free was a triumph to people, even though, as Annie Quigley used to say, nothing is really free. There's payment going on somewhere—taxes, advertising, lives. The crowds who flocked to the bars, tire shops, and music stores, whatever establishment had made a promotional contract with the radio station for a remote, did so because they wanted the prize give–aways; Khatia was just the body, the smiling face in control of *stuff*, stuff they deserved because of all the times they had to pay at some point. But they began to know her. "What's your name?" they asked. She recognized the regulars, the ones who showed up at every remote she ran, hands reaching out to her. She could give them something, and they were grateful to her. They joked with her, offered her cigarettes that she began to turn down as the months went by.

"Khatia! Marry me!" This from a woman, shorn–headed, pierced, tattooed, and heavy–set.

266

"Hey, dig it, Khatia."

"You're zee bomb, mon amour."

"When are they gonna give you your own show, Khatia?"

Khatia, bent over her bag of goodies, paused in her task at this question.

"You deserve your own show, Khatia," the person said again. Khatia looked at the middle–aged man with a graying pony–tail. His t–shirt was gauzy with age, and it had a Tom Petty and the Heartbreakers logo on it, a heart with angel wings.

"Yeah, Khatia," someone else said. "You do. When are they gonna let you DJ?"

She shrugged and handed a new CD of the Steve Miller Band to the old hippie.

"Soon," she said. The bag was only half empty. Or half–full, she reminded herself. One of the interns had another one in the van. He stood beside it, guarding the little scooter on which Khatia putted around the city, looking for cars with bumper stickers. Every hour or half–hour, she would call into the station and have an on–air conversation with the DJ, vaporous chatting:

"What's it like out there, Khatia?"

"No forms of intelligent life here in the Sunset District, Gus, but if your license plate reads 1–R–S–V–8–0–2, call in now because you've just won a trip to—*Cabo San Lucas.*"

"Cabo! Right on, Khatia. Power to you, and check in later."

"Right on, Magic Gus McGill."

She turned back to the crowd. They were like friendly seals, waiting for a fish. Pay attention to me, their faces seemed to say. She smiled back at them, paying attention, something she was learning to do little by little everyday.

Porter had moved to San Francisco right after his semester ended at the University of Rhode Island. He and Cree converted the little back porch into a bedroom, replacing the screens with panes of glass and putting in a space heater. Her little family of men, Khatia thought. She tried to hug her brother at least once everyday; it was awkward for them. They were like strangers, but they looked at each other, knowing they would like one another if they stayed quiet when it was right and talked when it was right. Someone was usually in the apartment when she got home from the radio station or the restaurant. Today it was Cree.

"I'm not going to be here long," he said, after giving her a kiss. "Gotta take my dad to an AA meeting."

"Oh, Cree," she said. "You mean he finally agreed to go?"

"Yeah. He's gone before, about three years ago, but he was still drinking. At least he hasn't had anything in a couple of weeks this time." He shrugged. "Hey, what are you gonna do? All I can do is not hold my breath."

She nodded. "Where's Porter? Doesn't he have to work tonight?" Her brother had taken over some of her hours at Simonetta's since she had started work at the radio station.

"He went over to your grandparents."

"With the cam–corder?"

"Of course."

Porter would start school at San Francisco State University in the fall, and he continued to work on the genealogy project until then, hoping to get some credits for it. Within a few days of arriving in the city, he found his way to the Chews, impressing them with his tiny Chinese vocabulary and his eagerness to spend time with them. They cried when they saw him; he looked like their son who had died of leukemia in China. They embraced him, calling him Little Son in Chinese.

Khatia could not bring herself to go over there very often. In the way Porter reminded them of the son, she reminded them of the daughter. She remembered her embarrassing flight from the gate of their house.

"What are you going to do with the rest of your afternoon?" Cree asked as he put on his pea coat. The day was sunny, although they were in the throes of winter. Across the street, the neighbors had strung Christmas lights on their shrubs and hung a wreath on the front door. Cree pulled mistletoe out of his coat pocket and held it over his head. She kissed him.

"I don't know. Porter said something this morning about craving *cha siu bao*."

"Mmm…" Cree's eyes got big and he licked his lips. "Barbecued pork buns. Save me some. Get some of those egg tarts too."

"Okay. Good luck with your dad."

"Hey, thanks." He attached the mistletoe to a thumbtack in the kitchen's doorframe, gave her one more kiss, and left.

Khatia watched him from the window until his Volvo had disappeared down the hill. The apartment was quiet. She could only hear the wind outside, finding its way around corners, and Artichoke snoring on the couch. She pushed him over and lay down on the cushions, draping her tired legs over the back. The dog lifted his head with a "why–are–you–bothering–me" look, and then he sighed, putting his head back down and licking the inside of his dog–lips. She rarely had time to be alone these days with her little family of men: brother, lover, dog.

In the bedroom closet, she kept two items, one opened and one unopened. The first was a letter from Shoshonah she had received two months ago. She was getting married to Mina. They would be married that month, in fact. At first, Khatia had looked at the letter as if it were mis–addressed, and the news it contained were sweet and amusing but belonged to a stranger. But as the wedding date drew nearer, the words it revealed seemed heavier. Just yesterday, she had written a postcard of congratulations to her old friend. On it she wrote: "All happiness to you. So much has changed. We're not in the gill net, are we? We can stay still now."

The Inuit drawing of the salmon hung in the hallway near the bathroom. She passed it everyday. It was a drawing, a gift from an old intimacy, an old friend.

The other item, unopened, was a box her father had sent soon after Porter moved to the city. It was addressed to both of them. Porter refused to open it, and Khatia waited for him. Their father sent Porter checks each month for the amount tuition would have been had he been in school. No letters. Her brother wordlessly set the checks aside in an envelope under his bed when they arrived. The unresolved parts of their lives. They could not expect to be perfectly happy. Cree recommended a counselor at the hospital, but Khatia's insurance did not cover those kinds of sessions, and she

269

wanted Porter to go with her anyway. He refused to see anyone, swearing off "head doctors." She continued to wait.

Today, she had achieved two things. First, her savings was finally built up enough that she could afford something a little extravagant. Second, one month had passed since she quit smoking. She had smoked cigarettes regularly for exactly a year, and then quit. It was harder than she thought it would be, but she promised herself that if she could do it, she would forgive herself of one thing.

The front door opened and Porter ran up the stairs.

"Hey," he said. He brought the outside with him in a cold wave, the smell of gray ice, vinyl bus seats, and humanity. "Lounging, eh? Let's go get bao."

"How ya doing, Little One–Track–Minded?"

"Come on, Khatia. I'm starving."

"I don't have the car so we'll have to bus it."

"Damn. I was hoping we'd go to Chinatown instead of Clement Street." Both areas sold Chinese food, and Clement Street was closer.

"We can go to Chinatown, if you promise to do something with me afterwards."

"What?"

"Just promise."

He shrugged in that way she recognized as part of what he called his "distractibility."

"Yeah yeah, sure sure. Let's go. I'm wasting away before my very wasted eyeballs."

They took the Metro downtown and transferred to the 30 Stockton bus. Khatia watched the faces of the passengers change as she boarded. Little old Chinese ladies and men got on the bus, shoving others out of their way in order to get a seat. The Self was sacred but not the Other. She and Porter stood, holding on to the metal poles. The people around them spoke in Cantonese, a loud, complaining language. Porter could not understand it since he was learning the Mandarin dialect from their grandparents.

They went to the deem sum shop with the best bao: steamed white-doughed buns filled with red, barbecued pork. They each ate two before buying another two dozen to put in the freezer, although that might not be necessary. Porter held the pink bakery box tied up with red string, and Khatia ordered some tarts for Cree and conal shaped sponge cakes for breakfast.

"There's this shop I want to check out before we go back," he said as they left the shop. "They told me about it today."

Khatia and Porter never referred to their grandparents by name or title, identifying them through pronouns and the context of their conversation. The same with their mother and father. Talking in veils was part of their understanding.

"What kind of a store is it?" Khatia asked.

"Junk and stuff."

"Junk and stuff."

They walked up a hill and over two blocks. Chinese people were everywhere, standing in doorways, shopping for duck, fish, and vegetables all fresh and alive, crammed into cages, tanks, bins. The street gutters were littered with cans, squashed bakery boxes, pink plastic bags, soiled tissue, old–man phlegm gobs. Cars and buses fought jay–walkers made up of locals and tourists alike. If you did not have black hair and golden hued skin you stood out as a tourist, even if you were local. Outsider. White–ghost. Black–white–devil. Khatia reminded herself that she was half inside. Half–gold. Would they accept her as valuable?

They arrived at the store. It was off the beaten paths of Grant Avenue and Stockton Street. No non–Chinese walked these sidewalks, and Khatia wondered if the locals could tell about her and Porter. With Porter, his elfin–shaped eyes, they probably knew; the eyes really did stand out. If she drew a rendition of her eyes next to Porter's the difference would show. Porter had looked up a statistic: the most common type of cosmetic surgery among Asians was having a fold cut in their eyelids. Eyes might be the windows to a person's soul, but eyelids were the advertisement of one's identity, at least for many Asians.

"Here it is."

271

Olivia Boler

Porter stopped in front of a dusty door marred with peeling paint. They went inside. A woman behind the counter stared at them. Porter walked up to her and spoke in a low voice. Khatia hung back by the door—something smelled strongly of menthol and earth in this room. She couldn't hear her brother's voice, and for a moment imagined he was speaking Cantonese, even though she knew this was impossible. He wanted to learn this culture; an intensity overwhelmed her as she watched him, his intensity. She looked around the store: it was full of jarred roots and books that gathered dust on rickety particle board shelves. In the back corner, near the ceiling above the counter, a porcelain statuette of a Chinese god, the face neither male nor female, the hair long and the flowing clothes adorned with gold and green paint, rested on a red–painted shelf. Two red electric candles were on either side of the figure, along with an orange and a rice bowl holding smoking incense. Khatia stared at this for some time, waiting for the small display to overwhelm her with connection. She felt nothing except guilt because she thought the plastic candles were tacky.

"Let's go," Porter stood at her elbow. He held a rolled up poster and a package tucked under his arm. "Want to go watch the sunset?" he asked when they were outside. Khatia did not ask him about his purchases. If he wanted to tell her about them he would. They still responded to each other's need for privacy.

They took the buses back across the town and got off in the hills of the Sunset District. Here was Turtle Hill, that hill where the fog rolled over the land even if the rest of the city was clear. That evening they were lucky and the fog stayed away, promising a good show. In Milford they would watch the sunset from a small outcropping of rocks in a farmer's fallow pasture. It was the point their father ran to on his morning runs. Khatia had not thought about those sunset–watching sessions in a long time, and she had never asked her brother why he had tagged along with her those few times.

Khatia loved this hill, and she like to think her mother had named her after it in particular.

"Bao?" Porter cut the string on the box with his pocket knife.

"Bao," Khatia said, taking one of buns into her mouth and biting off a mouthful.

"Yum." They both sighed in appreciation.

272

Golden Gate Park stretched below them in a green sash against the urban landscape. To the left, the Pacific Ocean waited to receive the sun, its waters stretching away to the land of their ancestors. Half of their ancestors.

Porter opened his package. It was a book of Chinese astrology, twelve animals, one animal for each year.

"The poster has the animals on it. I'm going to hang it in my room."

"What year am I?"

He flipped through the book.

"Rat. This was your year, in fact. Every twelve years."

"Rat?" she wrinkled her nose.

"You're 'blessed with great personal charm,'" he read from the book. "And you 'love to save money.'"

Khatia laughed at the truth.

"What are you?"

"A dragon," and he roared at her, his mouth full of masticated bao.

"That's what I should be with all the smoking I did this year."

"Good thing you didn't disappear into a cloud of nicotine syrup. I couldn't believe the way you sucked those puppies down when I first got here."

"Sick, isn't it?"

"Definitely." He shook his head. They gazed off in the direction of the ocean, chewing quietly.

"I'll never feel it, Porter," Khatia said after a moment. "I won't be able to force it on myself."

"What?"

"The culture. Being Chinese. I don't feel any different inside, but at the same time, something has changed. The way I look at myself has changed, even though I haven't. Does that make sense?"

"Yes."

"How do you do it?" she asked. "I mean, I know I love this food. I love

273

this pork bun in my hand. But what does that mean? How can you embrace all this so readily?"

Her brother looked at the bun in her hand.

"Because I want to," he said. "It's my choice now. We weren't given a choice as kids. Maybe it's better for us, although it makes me angry. I'm a clean slate in a way, Khatia. I can see it without all the bias of upbringing."

"Except the biases of *your* upbringing."

He nodded, but said again, "I'm a clean slate."

Her fingers trailed in the dirt.

"We can't really know why she did it. Dad meant more to her than anything else, I guess. We all have our little weak spots, but you could also call them our joys. This soil means more to me, to who I am, than knowing Mom was a full–blooded Chinese person. She was still an American, a San Franciscan. That's what I am, Porter. I know that now." She spread her arms wide, curving her fingers in. "I love this *place*. I love it even more because I love Cree, and cooking, and working at the radio station. And because you're here, Porter." She blushed a little, dropping her arms, and did not look at him. "It means a lot to me that we have each other."

Her words hung in the air. They watched the sun as it descended on the towers of a cargo freighter heading out to sea. Porter reached out and touched her hand lightly.

"We haven't lost anything new, Khatia."

"But we might," she said quickly. "If we're not careful, we might."

They did not speak for a few minutes. The ship disappeared in the blinding light of the sun. It reappeared when the sun was gone.

"I want you to do something with me. And you promised earlier to do it—"

"The box?" Porter interrupted.

"Yes."

He nodded, grasping her fingers for a moment, picking a bit of the dirt from under her nails.

Porter used his knife, but Khatia was impatient. She tore into the cardboard, ripping its yielding, gummy softness away. It split in half, and she stood up with it, jiggling the contents out. A pile of material came out of the ripped–out hole and landed on the couch in a quiet rustle. They stared at the pile for a while, taking in the colors. Copper, turquoise, dusky rose, magenta, ruby, ebony, chartreuse. Conventional names like brown, blue, and pink would not do to describe the banquet of fabric. Porter reached down a tentative hand and stroked the soft silk of the dresses. Khatia picked one up and held it out. It was hand–made, she was sure, custom–made, lined in silk charmeuse. Silk on silk. Silk on skin. The snaps and clasps were old–fashioned. The zippers looked a little rusty. They were Chinese dresses with mandarin collars and frog buttons as she had seen waitresses wearing in Chinese restaurants. Brocade jackets and crocheted sweaters to match.

Porter found a note in their father's handwriting: "These were your mother's, part of her wedding trunk. I've included the letters you would not take, Khatia." The packet was still wrapped in its chamois cloth.

Their mother's wedding trousseau. Had she put it together alone? Had she had her mother's help at all? Khatia could picture young Annie carefully folding the dresses, placing them between sheets of tissue paper, humming a song and giving herself advice for her wedding night, taking on a mother's role, mothering herself. Surviving abandonment.

"Here," Porter handed the letters to Khatia, but she shook her head.

"You take them. For your research."

She knelt down next to the couch and sifted through the dresses with her hands, the licking of the slippery material. One tear from each eye fell onto the silk.

"We could lose Dad, Porter."

He opened his mouth, and she knew what he wanted to say, what he had been mumbling almost every time the subject came up: "He should have slashed us too. He should have hit us." Would violence have made their father confess any sooner, perhaps when their mother was still alive and they could learn from her, and about her? Porter closed his mouth.

They looked at the dresses, touching them, the foreignness, the dying

275

shapes of a woman's body inside them. Khatia knew then what she would do with her money. She would celebrate the end of her year as a smoker. She knew from looking at ads in the Sunday paper's travel section that she had just enough money for two round trip tickets to Boston and one one–way ticket from Boston to San Francisco. After he returned from St. Petersburg, they would bring their father to this place they loved. Khatia Quigley. *Wu Shan*. She would do this for he father and brother. For Cree and for Artichoke. For her mother. For herself. For her family.

ACKNOWLEDGMENTS:

Thanks go to the first writing teacher who not only encouraged me, but challenged me, Anthony Giardina. To Clarence Major, Gary Snyder, Sandra Gilbert, and Jack Hicks for their guidance. To Jane Vandenburgh who saw the beginning of the journey. To my fellow writers of the UC Davis Writing Program for no-holds-barred critiques, among other things. To my editor, Jim Rankin, for making a life-long dream a reality. To Carol Marshall for endless enthusiasm, belief, and advice. To Susan Yue for telling me to suck it up and just write. To Theresa Hanna, Erin Callahan, Jen Flynn, Cessy Alcantar Barnes, and Anna Price for friendship. To Melissa Stein for good advice and commiseration. To Luna, Cernie, and Laume for the charm—Blessed Be! To my sisters, Kathy and Sarah, for their unceasing support and affection. To my Grandma Jane Forstner and Uncle Phil Roeber—I wish they could see this. And most of all, to my love, Paul Marshall for everything essential—perfect love, perfect trust, perfect fun.

Olivia Boler

About the Author

Olivia Boler is a native of San Francisco. She lives there with her husband, dog, and cat.

She received a BA from Mount Holyoke College and an MA from the UC Davis Creative Writing Program.

She is currently working on a short story collection and her second novel.

278